SHADOW AND SWORD

SHADOW AND SWORD

N. K. CARLSON

ISBN: paperback 978-1-956183-93-1
Ebook 978-1-956183-95-5

Library of Congress Control Number: 2021951561

Any references to historical events, real people or real places
are used factiously. Names, characters, and places are products
of the author's imagination.

Cover Design by Diana TC, triumphcovers.com
Edited by Melanie Doan and Ashley Olivier

First Printing Edition 2022

Published by Creative James Media
Pasadena, MD 21122

TERRA

For Andrew and Benjamin,

"The darkness is passing and the true light is already shining."

Chapter One

Smoke burned Reith's eyes as he dashed through the trees. The horror of it all brought tears to his eyes, and not just because of the smoke. They streamed down his face as he continued his headlong sprint deeper into the forest, away from the death and destruction behind him.

An aching stitch formed in his side as he ran and sweat and tears mingled with ash clouded his vision, but he could not stop his headlong flight through the woods. He couldn't. Not if he wanted to live.

"Run," had been the instruction. The singular word was simultaneously whispered and shouted from that horrible gray face, as if one man spoke and a thousand other voices joined in. Reith shuddered at the memory, trying to shake the image from his mind's eye as he ran.

He had no care in the world other than putting as much distance as possible between himself and the horrors behind him. Trees and branches flew past him, narrowly missing him as he dodged to and fro. A few grazed his arms, legs, and face, but thankfully, the midafternoon sun illuminated enough of the forest for him to avoid the worst of the sharp tree limbs trying to trip him.

Despite this good fortune, he was in unfamiliar terrain, completely lost. In all of his hunting trips, he had never come this far west. His trips tended to be east of Coeden, his hometown. He had always found the game to be more plentiful to the east.

Reith didn't see the stream before he hit it at full speed. The water pulled at his feet, tripping him. He stumbled and stepped on a slippery rock, lost his balance, and fell forward on his face with a splash.

He pushed himself up and stood in the midst of the cold stream for a moment, sputtering water out of his mouth. It was up to his mid-shin. All thought of the command to run was driven from his mind, washed away by the refreshing flow of the stream.

"At least nothing is broken," he muttered to himself.

Reith checked his pack, sighing in relief that it wasn't too wet. The two dead rabbits were still hanging off of it from his morning hunt and his bow and quiver of arrows were dry as a bone.

He surveyed his surroundings and he realized everything seemed foreign to him. *Where am I?* He shook the water from his shaggy hair. Then he remembered the map.

He opened his pack, thanking Heaven that the inside was dry. He pulled out a small leather tube with a string tied around it, holding it together. Pulling the string, a leather tube sprang open to reveal two small pieces of parchment. He removed them and spread the first one out on a flat rock. It was a map of the entire continent of Terrasohnen. He quickly rolled this one back up and unrolled the second. This one, he knew, was a map of the area. He saw the names of the towns, Coeden in the very center, Suthrond many miles south and east, Palander to the north. The southern edge and western edge were blue, marking the Great River, which flowed north to south and the Rammis River, which flowed down from the east to meet the Great River. Reith put his finger on a point a short distance from Coeden. *Here I am. But now what?*

He rolled the maps up and tied the leather roll around them before sitting down beside the edge of the stream. It was then that the weight of the situation hit him like a charging bull. Once again, tears filled his eyes, and hot water streaked down his check to join the bubbling stream, drops among many flowing toward the sea.

The loneliness of the forest was oppressive, like a blanket on a hot day. It pressed in on him from all sides. The vastness of the space between him and everyone and everything he had ever known made his head spin. He realized then just how alone he was, and the tears flowed harder. Everyone was gone. No one had survived.

He was all alone except for the wicked, horrible laugh that kept forcing itself into his mind. *The Gray Man*, he thought. The Gray Man's laugh was like a sinister song repeating over and over in his head.

When the tears dried up, Reith washed his face, arms, and hands. The water ran black with soot as he scrubbed. When he was finished, he plunged his face into the cold flow and took a long drink. Then he began setting up his camp. *This is as good a place as any to camp for the night,* he thought as he gathered fallen sticks to build a fire.

While the fire heated up, he skinned one of the two rabbits with practiced hands and washed the meat in the stream. He took the flat rock that he had unrolled the map on and placed the meat on it, then put that next to the fire to roast.

As the meat was cooking, Reith took inventory of

everything in his pack. He had a dozen arrows and his bow, a knife, flint and tinder, an extra shirt, a sweater, one whole dead rabbit, and a water jug. Water was no problem, as long as he was near the stream. If he went west, he'd run into the Great River and would have plenty of water. It was the lack of shelter that worried him. It was early spring, so the nights could still get cold. There was also the potential problem of rain, but he decided to simply ignore that worry for now.

The advice Vereinen had given him many times popped into his head. *Worrying about something you can't control is like shouting at the wind to quiet down.* Reith even imagined it as Vereinen would have said it, in that slow and even tone of his, while looking down and scribbling on a piece of paper. The thought of his master made him smile.

After dinner, Reith cleared a spot on the ground several feet from the fire of branches, leaves, and rocks for his bed. When he finished this, he took his shirt off and washed it in the stream, then hung it up to dry on a tree branch. He put on the spare shirt and sweater and laid back against his pack.

What he wouldn't give for a story from Vereinen right now. Vereinen's stories were legendary in Coeden. He told of long-ago wars, heroes, and villains. Many nights, the town tavern was full of children and adults alike, listening to the chronicler's stories.

It was at this moment that the loneliness struck again. Survival and flight had driven the ache from Reith's heart, but now it came back with a vengeance at the memory of those happy nights listening to tales surrounded by friends and family. Now they were all gone and he felt abandoned.

He hung his head, trying to control his emotions. A sudden rage came over Reith, and he hurled his knife at a tree, where it stuck, quivering. He screamed into the gathering darkness. Birds took flight out of nearby trees, but all too soon, the forest went still and silent, as if the scream were hanging over it like a fog. It was as lonely as ever.

Reluctantly, he began to sift through the events of the day. His mind began to play them like a vivid dream.

At dawn, he had packed his bag and went out hunting. He was sure to avoid waking up Vereinen. He tiptoed out of the house and gently shut the door behind him. The sun peeked over the horizon and the shadows were long. Dew covered the ground. He remembered how it had glistened in the sunlight. *It's strange what the mind remembers*, he thought. This was another piece of Vereinen wisdom, learned over a lifetime of talking to people about what they remembered.

He hiked through the woods, going east as always. For an hour, he remained on the main trail, a trail he blazed while hunting the past few years. Hunting was one of Reith's favorite activities. Just him, the forest, and the prey. It was simple, elegant. The long walks and the waiting gave one time to think.

He left the trail to check his traps, which were laid out in a large circle around an open glade in the midst of the forest. By now, sunlight poured down through the leaves and beams of light illuminated the ground. Two of his traps had caught rabbits. He hung the fresh kills on his pack and reset the traps. He remembered that he had made a mental note to move the traps the next morning. *I'll never do that now*, he thought. *Some fox will enjoy those rabbits.*

After resetting the traps, he walked down a smaller, less worn path, away and to the left of the main one. Ten minutes on, he came upon his favorite hunting tree. About ten feet up, the tree forked, leaving a perfect seat for a watching hunter. He hung his bag on a lower branch and swung up into the tree. After a few seconds of effort, he pulled himself up and settled in. And he waited.

To make time go by, he mentally reviewed his lessons with Vereinen. As a chronicler's apprentice, there was much to learn. The previous day, Reith had been hard at work memorizing the human kings and queens of the first epoch. *Ranab, Elza, Driden, Pire*, the names still came easy to his mind. But what useless information now that he was alone in the woods for the foreseeable future.

After a few hours of fruitless waiting at his favorite tree, he had set off further east, hoping that his luck would change. He found a spot, not quite a hole in the ground, but more of an impression in the soft dirt that was protected by fallen logs. It was a good place to see but not be seen. As with before, after a few hours he had nothing to show for his efforts. He stood up and stretched his limbs that were stiff from inactivity. He judged that it was slightly after noon. After a quick bite to eat, he started back toward Coeden.

Reith walked the well-worn, familiar path, lost in his thoughts about the morning hunt and of long dead monarchs. About a mile from the town, he reached the top of a small rise that had few trees. He paused for a break at the top of the hill, retrieving his water jug from his pack. As he tilted it back, his eyes caught a glimpse of the sky. Above the trees, in the direction of Coeden, he could see thick, black smoke rising. *Fire.*

He raced back through the woods. Fires in Coeden called for all hands on deck. He raced back to help put it out. As he jogged to town, the smell of smoke grew stronger. *I hope it's not burning anything important*, he thought.

Reith heard them before he saw them. Harsh, loud voices. They were not the voices he had been expecting.

He had expected the voices of the men of Coeden, perhaps the baker, blacksmith, or Vereinen, but these voices were strange. He could not make out what they were saying. He stopped running and crept to the fringe of the forest, fear coursing through his body. He stayed hidden when he saw who the voices belonged to. A group of men, soldiers by the look of them, though none were in uniform, were organizing and preparing to march out on the road heading north. There were roughly fifty that he could see. Some were loading a cart with bundles. Others were carrying torches, lighting anything that wasn't already on fire. Around them, the houses and buildings of Coeden were ablaze, spewing smoke to the heavens. No familiar faces were in sight.

Instinct told Reith to stay hidden. He slipped behind a large tree, his back against it, head turned and his ears strained.

He tried to calm his breathing and the racing of his heart so he could hear what the men were saying.

Reith struggled to make out anything specific before a cold voice pierced the air. "Is there any sign of him?" It sounded as if someone had squeezed every last drop of warmth and color from the voice. It was icy, sharp, and gray, if a voice could sound like a color.

"No, sir," a second voice replied. "We have searched the entire town, but there has been no sign of your man."

Reith slowly edged around his tree to try and catch a glimpse of the speakers.

"And what did you do with the rest of them?" the icy gray voice asked again.

"We killed them all. As you commanded, sir."

Reith's heart skipped a beat. *Killed? All of them? How? Why? Vereinen too?* All of these questions bounced around his head. Fear coursed through his veins, heightening every sense.

"I can't say I am entirely pleased," was the cold response. Reith remained frozen in his spot, not daring to move lest he be seen and killed too. "If Vereinen has escaped, it shall be your life for his."

I've got to find Vereinen, and quick!

Reith circled to the southern end of the town, creeping in the shadows of the trees and keeping out of sight. The voices of the men slowly died down as he got further from them. He only had two goals: remain alive and discover the truth of what had happened. He crept between two houses, both on fire, rather than by the road. There was no one around. All of the buildings were engulfed in flames. He walked down this side road, staying as close as he could to the houses to avoid being seen, but not too close to avoid burns. He soon reached the corner and carefully looked toward the town square. Here, most of the buildings were smoldering ruins. *These ones were burned first.*

Reith still hadn't come across any living person, aside from the armed men he'd seen earlier. Fear coursed through his veins, heightening his senses. He was ready to run at the slightest provocation. He pulled out his bow and notched an arrow, just in case.

He slowly walked down the road toward the town square. His eyes darted this way and that, looking for signs of movement. He saw nothing, but every so often he paused to listen. Aside from the crackling of the fire, he heard nothing.

At last, Reith carefully peered around the corner of a smoldering building and looked out into the square. His eyes immediately fell upon a large mound of bodies. He looked around for any sign of the men, and seeing nothing, he rushed forward. His eyes saw but his brain did not understand. There was the butcher, Ferrell and his family, the blacksmith, Brage and his wife, Kina, and a dozen other familiar faces. Bull, the tavern keeper, Jelp, the tanner, old Tom who's second best bow was Reith's.

In horror, he circled the pile, each step bringing to sight another familiar face. Some had been killed with arrows, which were still jutting out of them. Others were killed by swords and spears. Blood soaked all of the clothes and pooled on the ground around the pile. Reith sank to his knees, bile rising in his throat before spilling from his lips.

When he was finished throwing up, he dragged himself away. He couldn't bear to look anymore. He walked, with no plan of where to go, all thought of the men who had done this temporarily driven from his head by the grief they had caused. He found himself unconsciously approaching his childhood home, where he had lived with his father and mother until three years ago, when they had died of the fever and he had gone to live with Vereinen as his apprentice. As Reith approached, he could see the flames engulfing it. Sadness at the loss of his old house overwhelmed him, and he mentally chided himself for getting emotional over a building. He stood there for a few minutes, watching it burn.

Then a thought came to his mind. *Where was Vereinen?* He hadn't seen his face and body among the others. He turned and ran toward Vereinen's house, intent on finding his master.

Vereinen's home was set apart from the rest of the town, hidden by a grove of trees. Reith soon reached the house without being seen. It was, mercifully, unharmed.

He stepped in the front door and whispered his master's name, "Vereinen? Are you here?"

There was no reply.

Reith walked through the kitchen into the study. The

shelves were full of books, though three were conspicuously missing, the three volumes of the Epochs of Terrasohnen. Vereinen's life's work was a history of Terrasohnen in three volumes, divided by each epoch. As an apprentice chronicler, Reith was slowly learning all he could from his master.

Either Vereinen took them, or someone else did, Reith thought to himself. *And I doubt it was these attackers if they don't know where Vereinen is.*

He rotated on the spot, looking for anything else out of place, some sign of a struggle, some hint that Vereinen had escaped. Vereinen usually kept a cluttered study, but Reith was familiar enough with it to notice anything out of place. His eyes scanned the shelves, over the familiar spines of books and the curve of scrolls. Everything seemed in order. Then he noticed a green flower vase on the bottom shelf behind the desk, several inches away from where it normally perched. He stepped closer and noticed there was a circle with no dust where the vase had been. He picked up the empty vase and felt a rustle inside it. After reaching in, he pulled out a small piece of paper that had been folded over four times. Inside read:

R, meet me at Erador. Come quick. Bring map. V.

Erador, Reith thought incredulously. *He can't be serious. The ruined city?*

He racked his brain and remembered that it was a city jointly made by humans, elves, and dwarves in the Second Epoch. It fell in the Dragon War, a thousand years past, when the dragons had come and laid waste to the west coast of Terrasohnen. To this day, a large portion of the

West was a smoldering ruin called Dragonscar. Even grass couldn't grow there. *Why would Vereinen tell me to meet him in a ruined city?* Reith wondered.

He pulled a large map from Vereinen's map pile and spread it on the desk. This was Vereinen's map of the continent of Terrasohnen. He found Coeden, near the middle of the map. To the west was Dragonscar, a blackened section along the coast. Reith judged it to be 200 miles away. In the middle of Dragonscar, at the coast of the Western Ocean, Vereinen had marked where Erador had been. It was nearly due west from Coeden.

Knowing his direction, Reith rolled it up and selected a second map from Vereinen's collection. This one, he knew from a glance, was the one of the area around Coeden. Reith took the two maps from Vereinen's file and wrapped them in a leather tube, which he then placed in his pack. He surveyed the room once more and noticed nothing strange. He left the house, locking the door behind him. As he walked through the trees toward the town, Reith wondered if he could salvage anything worth bringing with him or maybe find a horse.

"Halt!" came a shout as soon as Reith reached the edge of the town. In an instant, he swung his bow around and notched an arrow, whirling to see who had called to him. He saw at least a dozen men with arrows trained on him.

"I would lower your bow, if you know what's good for you." The voice was terrifyingly familiar, cold and icy as it was.

A man stepped out from behind the line of archers. He was tall and thin, clean shaven, and his hair was long and shaggy. The strange thing about him was that he looked like all the color had been drained from his body, as if he had taken a bath one day and the color was pulled from his skin by the water. His face and eyes were grey, along with his hair. At first glance, Reith thought him to be elderly, but his skin was still smooth and fairly young. Reith supposed he could be anywhere from thirty to seventy years old. His eyes were piercing and intense, hyper focused on Reith. He looked just as his voice sounded.

Reith slowly assessed the situation, along with this new, intimidating figure. He lowered his bow but kept the arrow on the string.

"Now boy," the Gray Man said, his voice betraying his impatience. "Look at this reasonably. Don't try to be a hero."

"Who are you?" Reith asked, blurting out the first question that came to mind.

"Never you mind," said the Gray Man.

"Why did you do this?" Reith asked, gesturing to the ruined town. Anger rose in Reith. He wanted to get this man talking so he could figure out a plan. *One against fifty isn't good odds.*

"Enough questions. I don't like questions," the Gray Man said, his face somehow becoming more gray as if his cheeks flushed with anger and his very blood was gray. The Gray Man paced back and forth and with each turn came slightly closer to Reith.

"I am looking for someone. He is a historian by the name of Vereinen. Do you know him?"

"No," Reith lied instinctively.

"You're lying. I wish people would stop lying to me; it's terribly frustrating. I am a man of my word, and I hold people to that same high standard. Now, boy, put away your bow and let's speak honestly."

Reith held his ground, not moving to put away his bow.

"You must know," the Gray Man continued, his face contorting in rage, "that I am no one to be trifled with!"

His shout disturbed a flock of nearby birds. He raised his hand, and fifty bows were pulled back, aimed at Reith.

Seeing no way that his continued defiance would end without him looking like a pincushion, Reith cautiously took the arrow off the string and slid it back into his quiver.

"Good," the Gray Man said, taking a couple of steps closer to Reith. Seeing him more clearly, Reith guessed him to be in his mid-forties, though he still wasn't entirely sure due to the gray skin and hair.

"And who might you be?" he asked, his eyes gazing so intently on Reith that Reith felt like the Gray Man was peering into his soul so he had to look down to avoid the gray eyes.

Reith thought about telling the truth, but he decided to hide his identity from this murderer. "I'm no one," he replied.

"Oh ho!" the Gray Man said, taking another step forward, though this one was a joyful hop. "Did you hear that, boys? This is No One!"

The other men chuckled at some unsaid joke. The Gray Man laughed the loudest.

"No One," the Gray Man repeated, "I am a man of my word. I said so before. I always keep my promises. Always." The last word came out as a snakelike hiss. "You see, when we entered this pitiful town of yours, I told my boys, I said, 'Boys, leave No One alive.' So you said the magic words."

Reith, worried and afraid, and still not understanding what the man was saying, said nothing. His eyes jumped from the horrible gray face to the arrows still pointed at him.

This is it. I'm going to die.

"You said you were No One. I promised to leave No

One alive." The Gray Man let out a mad cackle. Now Reith was completely terrified of this laughing mad man. He looked around for an escape but could find none.

"And so, No One," the Gray Man continued, pacing in front of Reith now. "Take one last look around." Reith obeyed, glancing nervously at the armed men pointing arrows at him, at the burning buildings, and at the pile of bodies, rage bubbling up in him.

"Run," the word was almost a whisper, yet it rang out, louder than Reith could have thought possible. It beat against his ear drum as if someone had rung a bell by his ear. "Run. If you look back, we will shoot over your head. The next arrow will be right behind it, aimed true at your back. If you come back, we will kill you. I am a man of my word. If you come back, I will give you a name we can mark on your tomb."

Reith hesitated for just a moment, but then the Gray Man screamed, "RUN!"

The word hung in the air like the smoke from the smoldering town and Reith bolted. He pushed past the archers and rushed out of town, running in a headlong sprint, running for his life.

At the town's edge, just before he reached the forest, he chanced a look back and an arrow whizzed past his head, sending a short breeze across his face. He jumped behind a tree and heard the thud of an arrow hit the other side of the trunk.

Reith fled from the horror behind him, running faster than he ever thought he was capable of running. The Gray Man yelled after him, "If you see Vereinen, tell him I'm looking for him! Run!"

Chapter Two

That horrible gray face and voice haunted Reith's dreams that night. He slept poorly and awoke groggy. It took a few minutes to remember where he was and what had happened. And then it all washed over him again. He kept picturing their faces. Their lifeless, bloody faces, eyes open in fear but not seeing, never seeing again.

He spent the first few minutes of his day with tears running down his cheeks.

Reith washed his face in the stream and then ate some of the rabbit from the previous night. He packed up his few belongings and prepared to depart his camp. As he looked around to make sure he wasn't forgetting anything, a wave of nostalgia crashed over him. Despite only camping there one night, this clearing by the stream, in some small way, felt like a home. *I have no home now,* he thought sorrowfully.

The stream flowed from northeast to southwest. He knew he must travel due west to reach Erador and find Vereinen. But as the stream was his only source of water, he decided to follow it and hoped it turned due west somewhere downstream. If not, he could always leave its banks and cut across the land.

As he set out, the sun was nearly straight behind him, and when the trees weren't too thick, his shadow stretched out far in front of him, a guide leading onward.

He traveled along the northern bank of the stream. The water on his left bubbled and babbled. Despite the sound, he heard plenty of birds singing in the trees. Several times early in the morning, he saw a deer scamper away when it heard him coming. He thought about shooting one but decided against it. Killing a deer now would stop him in his tracks for the day as he would have to skin and clean it. Around midmorning, he came across a patch of strawberries growing along the bank, which he happily devoured, saving a few for later.

As he walked, his mind wandered to that which was behind him. Unbidden, thoughts of Vereinen came to his mind. He remembered a time, shortly after moving into Vereinen's house, when Vereinen had criticized his penmanship.

"What is this, a P?" Vereinen asked, squinting at the page Reith had written on.

"No, sir, that's an R. See the tail?" he replied, pointing to the letter.

"Humph," Vereinen grunted, "It looks like what one of my goats would write if they were able to grasp a pen."

As he walked, Reith smiled at the thought of that memory. On the outside, Vereinen was sometimes grumpy, but on the inside, he had a big heart. He loved telling stories to the children and any adult who wanted to hear at the tavern. At that thought, Reith remembered the flames that had licked it. And then the image of that horrible gray face swam into view. He shuddered, shaking his head to dissipate the figure.

By the late afternoon, the sun shone directly in his face, making it hard for him to see. Reith stumbled several times over rocks and sticks because of the excess light. When he almost tumbled into the stream after tripping over a log, he decided it was time to find a place to settle for the night. He spotted a small clearing about twenty yards away from the stream and set about collecting wood for a fire.

As the fire grew hotter, Reith pulled out the maps again. He had no books, so he decided that he would study the map of Terrasohnen. *I'll know this thing better than the back of my own hand at the end of this journey,* he thought.

He unrolled the map and gazed intently at it. There was Coeden, a bit southwest of the center of the map. Around it, and around him, was a giant forest stretching from near the mountains to the east almost all the way to the Great River. Before it reached the river however, it thinned out until it became a plain. He guessed that he had gone about twenty-five miles that day and perhaps ten the previous day. Reith looked for a stream on the map but could not find it. *Must be too small,* he thought. Still, he had a general idea of where he was.

It will meet either the Great River or the Rammis River, directly southwest of Coeden. If I follow this stream until then, I can follow the river back up to the point where I can cross closest to Erador, but that will make this journey longer.

Reith sat there looking at the map and decided that he must leave the stream the next day or the day after if it hadn't turned due west.

He put the map away and skinned the second rabbit. He figured he could make this one last all the next day and into the day after if he rationed it. But he knew that he would have to hunt again soon. As the rabbit cooked, he pulled out the map and studied it some more. This time, he looked toward the wider world. To the far north, farther than even Galismoor, the capital city, were snowcapped mountains. Across the center of the map stretched the open plains. On the far side of the plains were twin lakes, and the area was aptly named the Twins Region.

Reith thought back to the time Vereinen had first shown him this map when he was thirteen.

"And over here," Vereinen said pointing to the twin lakes depicted on the map rolled out on his desk, "are Rangit and Brendel. And between them, the great fortress city of Kal-Epharion."

"Have you ever been there?" Reith asked, leaning back in his seat hoping for a story from his master.

"Oh yes, several times," Vereinen replied. "And down here—"

Reith interrupted, "Can you tell me about it?"

"About Kal-Epharion? What do you want to know?"

"Everything! Why did you go there? What does it look like? What are the people like?"

"Well," Vereinen said, leaning back in his chair. Reith knew this was Vereinen's storytelling posture. "I went to Kal-Epharion as lad, probably two or three years older than you are now. I traveled there with a group of traders and soldiers from Galismoor, where I grew up. The king sent them, and I asked if I could go with them."

"And the king said yes?"

"Of course. The king had been there about six moons previous and knew of a scholar there who would help me in my studies. So I took a scroll of commission from the king to that scholar. I was very excited, as it was my first time traveling from Galismoor—and to Kal-Epharion, no less. The City of Treasures, one of the oldest cities in Terrasohnen. They say the first men founded it in the First

Epoch. I know it may be hard for you to picture it, Reith, but I was giddy."

"I don't believe it. You, giddy?"

"Oh, I was, Reith. In the days leading up to the trip, I could hardly keep still. My mind was so filled with excitement that I barely slept. And then the journey happened. The journey there took about ten days. We were on horseback, and we traveled the King's Road. We spent our nights under the stars and our days in the saddle. Over the plains we rode. And let me tell you, it was the most bored I have ever been."

"Why was it boring?"

"Well, the plains are so flat that you can see the curve of the horizon on all sides. I know that sounds interesting, but where there is nothing to see except your companions and your horses, the view grows stale rather quickly. And if you have ever tried to read a book while on horseback, you will know that it is a nearly impossible task, what with the swaying and jolting with every step. And the company wasn't great. The soldiers weren't much interested in talking to a young chronicler like me.

"Ten days we traveled like this. So when Kal-Epharion began to rise out of the plains on the horizon, I was more than ready to reach it. For nearly two days it is in view as you travel to it, a red tower on the horizon that at first looks like a mountain. As you get closer, you can see that it is man-made. The more you ride in, you can see the lakes off to each side, each stretching past your sight. The fortress looms above the world, impenetrable. They used red stone from the mountains south of the Twins Region. It's so red it looks like it's on fire. Especially as the sun sets behind it. The gates were open when we arrived, so we rode in.

"The city is built in concentric circles. That way, if

attacked, the defenders can retreat inward and have a wall to defend. In the very center, the fortress tower rises into the sky. We made our way to the fortress, riding along each curve and passing through another gate as we entered the depths of the city. We were given lodgings in the fortress and we stayed there quite comfortably."

"And what happened while you were there?"

"I wandered through the markets during the morning, where the merchants sold exotic foods, spices, fragrances, dyed fabrics, livestock, and wares. In the afternoon, I studied with Master Windek. He taught me all I know about the history of Kal-Epharion and allowed me free use of his personal library, which contained many hundreds of volumes. We also went to the city library, which is nearly as big as the one in Galismoor. And in the evening, there were such wonderful feasts. We feasted with the governor, Master Windek, the clerics of the Temple of Kal, and with the lords and ladies of the city.

"That region is very fertile, and they grow the most delicious fruits and vegetables in the entire kingdom. You wouldn't believe how scrumptious they are. The people are simply wonderful. They dress in vibrant colors and sing wonderful songs that are joyful and melancholy all at the same time. Someday, you and I shall visit."

"Promise?" Reith asked, excited at the possibility.

"Oh yes. They have a wonderful library that I shall want to visit, and you can help me research."

"I would love to, Master," Reith answered. "I just hope the traveling isn't as boring as your travels were."

"You can help on that count too, Reith. Company and good conversation make any trip more bearable. In fact, we brought back a boy and his mother from Kal-Epharion to Galismoor. The king had requested that we find a new maid. Her boy was a few years younger than I was, about your age now, but he was just what I needed on that return trip. I had more questions about Kal-Epharion, and he had questions about Galismoor. We stayed friends, too, in Galismoor, until he went back to live in Kal-Epharion."

Alone at his camp in the woods, Reith wished he had someone to accompany him. Company and good conversation was exactly what he needed.

The next morning, Reith awoke to the sound of some creature moving near him, close to the stream. He gasped in fear, thinking the worst, but the noise was drowned out by the nearby stream. He drew his bow and slowly raised himself to a crouch. Next to the water stood a huge buck. Reith decided right then that he needed to take it down. Carefully, he sighted along the arrow, aiming for the heart.

His arrow found its mark, and a second followed close behind. The buck fell with a grunt and went still. Reith spent the morning skinning and cleaning the animal. He ate a tremendous lunch of venison and cooked what he wanted to take with him before wrapping it in fresh green leaves.

The morning was gone when Reith finally began to march again, this time weighed down with meat. It was a burden he would gladly bear, especially if his prey happened to walk so close to him.

That night, instead of pulling out the maps, Reith practiced archery. Using his knife, he pinned a bit of the deer skin to a tree. The buck provided plenty of skin that would absorb his shot but not let the arrows penetrate the tree. From twenty-five paces out, he shot arrow after arrow at the skin, hitting his mark each time until the thing looked like a pincushion.

The smooth wood of the bow felt familiar in his hand, a source of comfort in this wild place of loneliness. With each arrow shot, Reith remembered the hours he'd spent shooting arrows at the archery yard in Coeden. His interest in shooting began when he was eleven and he witnessed a shooting match between two of the town guards. He had watched in amazement as each archer sent arrow after arrow into the center of the target from further distances each time. With every bullseye, the crowd would cheer. From that moment, Reith wanted to be one of those archers. So he started practicing with an old bow at the shooting yard. At first, he had trouble pulling it all the way back, let alone shooting it at whatever target he aimed for. But he grew bigger and stronger and eventually that old bow felt like a toy in his hands.

One of the town guards, Old Tom, loaned Reith his spare bow when Reith was fourteen. Old Tom was getting on in years, perhaps around sixty. Even at that age, though, he was the finest archer in Coeden. This bow was top notch and had a stronger draw weight. He quickly grew accustomed to the new bow and liked how it felt in his hand.

Old Tom had been impressed and one day had placed a bet. "Reith, I will give you this bow to keep if you can beat me in a shooting contest."

"Are you serious?" Reith asked, looking from Old Tom to the bow and back again.

"I am serious. You can have this bow if you can beat me. But what are you going to put up for the bet?"

"Uh," Reith said, thinking. He didn't really have anything. "I'll give you ten Eagles." Eagles were the silver coins used by the humans of Terrasohnen. They were worth ten Heads, bronze coins with depictions of the king's head, and 1/10th of a Crown, gold coins with a crown emblazoned onto them.

"Deal," Old Tom said, extending his hand to Reith. The only problem was Reith didn't have ten Eagles. He only had one and a handful of Heads. Still, he shook Old Tom's hand, confident in his impending victory.

"We're going to have a shooting match!" Old Tom announced to anyone nearby interested in such things. A small crowd gathered. Old Tom went first from twenty paces. His arrow hit the center of the target. Reith nervously stepped up to the line. He glanced at the crowd of onlookers gathered and felt his heart race. Then he closed his eyes and took a deep breath, trying to calm himself. *Just like practice.* Reith selected his arrow and notched it, drawing back the string. He sighted along the arrow, gazing intently at his target. He took one more deep breath and then he released and the arrow sped forward, hitting his mark.

"Beginner's luck," Old Tom said.

They backed up to thirty paces and then forty paces, each result the same as the first. At fifty yards, Old Tom lost focus and hit the target, but several inches away from the center. If Reith got a bullseye on this shot, he would win.

"No pressure," Old Tom said, winking at him. "It'd be a shame to get sweaty hands and mess this one up."

At the mention of sweaty hands, Reith's hands did indeed begin to sweat. His heart started beating faster, and he felt the shakiness brought on by a surge of adrenaline. He wished he could take a few minutes and run around to calm down. But he couldn't. He had to take the shot.

Nervously, he selected an arrow and notched it. Drawing back, he peered toward the target, which seemed smaller than before. It also looked like it was moving. He took a deep breath and closed his eyes to steady himself.

"You'll do better with your eyes open, lad," Old Tom said. Even with his eyes closed, Reith could hear the grin on his lips.

After another deep breath, he opened his eyes. The target had stopped moving. Everyone around seemed to melt away until it was just Reith, the target, the bow, and the arrow on the shooting lawn. He released and the arrow was propelled forward, seeming to gain speed in the air until it buried itself in the center of the target.

"Well shot, Reith," Old Tom said, nodding his approval. "You earned that bow, fair and square."

Now in the forest, Reith pretended that the deer skin on the tree was that target from years ago. He smiled at the thought of his victory and then sent another arrow into the skin, fired from that trophy bow he had won.

The next morning, about an hour into his journey, the stream took a bend toward the south. Reith knew that now he would have to leave its protective waters for the open country. He took a last drink and filled up his water jug, then set out. He based his path on the movement of the sun, behind him in the morning and ahead of him in the afternoon. Where he could, he followed animal trails, always going west. To Erador. To Vereinen.

That night, he camped beside a small pond in a clearing. He was glad for the water, as he had drunk sparingly during the day. He was hot, and his throat was dry. He bathed in the pond, delighting in the refreshing coolness.

By the light of the fire, he looked over the map again. He estimated that he had traveled nearly 150 miles from Coeden and he should reach the Great River in a day or two. *And then Dragonscar and Erador.*

The next morning, he left his pond and began his march west. After three hours, he noticed that the trees were thinner here and then all of a sudden he found himself blinking in the open air of the plain in front of him. He had reached the edge of the forest. With renewed vigor, knowing that he was closing in on the river, Reith set off again.

Late that day, with the sun pouring down into his eyes, he climbed to the top of a small hill to see what lay before him. At the top, his eyes were dazzled by the light bouncing off of the swiftly flowing river below. Perhaps a quarter of a mile further on splayed the might of the Great River. Its opposite shore was perhaps 200 paces across. The other side was dark and indistinct. In this section of the river, the water was choppy and disturbed by unseen rocks and logs lurking beneath the surface.

Reith gazed at this beautiful sight for a few minutes before deciding to camp at the base of the hill for the evening. He dropped his pack and lit a fire, and as the fire was growing hot, he took his water jug to the river.

He traversed the open ground with ease, glad to be rid of his pack momentarily. The riverbank was about ten feet higher than the river itself, and he looked for a place that he might scramble down to the edge to get water. About fifty feet further upstream, the bank was gentler and he was able to get down to the water's edge to fill his water jug. The water was freezing. Now that he was at water level, he knew that he would not be able to swim across here. The current was too swift and he would be dashed against the rocks if he attempted the swim from here. Looking upstream and down, there was no obvious place of crossing this massive river.

After filling his jug, Reith returned to his fire and his pack. He unrolled the smaller of the two maps, the map of the area around Coeden. He knew from looking at the other map that Coeden was about level with Erador. He had traveled slightly south with the stream, so he could walk upstream to see if there was a better place to cross.

He looked intently at the map, hoping for a clue as to a bridge or a ford or a narrowing of the river, anything that would make it possible to cross. In these wildlands, there was no city or village nearby to seek refuge and help.

Reith sighed, put the map away, and set about cooking some of his food.

In the morning, Reith set out along the bank of the river traveling north. It was a gray day, windy and cold. Reith thought about the Gray Man and shuddered. He had been doing his best to avoid thinking about the man, but now that was all his mind wanted to think about.

Why would the Gray Man want Vereinen?

Chroniclers weren't exactly the most helpful people on current events, such as rebellions or whatever it was the Gray Man was doing.

Why did the Gray Man need an expert about the past? What secret does Vereinen know?

Reith continued on, always on the lookout for a way to cross the river. The ground was grassy and smooth and much easier to walk on than the uneven forest floor. Around noon, he shot a bird that was standing on the bank of the river. It was white, with gray patches. It was a bird Reith had never seen before, being a little smaller than a chicken, and Reith hoped it would make for good eating that night.

Every time he came to a bend in the river, he hoped that around the curve he would find a bridge or a shallow ford to cross, but each time he was disappointed. As the day went on, the ground grew rocky, making it hard to keep up his pace.

The bird was not nearly as good as a chicken, but it was much better than nothing. Reith ate it without complaint. Then he went to sleep dreading the thought of eventually swimming across the fast-flowing river.

In the morning, Reith awoke, stiff from sleeping on the rocky ground. He stretched and then wandered down to the water's edge to drink and wash. The water was just as cold as it was yesterday. Back at the top of the bank, Reith looked forward, upstream, to see what was coming ahead.

The river looked just as wide and rough as ever, though there was a bend perhaps two miles ahead. Then he looked at his side of the river, along the edge where he would walk. The ground was littered with rocks and stones for about ten paces wide right next to the river but outside of that ten paces wide strip, it was clear, like the plain. His eyes followed this line between the clear plain and the rocky strip and he saw what looked to be some sort of path. It was just visible under the thick grass that had sprouted up between stones. He turned around and looked back the way he had come and saw the same pattern.

"Is this a road?" he asked of no one in particular. It sure looked like some sort of road or path from long ago. *If it's a road, then it must go somewhere.*

Reith moved over off of the rocky strip to the grassy plain, as it was easier walking there. He shook his head, frustrated that he had slept on the rocky strip rather than the soft plain the night before. In the gathering darkness, when he had made camp, he was too tired to look around and see what was right in front of him.

Come to think of it, I should have noticed I was on some sort of path.

All day he walked alongside this path beside the river. Every mile he went along, the road was clearer, more defined, as if he was getting closer and closer to where the road had originated and where it had been taken care of better.

Shortly after noon, the path climbed a hill, and the river fell away. Soon, Reith reached the top, and the river stretched out before him. It curved to his right, flowing from east to west. Facing north, he saw that the river made another bend back to the north. Below him, the river was slower and wider, as if the hill he was climbing was acting as some sort of natural dam, blocking the flow of the river. Below, the grassy plain disappeared into endless sand that gently sloped down to the river. Gone was the sharp bank.

The road was very well defined here. He could see that the road he had been traveling from the south met another road coming from the north, and each turned to the water. At the meeting point of the two roads was a large pile of stones, similar to those that littered the ancient path he had been following. There was no mistaking what it was: an ancient, ruined fortress and a ford.

Chapter Three

Reith jogged down the hill toward the ruined fortress, propelled by gravity. His heart beat fast with the excitement of exploration. He barely avoided stumbling over the rocks on the ground as he went.

He soon reached the bottom in one piece and walked up to the decrepit shell of a fortress. It was small, no more than fifteen aces per side. Its footprint was square. Whatever had been its roof or battlement had crumbled away a long time ago. The stones from the roof and battlement were piled together inside the structure. It's walls were mostly standing, though a few stones had fallen.

Reith walked around the entire thing once, and seeing no way in nor anything worth exploring further, he turned his attention to the ford.

As he had seen from the hill, the roads from the south and the north met here at the fortress and turned toward the river, which had a long, flat bank. The current was gentle here. If it were shallow enough, he could walk over with ease. If not, the swim shouldn't be too taxing.

Across the river, the land was dark and shadowy. For whatever reason, Reith had not yet paid much attention to the far side of the river, intent as he was upon finding a place to safely cross. Perhaps this was due to the fact that the other side looked so inhospitable. He hadn't given much thought to what exactly Dragonscar might look like, but it was clear now that Dragonscar was a place of waste and ruin. The ground was blackened, and there was no green thing to be seen despite it being springtime. *That's where Vereinen wants me to go?*

The sunlight shimmered on the water as he approached. It was midafternoon now. He had plenty of sunlight left to cross and travel some more that day, but something in his gut gave him pause. *This doesn't feel right*, he thought. There was something about that other side that felt foreboding and forbidden.

Reith glanced back at the old fortress and decided he would attempt the crossing in the morning. Part of his brain applauded this sensible action. The other half whispered, "Coward." He shook the thought away.

He decided to camp on the plain on the far side of the fortress, away from the water. The grass was free of stones here. He cleared some ground and lit a fire with some grass and old driftwood he found on the bank. Then he went to explore the fortress again.

This time he took his time circling the building, hoping to see or find something of use. He meticulously inspected every crack, crevice, and stone, noticing something he hadn't before. On the river side of the fortress, a stone door was set in the wall. Its hinges were long rusted away, but he decided to try it anyway. Reith pulled at the handle and then pushed his shoulder into it. Reith put forth a great effort and it gave way, falling back into the building with a crash. It raised a cloud of dust, and Reith coughed for a minute.

When the dust settled, he cautiously stepped over the door into the fortress.

I must be the first person here in hundreds of years, he thought. The idea excited him.

As he had surmised from the outside, the roof had fallen in. The entire room was covered in debris and rock. Nature had begun to reclaim this space, and grass was growing up between the stones. Beneath a pile of rocks in the center of the room was what looked like the remains of an old table. Unfortunately, Reith could not walk much into the room due to all of the rubble, but something near that old table caught his eye. It was a curiously shaped stone. He reached for it and began to tug it out.

At last, he worked it free and held it up to examine. It was a stone cylinder about a foot tall and a hand's width across. Despite the fact that it was stone, it was light. On top was a small hole with another piece of rock wedged inside. It fit so perfectly that it had to have been hand carved for just this purpose. He shook the cylinder, and he heard a faint sloshing sound inside. Reith had found an ancient water jug.

He opened the jug and poured the water out, not wanting to drink it if it had been in there for hundreds of years. He placed the jug in his pack, along with his other few possessions.

This will come in handy across the river, he thought.

There were legends that the water in Dragonscar was not fit to drink, but he had never asked Vereinen about it. Still, it was better safe than sorry.

One last glance around the room yielded no new information, so Reith stepped back outside to tend to his fire. He noticed a few more of those white birds milling about on the bank of the river, so he pulled his bow out, notched an arrow, and aimed at the most plump bird in sight.

Reith slept better that night, knowing there was grass to lie down on. As the sun rose, he prepared to make his way across the river. At the water's edge, he surveyed the way before him. The water was shallow, and he could see the sandy bottom for several paces out. *It's clearly a ford, but does that mean I can walk across? Or is it just a gentle place to swim?*

He removed his shoes and placed these in his pack. If he had to swim, he didn't want those on dragging him down. He was a competent swimmer, having learned at a young age with many of the other children of Coeden down in the pond. If he had to swim, he would. But his main concern was making it across and keeping his pack dry.

Reith stepped into the flow and waited a minute for his feet to warm to the icy water. It was still early in the season, and he knew the waters came from the north, where frigid runoff flowed down from the Frozen Mountains. Still, the intellectual knowledge of the water's origins did nothing to warm his freezing feet.

The ground was surprisingly sandy beneath his feet; he had expected large rocks. After wading and waiting for his feet to warm up, he decided it was about time that he was off, and he began walking in further. Everywhere the water touched that had previously been dry burned him as only the cold could. But he kept going. Soon, the water lapped around his waist. He took his pack off of his back and held it in front of him to prevent it from getting wet. His lower half was numb. He soon lost count of his paces, but judged himself to be at the middle of the river.

So far so good, Reith thought.

The water gently tugged at him, pulling him downstream, but it wasn't strong enough to pull him in. The water was at his mid-chest now, and he held his bag out in front of him above the rippling waves.

Reith took another step and fell forward. He had expected his foot to strike the ground at the same level as his other one, but his foot kept going. He stumbled and narrowly avoided falling in. He held his bag aloft, above his head now. The water was up to his shoulders. He paused to collect himself, shaken by the near fall. Then his arms began to burn. A few more steps and the water lapped at his chin. He lifted his face up to avoid getting water in his mouth and nose. He kept his bag straight overhead. At this position, he could barely step forward, so he shuffled another several feet. Luckily, he was just tall enough to keep his head above water and avoid swimming. He didn't know how he would keep his bag dry if he had to swim.

After what felt like hours, though was really only a couple of minutes of shuffling, the ground began to go back up and the water receded. His arms ached from holding the bag up, and as the water went down, he was able to take longer steps, gaining more ground until at last he was able to drop his arms from about his head and cradle his bag in his arms in front of him.

Reith stumbled forward onto the beach. The air on his wet skin and clothes was colder than the water had been. He quickly deposited his bag on the sand and removed his shirt. He slipped on his spare and then rubbed his shivering arms. He looked around and found some driftwood and set about making a fire, his teeth chattering from the cold. He could barely hold his flint and steel steady, but he did succeed in lighting a fire. He sat down next to it and warmed himself by its heat.

When he was sufficiently warm, he laid out his wet

shirt beside the fire to dry. By now, the sun rose higher in the sky and Reith judged it to be mid-morning. He took in his surroundings on the beach. The beach on this side was like that on the other, wide and flat. There was no fortress. Instead of the shell of roads going north and south, there was only one road pointing due west.

I'd bet my bag that road goes straight to Erador, Reith thought.

The road, or what was left of it, was on a gradual incline, leading to lands above the river. Beyond the sand of the beach, the earth was black and charred. No grass grew. It looked as if someone had begun a garden by digging up the earth and preparing it for seed, but never got around to seeding it. Perhaps 100 paces away from the river, the road vanished from view, lost in the sea of blackness.

Now sufficiently warmed, Reith prepared to embark on the next leg of his journey. He took one last drink from the river and filled both of his jugs with water. And then he set out into the darkness of Dragonscar.

If Reith had not had the ancient road to follow, he would have soon become disoriented and lost. Though there were no trees and no visible clouds, a gray veil covered the land, dimming the sunlight as if it were twilight, even at high noon. Reith could not decide if he cast no shadow or if his shadow was cast to all sides. In the same way, when he didn't look up, the light seemed to come from everywhere and nowhere. In these moments of confusion, he looked up to the sun, reminded himself of its presence, its light, and its warmth. He needed that reminder frequently.

Dragonscar was the sort of place where nothing happened and time seemed to stand still. Onward Reith went. The road wound around and between hills, over plains, and down into small valleys where he supposed water once ran. It was a thirsty sort of place. It had the stale air of a drought, and he guessed that it never rained here. Reith found his throat was becoming parched more quickly than it had on the other side of the river.

He made his best progress in the afternoon. The sun was in front of him then, and it gave him something to aim for, a goal worth pursuing, a beacon of hope in the darkness.

Ever since he had left the river, he had seen neither water nor animal nor bird. The only sounds he had heard all day were the thumps of his shoes on the ground and the sound of his breath as he hiked. He had felt lonely on his journey before, nearly every day, but this level of loneliness made the previous loneliness feel like being in a house with a friend in another room. Not only was he alone from any and all human company, he was separated from anything living at all.

That night, he slept beside the road. It wouldn't do to call it camping as there was no fire to be lit as there was nothing to light on fire around. Reith had been afraid that the darkness of night in this place of shadows would be absolute. He was surprised to discover that the darkest part of the night was barely any darker than it had been in the daytime. This land seemed to lie in perpetual twilight. Rather than taking comfort in this, Reith was disturbed.

"The natural order of things is death and resurrection," Vereinen had told him on several occasions. It was one of Vereinen's favorite sayings. "Each day, the sun dies and rises again renewed. Each month, the moon diminishes to nothing and then comes back to life. Each year, the world dies with winter and awakes again in the spring. They say even our bodies will come back to life one day."

Reith didn't know if Vereinen had made it up or if he was quoting something. He made a mental note to ask the next time he saw him.

In this shadowy place, there was no resurrection, only death. And yet, above it all, the stars and the moon were still visible, reminders of all that was good in the world.

———

In the morning, though Reith had to look up at the sun to remind himself that it was indeed morning, he began his walk again. The monotony of each step and the blackened landscape lulled him into a waking slumber. On and on he went, deeper and deeper into Dragonscar. He was incredibly thirsty but barely touched any water.

There was nothing here fit for humans. No greenery, no water, no animals, no birds, and no insects. It was a dead place, and yet he walked, seeking Vereinen and Erador.

He imagined dragons. He pictured them swooping overhead and breathing fire, igniting trees which were not there anymore. Vereinen had shown him a sketch of a dragon in a book. To Reith, it had looked like a large snake with arms and legs and giant bat-like wings.

"And they can breathe fire?" Reith asked his master, curious about these legendary creatures.

"Oh yes, they could. In fact, the dragons of old left a scar on the earth on the coast of the Western Sea. They say the fires they breathed raged for a hundred years, sparing no living thing. To this day, Dragonscar is a dead place."

He tried to imagine what Dragonscar looked like before the dragons came. *It must have been a lush plain. They wouldn't have built Erador in a desert.* He tried to picture the blackened fields as green with grass or with crops, as the valleys flowing with rivers and streams. He had to fight the utter dullness of the land to keep the picture in his mind. It seemed that the land did not want life, not even in his head.

The road led him down into a small valley. At the floor of the valley, it curved to the right, to the north, and wound up the hill on the other side. Just then, he felt the wind pass by his face. He realized that he had felt no wind since the river. The breeze brought another surprise as well. On the air was a scent that reminded him of the blacksmith's shop in Coeden.

It took Reith a second to place the smell, but then it came to him. It was the smell of brine. Brage the blacksmith used brine for quenching hot metal in his shop. But as soon as he had identified the smell of brine, it was gone, as fleeting as the breeze that brought it to him.

Then the smell of Dragonscar rushed back into his nose. It was the smell of smoke and charcoal and it burned, making him cough. He wondered how he had not noticed it before. Perhaps as he traveled further into Dragonscar, he grew more used to it. The smell of brine had temporarily driven the smell of smoke from his nose, and its brief absence made its return more noteworthy.

Reith continued on, following the road, and near the top of the hill, he felt the breeze and smelled the brine all over again. Puzzled, he trekked to the top and stopped short at the sight before him. Without realizing it, he had walked the entire day and now the sun was low on the horizon in front of him. The light shone and reflected off of the waves. The sky was red, orange, yellow, purple, and blue, a dazzling array of light, each color reflected by the water, like light through a colored glass. The effect was spellbinding. The water stretched out further than the eye could see. Reith had never seen the ocean before, and now he was stunned at its majesty and greatness. Suddenly, it struck him how large the world really was and how small he was in comparison.

After several minutes of marveling at the sun and the sea, he realized then that he was on top of cliffs overlooking the sea, perhaps 100 feet in the air above the water. To his right, on top of the cliff lay the ruins of some great city. The stones were blackened by fire, but many of the walls remained. Some of the walls stretched dozens of feet skyward. Reith guessed that this city had once been twenty, thirty, or even fifty times larger than Coeden. There was no mistaking it; this was the ancient ruined city of Erador.

The ruined city did not keep his eyes for long before he noticed a different wonder. Even nearer to him, inland from the cliffs, there was a small hill topped with twelve trees. Each of the trees was a different variety. He recognized several fruit trees that had grown near Coeden. The other trees were foreign to him.

Reith walked toward this small hill and found that a small stream bubbled out from under a rock on top of the hill and flowed down the hill toward the cliff and off it into the ocean. Wherever the stream ran, green grass sprouted up beside it. The water was perfectly clear. Reith realized just how thirsty he really was. He dropped to his knees and plunged his face into the refreshing coolness, sipping the sweetest water he had ever tasted. The water took away all of the weariness from his journey and washed him clean with ease. Reith felt strong and new. He stood back up and surveyed this strange hill again.

The twelve trees were arranged in a perfect circle around the hill. He walked among them, placing his hand on each trunk as he passed. When he touched a tree, it seemed to vibrate and move from some unseen wind. From seemingly nowhere, an apple from the apple tree presented itself to him, as if the tree were offering it as a gift. He reached for it and plucked it, wordlessly giving thanks to the tree by his touch on its trunk. This apple was golden and reflected the multicolored sunset. It seemed a pity to eat such a perfect specimen, but just then his stomach rumbled. He hadn't eaten anything since that bird beside the river. Reith took a bite, and juice gushed from the fruit as if it had been full of cider. As the water had refreshed him, the fruit reenergized him, invigorated him, and fulfilled him. Like when he drank of the stream, he felt braver, stronger, newer, and somehow, purer. The thought didn't make much sense to him, but he knew it deep down in his bones to be true. The water and the apple had a cleansing effect on his body, mind, and soul.

Reith sat on the hill beside the stream overlooking the sea as the sun set beyond the horizon. As the darkness gathered, he felt the trees sway inward, toward him, as if they were sheltering him from the night. By the light of the stars and the moon, he laid down in the soft grass and slept. It was the most peaceful night of sleep he had had since he had left Coeden.

His dreams were of the most pleasant varieties, the kind where you wake up and try to remember but they slip away like water through your fingers and all you are left with is the feeling of peace, restfulness, and joy. The trees watched over him as if they were his protectors. If a tree could have feelings, these trees felt a kinship with this boy who had come to him.

All through the night, Reith slept. The curve of a smile was on his lips, and for the first time in weeks, he felt safe. He was safe.

Chapter Four

Reith awoke feeling more refreshed and rested than after any night's sleep in his life. He yawned and stretched. The soft grass tickled his neck and the smell from the trees was fragrant and sweet. He sat up and looked around.

There were the twelve fruit trees and the stream. Each piece of fruit glowed in the morning sunlight. The stream sparkled as if it were made of diamond. They looked out of place in the darkness of Dragonscar, an oasis of life in the middle of the graveyard. But as he kept staring, something shifted within him. Now it looked like the only things that belonged were the trees, the grass, the stream, and even him, and the rest of Dragonscar was the intrusion.

Vereinen might have said this was resurrection in action, but Reith didn't think that captured the scene before him. *It's not resurrection because the trees were never dead. This is something new. This is New. Newness itself sprung up from the ground. This is the earth winning the war over death.*

Reith sat there, basking in the glow of this new space.

His mind shifted to the trees and the stream to Vereinen. *Where is he?* He hadn't seen any sign of any other living person yet. *I bet Vereinen rode here on a horse, so he has probably been here for a few days. But is he still here? Did he even make it here?*

He took a drink from the stream, which raised him to full wakefulness in an instant. He refilled his water jugs as well for the day's searching of the city. The trees offered him some of their choicest fruit. He accepted gratefully, eating some now and saving the rest for later. This time, he tasted a fruit he had never seen in his life. This one was an orange ball with a tough skin. He peeled this away, exposing the juicy flesh beneath, which he eagerly devoured.

Then he followed the stream down to the cliff, which created a waterfall just to the south of the city. He decided that he would walk all the way around the city in a large semi-circle and arrive at the cliff at the other side before committing to the harder task of traveling through the ruined city which may be impassable at spots. A full loop would give him the opportunity to see if he could find any tracks left by Vereinen, as well.

Before this, though, Reith laid down on the grass and scooted forward until his face was over the cliff edge. He watched as the water from the stream tumbled down into the ocean below. It was a moment of pure wonder. There was something about gravity having its way with a flow of water. He enjoyed the view for several minutes before getting to his feet and beginning to walk around the city.

At the southern edge of the city, right on the cliff, were the remains of an old tower. The ruins were thirty feet tall and stood right on the edge of the cliff. The remnants of a rampart were at the top, a place for watchmen. It looked to Reith as if a wall had come off this tower to encircle the ancient city, but the wall had crumbled away, either from time or by dragon, he could not be sure. Here and there the wall stood tall, fifteen feet in the air. But these places were few and far between.

Through the holes in the wall, of which there were more than the wall itself, Reith could see rubble covered streets. Or at least he imagined these to be streets. In all of the debris, it was hard to see where the street ended and the buildings began. He walked on, following the course of the wall, looking for any sign of Vereinen either inside the city or outside.

Soon, he came upon another fortified tower. Like the other, this one was perhaps thirty feet tall but in worse shape, as its entire outside facing wall had collapsed. Inside, beneath the wreckage and rubble, Reith could make out a few stairs leading to the rampart.

Continuing on, he soon passed by a third watchtower. This one was much like the second one. Here, the wall was completely gone, as if someone had knocked it down. He imagined a dragon whipping its tail and flattening this section. In his mind's eye, it was a rather impressive sight. He was nearly halfway around his semi-circular journey of Erador. He could no longer see the ocean due to the city. He could just make out the hill and the grove of trees. These stood out as green pillars in the black landscape of Dragonscar, even from a distance.

Ahead of him he saw what he guessed to be the city gate. Looming above the buildings and wall stood a structure three times as tall as the other guard towers. As he approached, he saw that it was actually two towers, connected by a gigantic arch. Standing underneath the arch, he gazed at the main street that led to the heart of the city. It was much wider than any of the other streets he had seen. The rubble from the ruined buildings on either side of the street covered the whole of the road. He could see that it would be quite easy to traverse this road if he so chose. Turning around, he looked out from the city into the heart of Dragonscar. There was a road like the one he had walked on from the river which led straight into the wilderness. This road was wider than the road he had taken and more well preserved.

Reith stooped down to inspect this road. He saw his own footprints, fresh and clear in the dust coming from the south to where he stood. But there were other prints, too. They were not as fresh as his, but they could not have been more than a day or two old. Reith worried that these were the tracks of several men, and not just the one he was looking for. There were at least four sets, maybe more, but they were confused and jumbled together, as if the men had walked in two by two or one at a time. These footprints went into the city, but he saw none returning.

There were at least four people here recently, and chances are they're still here. Who are they, and why are they here? Where's Vereinen?

Now more than ever, Reith did not want to enter the city. Not yet, anyway. It was possible that these footprints had nothing to do with Vereinen. He hadn't ever considered the notion that he might meet someone else at Erador, let alone several other people. He did not want to meet them suddenly. He wanted to see them first and glean whatever information he could from them.

He continued along the outside of the city and each time there was a gap in the wall, he peered in, looking for any sign of life. He was disappointed. He walked along, passing two more watchtowers before finally arriving at the last one, which was built right on the cliff on the northern side of the city. This one was nearly identical to the first one with one significant difference. This tower had what looked to be a huge lantern on top. He imagined this to be a signal of sorts for ships in the night.

On the north side of the city was a small bay. There was a gentle hill leading down to the bay, and he saw in his mind's eye docks and ships of old. There was nothing now. Any dock either burned or rotted away, and any boat likely suffered the same fate.

Still, Reith imagined what Erador was like in its golden age, with ships coming from all corners of Terrasohnen and the islands around it bringing goods, people, and their stories to Erador.

Now that he had circled the whole city with no sign of Vereinen, unless he was part of the group of people who came in through the main gate, he had a decision to make. It was now late morning, and the sun was nearly directly overhead. He could re-circle the city and go back to the trees or he could enter the city and see what he could find. He walked back toward the main gate and debated.

Vereinen told me to meet him here. What if I beat him here? What if he never made it? How long am I to wait for him? He kept walking, frustrated by Vereinen's absence. *And who else is here? Anyone I meet here is more likely than not to be bad news. I don't want to come across them.*

As he approached the city gate, another little voice popped into his mind. "Coward," it said to him in a sneering manner.

"I am not a coward," he said through clenched teeth, trying to beat that voice away.

In the end, Reith did what he knew must be done. He followed the footprints into the city.

"After all," he said to himself, "one of those sets might belong to Vereinen."

But then another thought came to his mind. *What if one set did belong to Vereinen and the others came after him, following him?* The thought caused Reith to freeze in fear for his master and for himself.

At the city gate, he paused and gathered his nerve. He took a deep breath and pulled out an arrow and notched it, then slowly followed the footprints into the city.

The shells of houses and buildings lined both sides of the main street. Every once in a while, there was an empty space between two ruined buildings, and it took Reith a few minutes to realize that there had probably once been a wooden structure there, burned by the dragons or rotted away over the years. He guessed the former as many of the buildings had black scorch marks.

Windows and doorways looked like eyes gazing out at him. The notion was disconcerting, and he stayed in the middle of the road. About 100 paces into the city, two side streets merged with the main one. These streets curved, matching the contour of the outer wall. Whoever had made the footprints was apparently unconcerned with the side streets, as they continued straight on.

Reith's every step reverberated on the stone, echoing down the abandoned streets and off the dilapidated buildings, coming back to him like a strange drumbeat. He was worried he would not be able to quietly approach whoever had made these footprints when he found them. He passed another side street and then another, but the footprints kept going forward. With the curve of the side streets, he pictured the city from above as similar to half of a wagon wheel with concentric rings moving out from the center. The scorch marks were darker the closer he got to the center of the city, as if the dragons had been fiercest at its heart.

Ahead of him rose the largest ruin he had seen yet. It looked like some great tower had crumbled in place. The rubble still climbed higher than all of the other buildings near it. *This is the Citadel of Erador, or what's left of it.* He could see beyond the rubble to the ocean.

Reith remembered when Vereinen had told him about the Citadel, earlier this year back in Coeden.

"The Citadel of Coeden was the tallest tower ever built in Terrasohnen. It stretched hundreds of feet into the air, a monument to the humans, dwarves, and elves."

"Why did they build it?" Reith asked.

"Why does anyone do anything like that?" Vereinen replied. "Because they could. It did not serve a functional purpose. They built the city and the Citadel because they could. They were showing off to the world."

"What happened to it?"

"The dragons came from over the sea and laid waste to the city and the tower. What's left is a crumpled heap of rock where it once stood."

Reith now stared at the heap of rock which towered over the surrounding buildings. He tried to imagine how tall it had been before it had collapsed. He pictured a stone pinnacle in the sky, hundreds of feet up. Then his mind's eye conjured an image of a dragon blowing fire and swinging its tail at the tower.

In front of the remains of the Citadel, the ground opened up, as if the rock disappeared down a chasm. Reith was confused by this until he reached the edge and looked down upon giant steps cut into the rock, descending down to a flat space.

It's some sort of gathering place. It's an amphitheater, for speeches and plays.

Reith was just about to walk down into it when he heard something that froze his blood. *Voices.*

He darted behind a pillar and hurled himself to the ground. From beside the pillar, he peered down and saw five men walk out onto the stage from the wall behind it.

He couldn't see their faces as they looked away from him toward the Citadel. By the design of the amphitheater, he could hear exactly what they were saying as if he were standing near them.

"I told you we couldn't get in through there," one man said in a wheezy voice.

"Oh, shut up," a second voice, this one rough and harsh, replied. "There's no use going on about who said what."

The first retorted, "All I'm saying is—"

"Shut up, both of you," interrupted another, whom Reith recognized. The sound of that colorless, cold voice made the hairs stand up on the back of his neck. "I'm trying to think," the Gray Man said.

There was silence as the Gray Man thought and Reith lay there in horror. *The Gray Man, here? How is that possible? What is he doing here?*

"There has to be some way in," the Gray Man went on. "Everything I've read, everything I've studied, there's a way. He told me it was here."

Reith wondered who 'he' was.

"We could try going back up and having a nice look around," a fourth voice offered.

The Gray Man thought for a moment and finally said, "Alright, we'll go to the top and look for another way in."

The men began to move, and it took Reith a second to realize they were going to climb the steps. *They'll run right into me, and when they do, I'm dead.*

Reith stood, doing his best to remain behind the pillar and out of sight. He hunched over, and keeping the pillar behind him, rushed forward, toward the first building he'd spotted. This building was large, only a single story, and largely undamaged, other than the occasional scorch marks on the stone walls, though these were few and far between.

The door was gone, and Reith dashed inside and hurled himself sideways. He fell to the floor in a heap, surprisingly sweaty from the short amount of exertion. In the wall above him was an empty window, and he raised his head to spy on the men.

He had only just reached the building in time, as the men were now at the top of the steps. One of them looked his way, but it was not the Gray Man. The man stared at where Reith had hidden, looking for any sign of movement. After a few moments, he must have thought he imagined it and returned his gaze back towards his companions.

Reith could hear the men talking, but without the aid of the amphitheater, he couldn't make out what they were saying. He made himself as small as possible so he would not be seen and waited for them to move on. His mind began to race and his heart thumped loudly.

Why is the Gray Man here? What is he looking for? Where is Vereinen? Could he be the mysterious person the Gray Man mentioned?

The voices came in through the window, sounding like the buzzing of distant bees. After a minute or so, they grew fainter, so Reith carefully looked out to see. The men were walking along the edge of the amphitheater away from him. He breathed a sigh of relief and slumped down to the floor with his back against the wall. It was then that he noticed what sort of building in which he found himself.

Row upon row of high shelves filled the room, each covered in stone and clay jars and boxes. He stood up and went to the nearest of the shelves. With a nagging suspicion as to the identity of this strange building, he selected a clay jar and removed its top. Inside was a well-preserved scroll. He unrolled a few inches to see ancient parchment with words written in some unknown language.

At the edges of the scroll were small markings, elegant lines and shapes, which acted as an ornate border around the text.

Reith put this scroll back and placed the jar back on the shelf, then found a stone box next and removed the lid to reveal a leather-bound book. This book was also written in some unknown language. The leather was still fresh, even after all these years.

The Library of Erador.

Vereinen had told him briefly that the library of Erador was second only to the libraries of Galismoor, the human capital city, and Sardis, the elven capital city.

There was some magic about the place, something in the air that preserved these works from time and from the dragons. Reith began walking along the shelves, occasionally opening a box or jar that caught his eye. He found more well-preserved books and scrolls. In one clay box, on which was a table set for a king painted in bright colors, Reith found a book written in his tongue. He flipped through a few pages and discovered that it was an ancient book about cooking.

In the center of the room, sunlight poured inside from the ceiling. This was no cave in, however, this was by design. Beneath the hole in the roof was a squared in area surrounded by a short stone wall. Reith guessed that at one time, this hole was actually a pond of sorts, holding the rain water from above. So enamored was Reith with the Library of Erador that for a moment, he forgot all about Vereinen and the Gray Man.

He walked through the entire library, taking in the wonderful sights and smells of the old books. *I wonder how it is still preserved when the rest of the city looks so dead.*

On the opposite side from where he had come in, he found another door. He walked in and found himself overlooking a sunken courtyard. To his right, steps led down to the courtyard floor. Down below, he found more shelves under the staircase. These shelves were different. They were smaller and deeper, with slots that looked like they would hold individual scrolls. A desk of sorts was carved into the wall.

Reith pulled a few scrolls out to take a look at them, and they were largely like the ones he had found inside. One was different. This scroll was small, slightly longer than his index finger. He unrolled it and placed it on the desk. All told, the parchment was only four inches tall and about six inches wide.

The top left corner of the scroll was completely blank. Going from bottom left to upper right were what looked like stairs. Underneath this stair line, a grid system was drawn on the parchment. He took a few steps back and saw that it was a map of this system of shelves, probably for the librarian keeping track of the scrolls.

In some of the boxes were small symbols, letters, or numbers in some foreign language. He checked out a few of these and, sure enough, where there was a mark on the scroll, there was a scroll in the corresponding slot in the wall. He was fascinated by the working of this ancient library. He had never been to a library other than Vereinen's, and it was interesting to him to see how this one worked, or at least this small part of this library. He imagined what it must have been like a thousand years ago, with humans, elves, and dwarves perusing the shelves and reading and the librarians cataloging and shelving books and scrolls.

He was just about to roll up the scroll again when he noticed something different about one of the small squares. The square on the bottom left corner did not have a symbol in it. This one had three vertical lines. Instead of black ink like the rest of the scroll, these lines each had their own color: gold, silver, and copper.

Reith walked to the edge of the stairs and knelt to look at what was in this slot, reaching in and pulling out a long, shiny box. This box looked to be wood overlaid with gold, silver, and copper triangles, each alternating, coming together to form a pattern. The box was about five feet long, a foot wide, and three or four inches tall. On the side was a golden clasp, which he opened.

Reith was dazzled by the sunlight striking the metal inside. In the box sat a sword in a scabbard. Its hilt looked like it had been woven together from three different metals, just like the box. These three twisted together into a metallic braid. The cross guard was similarly woven together. A soft, leather grip covered part of the handle for ease of use. Diamonds adorned the hilt and the pommel. The scabbard was black leather with lines of the three metals inlaid upon the edges.

He lifted the sword out and held it in his hand. The grip was warm, as if someone had just set it down. It felt light, like it was part of his arm and not a foreign object. The strangest thing though was that it felt like it was vibrating in his hand, as if he had just clashed it against another warrior's blade.

Reith lifted it to his face and saw that the edge was sharp, as if it had just been sharpened and shined the day before. He slashed the air in front of him experimentally, and the sword hummed through the air. Strange as it seemed, he felt like he was meant to have this sword.

He sheathed the sword again and strapped the scabbard at his waist, with the sword on his left hip for easy pulling with his right hand. Even here it felt like it belonged, like it was part of him. He felt stronger and less afraid.

Reith closed the box and placed it back on the shelf.

It's a shame I can't keep it; it's so beautiful. If I ever can come back, I swear I will take the box with me.

He also rolled up the librarian's scroll and placed it back where it belonged as well. Then he climbed the steps and walked back through the library, determined to find out about Vereinen. *I wonder why the Gray Man is here. Maybe I can put an arrow in him.*

The thought made Reith smile.

Chapter Five

The sword swayed at Reith's side as he walked, giving him a feeling of strength and power, though he really had no idea how to wield a sword. For now, he would trust in his bow and knife.

Seeing no one in the deserted city, he scurried to the pillar he had hidden behind earlier, nearly bent double to make himself as small as possible. He paused to listen and heard no sign of the Gray Man or his companions. Judging the coast was clear, he walked as silently as he could around the top lip of the amphitheater, taking great care to step lightly so his footsteps would not resound on the rocks. He could clearly see the footprints of the men, and he followed them cautiously.

Presently, the tracks came to the top of a flight of steps leading down toward the Citadel. At the base was a gaping black hole in the wall. Here was an entrance to the Citadel.

What are they looking for here?

Reith tip-toed down the steps and took a moment to listen in the doorway. From far away, he heard the muffled voices of the men, but he could not make out anything they were saying.

The passage before him was dimly lit by light coming down from small holes and cracks in the roof. He was relieved because he had no torch nor any way to make one. He began to silently creep down the hall toward the voices.

The passage led straight toward the heart of the Citadel. After several dozen paces, the path came to an intersection of sorts. Three passages branched off from the one he was on. He listened to determine which passage the voices were coming from. The sounds echoed off the rocks and sounded like they were coming from all three at once. Thinking the voices most likely came from the center passage, Reith moved forward.

He had hardly gone a score of paces when the voices had all but died out. He retraced his steps and took the path to his right, which was left from his original course. A dozen paces confirmed that this indeed was the right path. The voices were louder now, and he could make out the occasional word, though individually they still made no sense.

He came at last to a wall. To the left and to the right, a dozen stairs went up to landings and turned at a right angle, leading back the way he had just come.

"Fool ... push ... door ... him ..." floated down from above. The sounds were stronger on the right, so he took this staircase. He knew he was getting close, so he took the stairs slowly, one every few seconds, to ensure near total silence. He reached the turn in the stairs and waited, listening. Now he could make out the voices.

"It won't budge," one of the men said, slightly out of breath.

"Push harder," came the unmistakable voice of the Gray Man. It gave Reith goosebumps.

"How do you know it's here?" another man asked. "And you still haven't told us what you're looking for."

"None of your business," the Gray Man hissed. "All you need to know is it is important for our cause. Now push!"

There was the sound of grunting and panting as the men set about pushing against whatever it was that the Gray Man wanted moved. After a few seconds, the sound of stone grinding on stone rumbled through the air, and the Gray Man cackled in triumph.

"One step closer to the key."

"What key?"

"I said never you mind," the Gray Man said harshly, evidently frustrated with himself that he had let it slip. "Let's go in."

The men's footsteps grew fainter as they entered the room. Reith peered around the corner and saw no trace of them, though he did see the doorway they had gone through. Quietly, he ascended the stairs, ears straining to hear.

"What's this key look like?" one of the men asked.

The Gray Man paused, and Reith realized he was torn between the desire for secrecy and the desire for finding this key he was so intent on finding.

What is this key that he won't even trust his henchmen with it?

Finally the Gray Man spoke again. "It's said to be one of the treasures of Terrasohnen. His instructions said it might not even look like a key."

"Whose instructions?" the wheezy voiced man asked.

"That's none of your business," the Gray Man spat. Reith could feel the danger in his voice.

"Then how will you know if you find it?" the wheezy voiced man asked.

"I was getting there," the Gray Man hissed. Then there was a thud, and one of the men yelped.

"Whatcha throw that at me for?" the wheezy voiced man said with a whine.

"That'll teach you for interrupting me," the Gray Man snapped. "Now, as I was saying, it might not look like a key. But it will unmistakably match this."

There was a pause before another said, "What, it looks like your bloody ring?"

Next came another thud and yelp.

"It will be like my ring, you idiot!" the Gray Man bellowed. "Do you see it? Do you see what's on it?"

"Uh, metal?" one of the men offered.

There was a third thud and yelp.

"Of course it's metal, you metal for brains son of stupidity itself! Three metals. Gold. Silver. Copper. This key will unlock a source of ancient power. Just the power I need to make myself emperor. So look for something made of those three things."

The men set to work, and Reith heard thuds and scrapes as the men moved around the room looking for the key. He looked down at his newly found sword's hilt, still hanging from his left hip. The gold, silver, and copper shone and danced in the light. They were clearly looking for his sword, or something just like it, so escaping now while they were distracted probably would be best. But at the same time, he wanted to know more.

Is it my sword? What will it unlock? What sort of ancient power? Who sent the Gray Man here to look for it?

"Hey, I think I found it!" one of the men said excitedly.

"Let me see," the Gray Man ordered.

Reith heard footsteps and then silence.

"In all my days," the Gray Man began slowly and

softly, "I have never seen anything like this. This is the most wonderfully ordinary piece of dung, you idiot!" His voice rose to a shout. "I said gold, silver, and copper, did I not?" His voice echoed along the stone passages, and the whole Citadel seemed to shake with his fury.

"And what is this cup made out of?"

There was silence as the man, it seemed, was too afraid to answer the question.

"This cup is made out of *bronze*! By the dragons, are you really that stupid?" the Gray Man continued on his rant. "Are you really such an imbecile that you can't tell the difference between something made of one metal and something made of *three*?"

The was a clang as the Gray Man threw something.

"Get back to work, you stupid, stupid ..." His voice trailed away into muttering that Reith could not hear. There were footsteps and more sounds of thuds and scrapes as the men began their hunting again.

After several minutes, the Gray Man spoke again.

"Come on, let's try another room." Footsteps grew closer to Reith as the men exited the room. He tensed, ready to flee if the men came toward the stairs. "That dang chronicler couldn't have given me more to go off of?"

Reith's heart raced at the mention of a chronicler.

That has to be Vereinen, right? Did they find him? Did he know about the sword? Where is he now?

"Let's try this next room,' the Gray Man said after a few moments of silence. "We can't stay here forever. We have to go back and finish off the remnant of Suthrond. Let's look today and tomorrow, and the next day. If we find the key, great. If not, we rejoin our host at the river and march on the refugees from Suthrond. Those fools will feel our fury."

The footsteps receded down the hall and Reith heard the sound of a door being forced open. They must have been further away now as their voices were swallowed by their new room.

This news about Suthrond was bad tidings indeed. Suthrond was a town similar to Coeden, but several days journey east of Coeden. Occasionally, merchants from Suthrond came to Coeden with goods to sell.

A remnant of Suthrond means that the Gray Man attacked them too. And he wants to finish them off, but he came here first. This sword must be of infinite value. It means I am in big trouble if he finds me.

He decided that his best course of action was to leave the city and retreat to the trees. There was a sense of peace and safety there, things he desperately needed with the Gray Man so near at hand.

Reith slowly walked back the way he came and presently found himself in the open again. The sea breeze blew salty air into his face and refreshed him. He could hear the distant crash of waves at the base of the cliff.

He took the main road, past the library, out of the city. He tried to walk along the edge of the buildings, away from the center of the road where his own footprints had mingled with the footprints of the Gray Man and his men. He didn't think that the Gray Man would notice his tracks, but he wanted to be careful just in case.

At the city gate, he paused to look back. There was no sign of the Gray Man. Ahead of him, the ancient road led away from the cliffs and into the heart of Dragonscar. *At the end of this road, by the river, are the rest of the Gray Man's men.*

In the distance, he could just make out the grove of trees, so he trudged towards them. As he approached, the afternoon sun sparkled on the fruit and the stream. A peach seemed to present itself to him out of nowhere, the brightest orange peach he had ever seen. He plucked it and ate while sitting by the stream. As he sat and ate, he thought.

Where is Vereinen? I don't think he came here at all. Where did he go? It didn't sound like the Gray Man captured him.

He drank some water from the stream, shocked once again by its freshness. As he drank, he imagined the water bursting into being just before it gushed out on this hill.

Reith thought about the people of Suthrond, and the Gray Man's vengeance upon them. *They didn't deserve to be attacked, just like Coeden. But some of them escaped. For now.*

The trees rustled in the breeze, but to Reith, it seemed like they were reacting to his thoughts. Not for the first time, though; he had the feeling that the trees could see and hear him and even connect with his thoughts. So he did what some might call crazy.

"What should I do?" he asked aloud. The trees stopped rustling and stood still, as if captured in a painting. Their attention focused on him, he could tell.

He slowly rose, dropping the peach pit on the ground, and instinctively held the hilt of his sword, which again felt warm, as if someone had just set it down. Then it felt as if he was not alone in his mind. Strange beings slowly wiggled their way in. They felt earthy and foreign. They did not care for the days but for the seasons. They were longer than he was, longer in regard to time, with long memories and long foresight, and this is what felt strange to his mind. They were not unfriendly; they were simply there. Then a singular voice, deep and slow, came to his head.

"Save them," it said, each word long and drawn out, lasting much longer than ordinary speech. "Serve them. Fight for them. Then find me."

The voice faded, and the other consciousnesses drifted away as a leaf on the wind. Reith staggered and fell to one knee. He was sure that the trees had invaded his mind. It was not an attack, though. *No, it was the roots of thought digging through soil to find water. Or that's how a tree would say it. And now I'm thinking about what trees think. But that voice was not the voice of a tree. That voice was older still than the trees, and longer. It had a memory from the dawn of time and it could see into the future. Who was it?*

"Save them. Serve them. Fight for them. Then find me," he repeated. Reith wanted to remember. He had no doubt as to the identity of 'them.' It had to be the surviving people from Suthrond.

But who is the voice? And how will I find them?

Still, he knew what he must do for the moment. The trees seemed to understand and presented him with their finest fruits. Of these, he filled his bag with the various types, fruits that were shades of red, orange, yellow, and green. He refilled his water jugs in the stream and took a long drink. Any weariness in him fell away as a garment, and he felt he could run through Dragonscar to the river.

He rotated for one last look around at this paradise in the midst of despair. The trees seemed to all be turned toward him. Beside the stream, the earth seemed to shift, and a small shoot grew up from the dirt. It rose to a height of two feet, then branches sprouted from its end. It was now a small tree, maybe three feet in height. From the branches, pink flowers blossomed.

Reith looked on in wonder at the strange sight. The flowers released a sweet fragrance into the air. Soon, the flowers disappeared, and in their places were small, round, green balls. These grew in size as the tree grew. Then the green changed to a glorious orange and red, like a sunset.

Before him stood a small peach tree, which had sprouted to bear fruit within the span of minutes.

He stepped forward and gently squeezed a few of the peaches. They were perfectly ripe. As the other trees had before, this tree seemed to present him with a particularly juicy peach, which he gladly accepted.

This is where I dropped the peach pit just minutes ago, he thought. *What is this place?*

The oasis in the midst of the black scar on the land seemed to radiate the emotion of joy toward him, and he felt it swell up in him, from his toes to his throat, as if he had plunged into a pool of joy. The joy soon covered his head, and he felt slightly dizzy, but in a good way, like he had felt when Vereinen had let him try a glass of wine several months before. It was a good feeling.

With the joy engulfing him, he turned and left Erador behind.

He jogged down the road, back toward the river. As he went, he planned his next few days. The Gray Man would not find the key he was looking for, as Reith was pretty sure that it was his sword. He would search today and then next two before going back to his men empty-handed. This gave Reith a few days advantage.

But Suthrond is further from here than Coeden. Even with a few days head start, I can't possibly beat them there. They have horses.

He kept jogging, impressed with how the miles seemed to slide past. *There's something about that water that strengthens and renews,* he thought.

Even with this fresh speed, he was no match for the Gray Man's horses. He contemplated what to do as he ran. He couldn't race horses the many miles to Suthrond. The horses seemed an insurmountable obstacle.

As Reith ran through Dragonscar, he found that the

dreariness of the place had no effect on him this time. While on the way in it had felt like a waking dream, he remained on high alert with a clear mind. His eyes took in the ruin and deadness, but it did not consume him. The fruit and the water sustained him and protected him from union with the despair around him.

Something had changed for him. Indeed, something had changed for all of Terrasohnen. From dead land, streams flowed. From dead earth, fruit ripened on the tree. Trees spoke. Lost swords were found. That which was old is made new.

As he ran, he found himself spontaneously singing.

What once was dead now bursts with life
Parched land with streams do flow
And the trees speak long and slow

What once was lost now can be found
All that is broken is proven untrue
And all that is old is now turning new

What once was gone now comes again
Where hope had failed we see the light
And an end to the endless night

Still, it was a surprise to see the river around a bend. It had taken Reith nearly two days to traverse Dragonscar the other day. Now he had done it in a single afternoon. He realized now that he had probably walked incredibly slowly

through desolate wasteland of Dragonscar on his way to
Erador, weighed down as he was by the darkness and
despair around him. Now, though, the water and the fruit
kept him sharp, fresh, and new. He forded the river with
little difficulty and made camp by the old abandoned
fortress again. He ate an apple and threw the core out onto
the plain.

As the sun rose over the horizon, the light pressed against
Reith's eyelids, but he kept them closed, content to lie
there on the grass. His other senses were attuned to the
world around him. The river rushed by, and he heard each
splash against the rocks. The air smelled sweet, and it
reminded him of the grassy hill with the fruit trees in
Dragonscar.

He opened his eyes and looked around. There, out on
the plain where he had thrown the apple core the night
before, stood a small shoot of a tree, about two feet high. It
had no fruit, but from its blossoms, Reith saw that it was an
apple tree.

That fruit is magic, he thought. *It will grow quickly anywhere.
But we are further from the water and the magic of that grove of trees,
so it doesn't grow nearly as fast.*

As he set about making his breakfast, he gained clarity
about his next step. Instead of continuing east, he decided
to turn north and follow the old road. *I will go to the Gray
Man's camp. If I can get one of their horses and maybe spook the rest
and get them running, I might beat them to the Suthrond survivors.*

After a breakfast of fruit, this time trying one that he
did not recognize, he dug a small hole near the apple tree
and planted the seeds. This fruit was unknown to him. It
did not grow near Coeden, so he had no idea what it was

called. He covered the seeds with earth and stood up, brushing his hands.

"There," he said. "Someone will eat from these two trees in the future."

He followed the river on the ancient road. Very quickly, the river narrowed and became impassable. The bank grew steeper, so that it would have been nearly impossible to reach the river safely. *It must widen out again further north into another ford,* he thought.

At each hill, Reith slowed down, as he wasn't sure what was on the other side. The last thing he wanted was to announce himself to the Gray Man's men by standing on top of a hill overlooking their camp.

As the morning wore on, a cold wind from the north sprang up, and Reith pulled his extra shirt on to shield him from the dropping temperature. Dark clouds loomed, and Reith guessed it would rain soon. He was not wrong, as great drops of rain began to fall, a few at first, but then multiplying into a heavy shower. Within minutes, he was soaked through. Nonetheless, he pressed on, albeit with head down and slow steps.

With the rain still pouring, he came to the top of a hill and saw below him about a hundred tents. Many horses were tied to the tent stakes. Next to the camp, the river was flat and wide. It was the other ford. Reith laid down on his belly to spy on the camp below. He saw no men, and he guessed they were all in their tents trying to stay warm and dry. Nearly all of the horses were unsaddled, except for three on the north side of the camp.

I bet those horses were out with scouts and they came back when the rain started. That's cruel, making them stand out in the rain all saddled up. But it's good for me. A plan formed in his mind.

Reith jogged back down the hill, out of sight from the camp. He turned and kept jogging out onto the plain. He made a large loop and came toward the camp from the north, being careful to avoid making noise. With the men all in their tents because of the rain, the only thing that could give him away would be a loud 'neigh' from one of the horses.

As he got closer, Reith took a better look at the three saddled horses. One was black, another was chestnut, and the last one was a smaller white mare. All were saddled and ready, but of the three, only the mare seemed to not mind him. The black and the chestnut stamped their feet in the mud and shied away from him.

There was a cough in a nearby tent, and Reith froze. His heart pounded in his chest, and adrenaline surged, preparing him for fight or flight. Mercifully, no one came outside to see what he was doing.

Reith took an apple from his bag and held it out in front of him. He slowly began to walk toward the mare. She eyed the apple with interest and took a step toward him too. The black and the chestnut horses looked at the apple as well, but they did not step any closer. Slowly he inched toward the horses, making no noise. His ears were straining to hear any sound of movement from the tents, but the rain outside drowned out any. At last he was close enough that he could reach out and touch her if he had wanted, but he held firm, holding out the apple to her.

She sniffed it, and her nostrils flared. But then she stretched out a bit further, taking the apple in her teeth and munching happily. Reith stroked her mane and stepped next to her. The rope that tied her to the tent peg had a thick knot, so he pulled his knife and slashed it. Then he led the horse away, patting her neck as they walked. His heart was pounding, but he knew he had to stay calm to keep the horse calm.

Reith did not try to mount her, not yet. He wanted to

be well away from the camp so he could avoid making any noise. The rain continued to fall gently, and for once, he was glad of it. He made his way out into the plain, and then pulled on the horse and circled back to the south. She responded well to his touch. They rounded the hill and finally were out of sight from the camp. Reith pulled out another apple and gave it to the horse.

"Here you go," he said, patting her side as she ate. "Good horsey, good girl. I bet you love that apple, don't you?"

The horse let out a soft whinny, and Reith took that to be an affirmative response.

"Now, what to call you?" he wondered aloud, thinking of a name for the horse. He worked at the knot on the piece of rope he had cut as he thought. "I can't ride you off without giving you a name. It would be the height of discourtesy."

While his mind raced, the knot he was working on came apart, and he placed the piece of rope in his bag.

"Well, you kind of look like the moon. Moonlight?" The horse merely stood there, which he took as a bad sign on the future of the name 'Moonlight'. The rain lessened slightly. "Okay, not Moonlight. Starlight then?"

The horse again did not respond.

"Uh, Pearl? Poppy? Dang it, I'm stuck on P names. How about Whitejoy? Or Lady?"

The horse stood as stoically as ever.

"Let's see, what else is white? Snow? Lily? How about Aspen? Aspens are white."

At Aspen, the horse nuzzled his hand. Just then the rain stopped.

"Alright, Aspen it is. Here's another apple, and then we had better leave. Would you let me ride you?"

Aspen whinnied, and he clambered up. Then she grunted at his inexperienced mounting.

"Don't worry, I'll get better." Reith sat tall and proud in the saddle before hearing a shout from the camp.

"Uh oh, Aspen. They noticed you're gone. We have to go!"

And with that, the horse and rider cantered off along the edge of the river.

Chapter Six

Wind whipped through Reith's hair. Aspen was making good progress, and the land was flying underneath them. They stayed next to the old road, going along on the soft turf beside it. Occasionally, Reith looked back to see if there was any sort of pursuit. So far, there was none.

He assumed that the men would deduce someone had cut the rope and made off with the horse rather than the horse simply escaping on its own. *But if these men are anything like the ones I overheard in Erador, they might not be smart enough to figure it out,* he thought with a grin. At the very least, he knew the whole company would not come and seek him because their instructions had been to wait for the Gray Man to return. *Still, they might send one or two rangers out to look. And there is a good chance we left tracks.*

He pulled up on the reins and brought Aspen to a walk. He guided her to the path, where they would not leave any more tracks. "We can walk on the path for a bit, so they can't track us," he told her, patting her neck. She gave a soft neigh, appreciative of the rest.

They continued on, and in a short while, he saw the old fortress below them beside the ford. To his delight, the apple tree was taller than he had left it, and several bright red apples were visible on it, even from a distance. Aspen noticed these too.

"Alright, have at them," he said, and she pranced over to the apple tree. Reith plucked one of the apples, and Aspen began munching on the rest. The other tree had already begun to grow as well, already a foot tall, with the faintest hint of blossoms. After they had eaten the apples, Reith planted his core beside the other tree. Then he led Aspen down to the water to drink. As she drank, he refilled his empty water jug. One of them, the one he had found at the old fortress, was still full of the water from the stream by Erador. *I don't know what magic is in that water, but I think it would be helpful to save it as much as possible.*

"Alright girl, take a good long drink. We have to make it to the forest's edge by nightfall." Aspen raised her head and water dripped down her face. He mounted her and pointed her away from the river. "Let's walk to the edge of the road, and then we can gallop. How does that sound?" Aspen eagerly shook her head and began walking forward. As they continued on, he looked north. Still no sign of anyone.

Once we're on the grass, they will have a harder time finding our trail, especially because they should have no idea where we left the road.

"Okay, Aspen, let's go." Aspen jumped forward into a gallop, and Reith held on for dear life. The ground flew beneath them, and Aspen's hooves seemed to barely touch the ground. Reith bent low over her neck and urged her on. He imagined that if anyone could see them now, they would look like a blur shooting over the grass.

The same feeling of joy that had overwhelmed him at Erador came over him again. He felt free. The Gray Man was far behind him, and he was going to save the people of Suthrond.

After the hard gallop, Aspen slowed to a trot and then a walk. Reith swung down from the saddle to walk beside her, easing her burden. For several minutes they walked, horse and boy, with his hand on the pommel of her saddle.

They alternated between a trot and a walk several times, and with each walk, Reith dismounted and walked beside Aspen. They made good progress, much faster than if Reith had been walking by himself. The air was cool but not cold, thanks to the day's rain shower.

As the sun set behind them, the trees of the forest came into view on the eastern horizon. "Almost there, Aspen," he said. "Then we can rest for the night."

With the end in sight, they rode a little faster and longer on this leg of the journey. About a hundred paces from the edge of the woods, Reith dismounted and walked Aspen onward. "Let's go in a few hundred paces," he said. "Then we can light a fire and no one from outside the wood would see it."

They found a clearing near a small pond. There Reith dropped his bag and set about removing Aspen's saddle. He had never saddled nor unsaddled a horse before, the task usually being reserved for others. Still, he looked at where the straps came together and determined that getting it off would be easy. "It's getting it back on you in the morning that will be tricky."

As he unbuckled it, he tried to mentally catalog each and every step in the process so he could put it back on in the morning.

"Don't walk off now, okay?" Reith said as he undid the

last buckle. Aspen grunted, but deep down, Reith knew she was loyal and would stay near him. When she was finally free, Aspen walked to the pond and drank deeply. Reith set about making a fire in the gathering twilight. When the fire was going, he tossed a pear to Aspen, who happily gobbled it down before grazing. He chose for himself one of the orange fruits with the skin that needed to be peeled. He happily munched it as the fire glowed red, orange, and yellow in the clearing. When he had finished eating the fruit, he had several seeds in hand, which he planted in the ground around the clearing.

At sunrise, Reith awoke to find Aspen grazing a little ways off. There were several new shoots coming out of the earth, one for each seed he had planted the night before. He shook his head in amazement at the power of those fruit trees.

"Pretty soon all of Terrasohnen will be bursting with new life from that grove of trees at Erador," he said to himself.

He picked up Aspen's saddle, and for a minute his mind's catalogue from the night before completely disappeared. He stared at it with ever worsening dread, afraid he would be unable to saddle Aspen again. But then he saw a particular strap and it brought everything back to mind. Aspen patiently waited while he circled her and buckled and tightened all of the straps. In a surprisingly short time, she was ready to go. They took a last drink from the stream and set off toward the sun.

Where they could, they stuck to game trails. On these, Aspen could trot with little difficulty. When the trees grew too close together or came down too low for Reith to ride, he dismounted and walked in front, leading her on.

Reith guessed that they were able to cover about twice or thrice as much ground per day as he had all by himself.

"We'll be near Coeden in three or four days, and then Suthrond a day or two after that," he told Aspen.

That night by firelight, he inspected Vereinen's maps again. Suthrond was east of Coeden, and a road went from the north side of Coeden nearly straight to it. It was more of a trail than a road, as it was unpaved. Someone had cleared the trees and brush and traffic over the years had left the ground hard and without grass. Reith aimed to hit the main road, the one that went from Coeden to Palander, and then ride down to Coeden and take the road to Suthrond.

Still, he was weary of the travel. He had been on the road for weeks now and hadn't slept in an actual bed since the night before Coeden was razed. The ground had been his mattress and his arms had been his pillow. *Maybe I can spend a night at Vereinen's house and sleep in my own bed.* The thought warmed him, and he eagerly looked forward to it.

On the third day after entering the forest, Reith and Aspen came across the stream he had traveled beside so many days before. They turned to follow it northeast. Reith guessed that if it continued in this trajectory, it would intersect the road some miles north of Coeden. Plus, following it gave them a ready supply of running water, which he and Aspen greatly appreciated.

Around noon the next day, they found themselves going uphill. They stayed beside the stream, but the bank was significantly higher than before. In the distance, Reith could see a stone bridge spanning the stream.

"We have found the road, Aspen!" he said excitedly. He

led her forward, up the hill to the end of the bridge. He
cautiously looked both ways, making sure they were alone
before guiding Aspen onto the road.

Riding on the road was easygoing, and Aspen made
great speed. Reith was eager to arrive and sleep in his own
bed. Presently, Reith began to see the telltale signs of being
close to home, but before Coeden came into view, its odor
came first. The first smell was the smoke. The acrid aroma
overwhelmed and overpowered everything around,
hanging in the air like a fog. Reith could feel Aspen's
unease beneath him. He took a sip of the water from the
Spring of Erador and dripped some into Aspen's mouth as
well.

The next odor was the rancid smell of rotting meat.
Aspen stopped dead in her tracks and Reith retched, barely
holding down the food and water he'd had that day. Aspen
would go no further.

"Wait here, girl," he said, hopping down from the
saddle and rubbing her nose. He loosely tied the reins to a
tree branch and continued on alone. Then he buried his
nose in his arm and walked slowly into the town.

Except there was no town. All that remained were the
blackened and charred remains. Reith could discern no
standing structure, and it was only from his keen
knowledge from growing up there that allowed him to even
visualize where things had been.

It was clear that the Gray Man and his men had
finished the job before they left. Every building was
torched, and nothing was left standing. The destruction
was complete. There was nothing worth salvaging, no
wood from a house of structure that could be reclaimed to
fill a similar purpose again.

The smell of rotting meat grew stronger with every
step he took, even with his face buried in his arm. It came

from the remains of the townspeople, still heaped where they had been the day he had found them. He could go no closer than fifty feet, for the smell overwhelmed and overpowered him. Even from this distance, he could see no recognizable face. Where there had been flesh, bone could be seen poking out. Heads contained empty holes where eyes had been. There were crows and vultures about, and they paid him no mind. They were feasting.

Tears welled up in Reith's eyes, and he turned from the sight and the stench. *Even if I could stand the smell, it would take days to bury these bodies,* he thought dejectedly.

He walked away from the horror and went toward Vereinen's house, hopeful of respite. He gasped as he approached. The house was completely gone, and all that remained was a black mass on the ground. Ash and coals littered the clearing where the house had been. The Gray Man had found it after Reith had left and burned it along with all the rest of the town. There was nothing recognizable in the wreckage, no sign of the life that Reith and Vereinen had lived. The hope of a comfortable bed died in him, and he felt more weary and defeated than ever.

The emotion overwhelmed him, and tears came to his eyes, flowing freely down his face. He fell to his knees, despairing of ever having the strength to move on. As his well ran dry, he heard the sound of hooves and soon, Aspen came into view. She nuzzled his shoulder with her nose. He hugged her tight, holding onto her mane, and his tears flowed onto her.

Using Aspen for support, he surveyed the wreckage before him. Between the wood and the paper, Reith supposed that the house had burned quickly. *I wonder if the Gray Man looked around and took anything?*

There was nothing left of Coeden. The place Reith

was born, the place he was raised, that place was gone now, lost forever to death and destruction. *The forest will reclaim this land and in a hundred years, no one will know that Coeden was ever here at all.*

Aspen began tugging at him. She was ready to leave this place of death. He slowly pulled himself up into the saddle and directed her toward the road to Suthrond. With each step, he felt like he was leaving part of himself behind. He had not really gotten to say goodbye the first time. He had been forced to run, thinking of nothing other than reaching safety. Still, in the back of his mind in the time since then, he had held onto the slightest hope that Vereinen's house had remained untouched and that he and the chronicler could make their home there again someday and rebuild the town. Now, that dream was as dead as the people of Coeden.

What evil drives a man to commit such atrocities?

He prodded Aspen into a gallop, and off they went, the two of them fleeing from the wreckage of his past life, hurtling toward something new.

The trees were budding, and branches hung low over the road, forcing Reith to duck several times. One caught him square in the face, drawing blood and leaving scratches on his cheeks and forehead. He wiped blood onto his hand, flinching at the sting pulsing beneath his skin. And still, they galloped on.

Aspen needed rest, so Reith brought her to a stop and hopped off her back. Tall grass pressed at the road from both sides, and the trees hung down over them. The leaves were beginning to bud, and the spring air here held no memory of smoke. Beside the road, purple wildflowers grew in abundance, spreading their flowery scent and punctuating the green landscape with bursts of color.

Reith selected a pear from his pack. It was large, nearly

twice as big as his fist. With each bite, he found the sorrow being driven from him, replaced by the contentment good food brought. The tears dried from his eyes. He planted the pear seeds beside the road among the wildflowers.

"May you nourish the weary, give strength to the burdened, and respite for the restless," he said as he folded the dirt over the small hole he had made. Aspen finished grazing, and the two of them walked for a while, as the trees were too low overhead to ride.

Before long, the path began to climb. It was a slow and gentle climb, yet after many steps, his legs felt heavy. He rested one arm on Aspen's neck and looked ahead to see the top of the hill and blue sky beyond it.

When they reached the top, Reith gazed below, seeing the land stretch out like a scroll unrolled. A range of hills fanned out to the north and south. The forest continued to the east, but in the distance, the trees became less numerous. The sun reflected on the world as on water.

He turned and looked back west. He thought he could just make out the black shadow in the land where Coeden was, but he was not sure. Turning back east, he saw that the road went down before them and turned first to the north and then back to the south, winding through the hills like a snake. The setting sun behind them cast their shadows down into the valley.

He mounted Aspen, and she carefully made her way down the slope of the hill at a walk. When the road flattened out, he urged her to a trot, and they made good progress all the rest of the day. Reith attempted to mentally prepare himself for another night of sleep on the ground, but the preparations did no good. The disappointment was like a tangible thing, hovering over him like a cloud.

I shouldn't have gotten my hopes up.

The next morning, Reith awoke to an unfortunate spring rainstorm. He was soon soaked, cold, and miserable. His fire had gone out during the night. Aspen's saddle was soggy and heavy. His face was sore where he had been cut by the tree, and weariness coursed through his veins. He and Aspen hunkered down, hoping that the rain would soon pass.

Each raindrop on his face felt like a dagger of despair, piercing him and surrounding him in misery. By midmorning, there was no hint of the rain stopping, so he gritted his teeth, saddled Aspen, and the two of them began the day's slow, sloshy journey.

They walked more than anything, and even the walking was slow. The dirt from the path mixed with rainwater to make squelchy mud that sucked Reith's shoes down with each step. It was twice as hard as normal to walk, even for Aspen, who kept her head bowed beneath the pelting rain. The day dragged on, and the scenery rarely changed. All they could see was the muddy path at their feet and trees to either side of the path.

Around midnight, the storm finally stopped, and Reith was able to mercifully fall asleep in a dry spot under trees, just off the path. The following day, he awoke cold and damp, and his neck ached from the head-bowed trudging of the previous day's walk. All he wanted to do was collapse into a real bed with actual pillows and sleep for a week. He reluctantly got to his feet and readied himself for the day.

The road was still muddy, and rain had been replaced by humidity; it was rather warm for a spring day. Reith wiped sweat from his brows, frowning at the heat. Aspen seemed about as miserable as he felt. She hung her head, and each step seemed to cause her a great effort.

They camped and Reith managed to light a fire with brush kept dry under a thick grove of trees. That evening, the bugs came out. Reith spent half the night swatting unseen biting insects away from him and barely slept. In the morning, itchy red welts were all over his body. He could go no more than a few seconds without having to itch one appendage or another.

With each step, the anger and the bitterness grew in him. They were not directed at any one thing. Instead, they were directed at everything. *This stinks. By the dragons, I have never been more miserable in my entire life. In all of Terrasohnen, I must be the most miserable creature alive.*

In all of his misery, he forgot the errand upon which he had set out. Gone from his mind were the words spoken to him in Erador. Gone were thoughts of the people of Suthrond and their safety. Gone was any remembrance of the Gray Man. All that was left was the trudge, the bugs, the heat, the rain, and the misery.

"I wish I was home," he said aloud.

And yet home was gone, lost forever in smoke and death. There was no home. There was nowhere to return, nowhere to belong. Each marker of his identity had been swept away by the tide of events out of his control. He was no longer from Coeden, as Coeden was no more. He no longer was a chronicler's apprentice, for the chronicler was absent and silent. Everything he had been was now stripped away so that all that remained was himself.

But who am I?

The question brought to mind another one of Vereinen's lessons.

"Why are you a chronicler?" Reith had asked one day

while copying down some facts about trade routes or taxes or something like that.

"That is an interesting question," Vereinen said, looking up from his work. He set his pen down and brought his fingers together in front of his mouth. "Do you want the short answer or the chronicler's answer?"

He chuckled at his own joke, and Reith groaned.

"Very well, the chronicler's answer it is. It all starts at the very dawn of time itself," he began.

"Oh, brother," Reith retorted as he rolled his eyes.

"Oh, alright, maybe not that far back," Vereinen said as he smiled at him. "It all started with my questions. I see much of myself in you, young Reith. I questioned everything. Why do the seasons change? Why is Galismoor situated where it is? Why is Galismoor the capital city? Why are we here? Who am I? All of these questions were ones I asked, and more. I searched for the answers, and you know what I found?"

"Answers?" Reith asked, rolling his eyes.

"Stories," Vereinen said, ignoring Reith's sarcasm. "I found stories. The ancients had a myth about the death and resurrection of the earth each year, which brings on the seasons. Galismoor is where it is because old Queen Mallifar desired a city on the inland sea to vacation in, and soon everyone in her court preferred the vacation city to the old capital city at Dunbar.

"I found stories and I found myself in the stories. Each morning, we awake refreshed and ready for the day, by noon we are at our peak, and through the afternoon we decline until we fall into the daily winter of sleep, only to wake up in spring each morning. I imagined myself in the court of Queen Mallifar quite preferring the vacation city to the dreary, everyday city. It is the story of our past that informs the character of ourselves in the present, and our character today shapes who we are tomorrow. That is why I am a chronicler. And I hope that one day you find yourself in these old stories."

"You think I will?"

"Oh, I don't doubt it. You and I are a lot alike. You will find yourself in the silly stories of vacation cities. You shall find yourself in the tales of valor and great deeds. Your life is but one chapter in this great story. All that is left is determining what sort of character you will be."

———

Back in the present, while riding Aspen, he wondered, *What character will I be?*

He thought back on all that had happened these past few weeks. The hunting trip. The smoke. The dead bodies. The Gray Man. The hunt for Vereinen in Erador. The grove of trees and the stream. The sword. The Gray Man again. Finding Aspen. The trek to Coeden and now to Suthrond.

The path Reith was on had taken him to the ocean and back again, first from danger, into danger, and deeper into danger. His future was bleak and murky at best. And yet he could do nothing but go on. Resolve rose within him, and with renewed intensity, he focused on his task at hand: rescuing the refugees of Suthrond from the wrath of the Gray Man.

"You know, Aspen, in all of Vereinen's old stories, it is fairly clear who are the good guys and who are the bad guys. I think we have found ourselves in one of those stories. We're the good guys."

Aspen gave a loud neigh.

"That's the spirit, Aspen," he said, rubbing her head between her ears. "Now, let's gallop." The horse obeyed, and boy and horse flew down the road, as the great heroes of old would have done.

The forest opened up into farmland, and they were able to see Suthrond from a mile off. From a distance, Reith could see, like Coeden, the homes and buildings of Suthrond had been torched so that nothing recognizable remained. Reith had never been to Suthrond, so the layout of the town was unfamiliar to him. That did not matter, as Suthrond went the way of Coeden.

The smell of smoke still clung to the air. The smell of death was less prevalent, and Reith was thankful. As he made his way into the center of the devastation, he noticed there was no massive pile of bodies in the town square.

I suppose if much of the town escaped, that would explain it.

There were bodies at various places around the town, and Reith supposed they remained where they fell in battle against the Gray Man.

But where did the survivors go?

He and Aspen slowly made their way through town, looking for any trace of those still alive. At the southern end of the town, the land opened up again into more farmland. It was still early in the season, and very little was growing. But at the beginning of one of the fields, Reith saw the unmistakable sign of a multitude of footprints.

"Come on, Aspen," he urged, "we need to follow those tracks."

The multitude of footprints and the general disturbance of many people walking through the forest, the broken twigs and bent grass, were quite easy to follow, even after the recent rain. Reith had no idea how many survivors he was following, but it had to be at least fifty.

Could be several times that many, though, because of the sheer volume of footprints.

For several miles, the tracks were easy to follow in the soft dirt of the fields, but then the fields ended abruptly at the forest's edge. Reith dismounted Aspen and bent down to inspect the ground. The tracks entered the wood at what appeared to be a natural path. The dirt was packed down from feet over a long period of time. *Looks like a game trail used by hunters.* The footprints were fainter here in the forest but were still visible, with a great number of feet having trampled this ground.

Reith led Aspen by the reins. For a mile or two, they followed the tracks until at last they came to the base of a small hill devoid of trees. Reith climbed to the top to see what he may. His effort was rewarded. To the south, in the distance, he saw the smoke of several fires gently drifting into the air. *Found them!*

He judged the smoke to be about a half mile off, so he mounted Aspen and they soon came near to the smoke. In front of him, the trees thinned out and the land dropped into what Reith assumed was a valley, though he couldn't be sure until he reached the edge. He dismounted and led Aspen to the hill to their right, leaving her to graze at its base. Reith crept to the top, bending over to avoid being seen.

As he came to the top, his eyes beheld the scene in the valley below. Sunlight bounced and shimmered off of a wide river. On the near bank, the northern bank, was a town made entirely of tents. They were laid out in a grid system that reminded Reith of town roads. The smoke he had seen came from campfires near the mouths of tents and a bigger fire in the center camp. There were nearly a hundred tents spread out on the land. There were few people out of their tents, but the ones he could see were women and children. Two or three horses grazed nearby.

Here were the survivors of Suthrond.

As he stared, he heard a twig snap behind him. He instinctively reached for his bow and quiver, but before he could, a rough voice said, "I wouldn't do that if I were you, boy."

Chapter Seven

Rough hands grabbed Reith's shoulders and pulled him to his feet, spinning him around to face the speaker.

His sword was pulled from its sheath, and as was his dagger. His bow and pack were removed as well. Reith saw that it was a group of five, three men and two women, all armed with spears or swords. They had dark circles under their eyes and they appeared beaten down and weary, like they hadn't slept well in weeks. Their clothes were ragged, with small holes and patches.

Two of the men had picked him up. One had a crooked nose that looked like it had been broken and dark, beady eyes. The other had dark skin and had a bloody bandage around his left forearm. The two women seemed to be a few years older than Reith and they held their weapons with practiced ease. One was fair with long blonde hair, and the other had dark skin and hair like the night sky. They admired his sword, which shone in the sunlight.

The man who had spoken was a grizzled man, perhaps

in his fifties. He asked, "Who are you and what are you doing snooping on us?"

"My name is Reith," Reith said, looking the man in the eye. "Are you the survivors of Suthrond?"

"I'm the one asking the questions here, not you. I'll ask again, what are you doing snooping on us?"

"Are you the survivors of Suthrond?" Reith repeated, his voice louder with urgency.

"What's it to you?" the man demanded, looking him over.

"Please, I need to know. I have a message for the survivors of Suthrond."

The other four looked at the elderman, waiting. He sighed and said, "Alright, you found us. What is your message?"

"The Gray Man is coming."

The statement hung in the air, and all five of his captors looked at each other. *Was that fear in their eyes?*

"We'll take you to our leader," the grizzled man said finally with a sigh. "You can tell her your tale."

"Wait, my horse!" Reith exclaimed. "She's at the bottom of the hill."

"Hilda, go get the horse," the grizzled man ordered.

"No, she won't go with you. I need to get her."

"Fine. Hilda, go with him. If you run, you'll get a spear in your back."

Reith slowly walked down the hill toward Aspen. She fidgeted and stamped her feet, nervous because of the strangers, and it took a few minutes of coaxing for her to trust him and go with him. He walked beside her with a hand on her neck. Hilda walked beside him, and she took care to ensure her spear was in his peripheral vision at all times.

The two men walked beside Reith and Aspen and

escorted them down the hill. The grizzled man was in front leading the way, and the two women followed behind.

Reith felt the tenseness in Aspen. She wanted to bolt, but out of loyalty she stayed beside him. They walked through the camp, and Reith was on the receiving end of stares from the people. From beyond the camp, the sound of the river was a constant low roar.

He saw that most of the men were on the older side of things. Mostly, he noticed women and children. The women were cooking or washing and the children were running around amongst the tents playing. Everyone appeared worn out, and the state of their clothes matched their faces. There was an air of sadness about them.

In the center of the camp stood a large tent with its flaps open. The grizzled man told the rest of his party to wait while he went inside. Reith heard voices but could not understand what was being said. After a few minutes, he heard the man call out, "Bring him in."

His guards escorted him in, then turned and left. He blinked several times in the darkness of the tent, and it took him a few seconds for his eyes to adjust. He saw an elderly woman seated on a cushion and the grizzled man standing next to her. The woman had pure white hair that seemed to gleam even in the gloom of the shadows. A plain, well-worn sword hung at her side, sheathed.

She put her elbows on her knees, folded her hands in front of her mouth and looked up at him. "Well?" she asked, "Who are you, Reith?"

"I have come to warn you. The Gray Man is coming."

"But who are you?" the woman asked again. "Where are you from? How do you know this information? How can we trust you?" Her voice was slow, steady, and firm. She chose her words deliberately. This was a woman to take seriously.

Reith took a deep breath and launched into his story.

"My name is Reith. I was a chronicler's apprentice in Coeden. I was out hunting a few weeks ago, and when I returned, smoke was rising in the sky. I ran back to find that the town was destroyed, burned, and everyone was killed. They piled their bodies in the town square ..." His voice trailed off with the sadness of the memory.

After a moment, he composed himself and continued.

"I saw the men who did this. They were led by a man with gray skin and hair. I did not see my master's body, but I found that he left me a note to meet him at Erador."

"Erador?" the woman asked sharply. "Why would he have you go to Dragonscar?"

"I don't know," Reith said, still puzzled himself by that part of the story. "But I went. I hiked through the forest, across the plains, and forded the Great River. I traveled through Dragonscar and came to Erador. I didn't find him there either. But while I was there, in the ruins, I found the Gray Man again. He was looking for something."

He hesitated, not sure how much to divulge. It came to his mind that his sword might be dangerous, not only for its sharp blade but for what it was and why the Gray Man wanted it.

"What was he looking for?" the woman prodded, seeming to sense his hesitation.

"I don't know for sure," he admitted, which was partially true. "But he hadn't found it. I heard him tell his men he would only look for a few days before going back to finish off the survivors of Suthrond."

Dismay and despair came to the faces of the Suthronders. The gravity of the situation weighed them all down, and no one spoke for a few moments.

After a pause, Reith continued his tale. "I took one of their horses, and we traveled here. Her name is Aspen. We

left Erador with a two-day head start on the Gray Man.
But he's coming."

She stared deep into his eyes, looking right to the
depths of his soul to see if he was lying. He had the odd
sensation that she could read minds. At last she nodded
and said, "Alright, I believe you." She stepped forward and
offered him her hand, which he shook. "My name is
Heth."

"I wish we were meeting under better circumstances,"
Reith said. "What are you going to do?"

"That remains to be seen. We have discussed our long-
term plan at some length. But our people have been too
young, too old, too scared, and too injured to do anything.
This news you bring will force us to move."

"Tell me, how did you escape? No one from Coeden
survived as far as I know."

"We had an early word. A traveler on the road came
bearing tidings of an approaching group of soldiers, none
bearing the sign or sigil of the king. He said they were led
by a man who was strangely gray, like a ghost. We
evacuated women, children, and the elders to the forest,
where we waited for word. None came, but we saw the
smoke rising up. We waited all day and all night. In the
morning, Trigg here,"—she gestured to the grizzled man
—"took on the risky task of going back to town to see what
had happened."

"They slaughtered our men and burned the place. My
son ..." Trigg trailed off, lost for words, and tears began to
fall.

Heth patted Trigg's arm comfortingly.

"Who is the Gray Man?" Reith asked, hoping to finally
get an answer to this puzzle.

"We don't know," Heth said sadly. "We don't know
who he is, where he's from, or what he wants. All we know

is that he has slaughtered our people and burned our town. And now we know he has done the same to Coeden. Tell me, what is he like? All we know is what the traveler told us, that he was like a ghost."

"He's middle aged, though it's hard to tell. His hair is gray like an elder. But his face doesn't bear the lines of age. His skin is gray, like the color washed away in water. His voice even sounds gray, though I don't know how to describe it. It's like he's not quite human." Reith shuddered at the memory.

"It sounds like you spoke to him," Heth said. "How can this be?"

"He's one of them," Trigg said, stepping forward in anger.

"Peace, Trigg," she ordered, holding out her hand. "Explain yourself. Did you speak to him?"

"I did. They found me as I inspected the ruins of Coeden. He laughs like a madman. I thought he would kill me."

"And yet, here you are. How?"

"He asked for my name," Reith said, his mind taking him back to those cold, gray eyes. "He asked for my name, and I said, 'No one.' And then he laughed." Even now, icy fear coursed through his veins. "He laughed, and his men laughed too. He said that he had to let me live because he is a man of his word."

"I don't understand," Heth said, looking at him like he was mad.

"You see, he told his men before attacking Coeden, 'Leave No One alive.' No One."

"I see," Heth said, nodding.

"What?" Trigg said.

"He said to leave No One alive, Trigg," Heth explained. "And Reith said he was no one."

Trigg blinked and then understanding crossed his face.

"He toys with people's lives based on his own bloody jokes?" Trigg asked angrily.

Both Heth and Trigg pursed their lips and widened their eyes in a mixture of anger, sadness, and fear on their faces.

"And he is all the more dangerous because of it," Heth replied. "A man that treats life and death as a joke is a man to be feared above all others."

They sat in silence, each lost in their own thoughts about the Gray Man. Finally, Trigg broke the silence.

"Gray or not, I bet he bleeds red all the same if I get my sword in him," Trigg said with a growl.

"Thank you for bringing us this information, Reith," Heth added.

"What now?" Reith asked. "He's coming. And he'll be here soon. He's got horses."

"We cannot defend ourselves against an open attack. We have a few who would be handy in a fight, but we would not stand long against a force big enough to kill all of our men."

"We could take them," Trigg argued, his hand resting on his sword hilt, poised to pull it out as if battle were to be joined in mere minutes.

Heth shook her head. "No, we can't Trigg, and you know that. There's only one thing to do. We have to cross the river."

Of all of the things Reith expected her to propose, this was not one of them. They were at the southern end of human territory, right in the wilds between the humans and the elves. The river was the boundary that had not been crossed by either race in hundreds of years, as far as anyone knew.

Trigg was incredulous.

"Cross the river? Into elven territory? That's madness."

"It's the only way. The Gray Man will follow us anywhere in our own land. He is a dangerous and unpredictable enemy. He has horses for his men, and we have only a few pack horses. We cannot hope to make it to Galismoor or even Palander without being caught. He is faster than us. In the wild, we are sitting ducks. Along the road, we are served up for slaughter. No," she said with resolve, "the only way to save our lives is to cross the river and throw ourselves upon the mercy of the elves."

"But they hate us," Trigg said, his face now completely red with anger and fear.

"We don't know that," Heth retorted, unshakable in her determination. "Maybe their ancestors hated ours. But if we stay, we will surely be killed. If we cross, we have hope. And hope is the only thing keeping us going right now."

"I have to agree with Heth," Reith said. *Anywhere in our own land, we will be hunted. It's a death sentence.*

"Don't you jump in," Trigg snapped.

"He has every right," Heth said. "He risked his life to come and warn us. He is the reason we have this opportunity. A few more days and the Gray Man could have killed all of us, right here."

"And what if the elves kill us?"

"Then we will die knowing we did everything in our power to save our lives and the lives of the only ones we love left in the world."

"Fine," Trigg said after a long pause. "Fine. We will do it your way. And when the elves kill us, I will tell you 'I told you so.'"

"So be it," Heth replied. "Now, Reith, what is your plan? Do you want to try and make it past the Gray Man and escape to Galismoor? Or will you throw your lot in with us?"

Reith hadn't thought about this question at all. His sole purpose had been to warn the people of Suthrond. Vereinen's face came to his mind. *Where is he? I need to find him.*

Then, unbidden, the voice he had heard by the trees at Erador came to his mind.

"Save them. Serve them. Fight for them. Then find me."

Well, I have saved them. Now I must serve them.

"I will come with you," Reith said. "Where else can I go? I am an enemy of the Gray Man, just as you are." *And perhaps more so,* he thought, thinking of his sword and how the Gray Man wanted it.

"Good." Heth nodded as she spoke. "We will be glad to have you. Trigg, give him back his things."

Trigg handed Reith his pack, bow, and sword, which had been laying on the ground at the edge of the tent.

"Now," Heth said, rubbing her hands together, "let's tell everyone."

In a matter of minutes, the survivors of Suthrond were gathered around in a semi-circle around her tent. Each face looked tired, haggard, and weary. Sadness was in each of their eyes and Reith could read the evidence of their suffering like a book. *These people have known death,* he thought.

Reith stood off to the side, absentmindedly stroking Aspen's mane. When all were gathered and quiet, Heth spoke.

"My people, this is Reith," she said, gesturing to him. He became instantly self-conscious as everyone stared at him. He did not like being the center of attention, especially after so much time on his own.

"Reith is from Coeden, and he has brought us news. The same men that attacked Suthrond also attacked Coeden. They left no survivors. Reith survived because he was out hunting when the Gray Man attacked."

At the mention of the Gray Man, the crowd gasped as one.

"We still don't know who he is or what he wants. But we know that he is a murderer and a villain. Furthermore, Reith has brought other news to us as well." She paused, and took a deep breath. "He is coming here. He wants to kill us all and finish what he started. We are all in grave danger."

A chorus of muttering rose up in the crowd as each person turned to their neighbor to discuss the news. Heth held her hand up for silence, and the whispers slowly died away.

"We cannot stay here; we would be killed like our husbands, fathers, brothers, and friends were in Suthrond. We cannot attempt to go to Palander or Galismoor. We would not make it to safety before the Gray Man attacks. We would be assaulted on the road. That leaves only one chance for escape, one hope of life. We must cross the river."

The whispers rose like a hive of bees waking up in anger. Someone yelled from the back of the crowd.

"But the elves will kill us!"

Heth again held her hand up for silence.

"If we stay on this side, it means certain death. The Gray Man is a terrible foe. Perhaps the elves will have mercy on us."

There was more grumbling and muttering.

"It may seem like our situation is hopeless. But as long as there is breath in our lungs, we do have hope. Our lives hang in the balance. If you wish to stay on this side of the river, you may. No one will carry you across. But I am going. It is our only hope in this hour of peril. Now go, pack your things. We will leave in two hours."

There was more grumbling and muttering, but the survivors of Suthrond dispersed and packed up their meager belongings. Reith stuck with Heth and Trigg. Even though he had only just met them, he craved their familiarity amid such new surroundings.

"Is there anything I can help you with?" Reith asked Heth.

"Why don't you take your horse and ride downriver a few miles to see if there is a better place to cross. If you don't find one, go a few miles upriver and look. I think we might be able to cross here, but it will be difficult."

Reith jogged over to Aspen and swung up into the saddle, then walked her through the camp toward the river. Everywhere he looked, fires were being extinguished, tents were being taken down, and bundles of clothes and supplies were tied up. As he passed, it seemed that every eye looked up to him, appraising him. Their eyes asked, "Are you saving us or taking us into greater danger?"

At the river's edge, he dismounted in order to get a better look at the potential crossing. The bank here was wide and flat, covered with small rocks and pebbles. The river flowed swift, and there was some whitewater, signaling danger lay beneath the surface.

"It would be dangerous at best to cross here," he told Aspen.

I could do it, but what about all of these older people and kids?

He mounted Aspen once more and rode west along the river bank. The bank rose and below him, the river grew immensely choppy. Presently, he found that the river entered a canyon, with steep cliffs on either side. He turned and went back.

The camp was a flurry of activity when he arrived back. From across the camp, Heth gave him a questioning look. He shook his head and pointed upriver. She gave him a thumbs up and continued bundling her possessions.

Further upstream, the river seemed to move slower than below. But the river was too rocky and choppy to consider a crossing here. About two miles away from camp, Reith noticed the roar of the river was increasing. He rounded a bend and saw a waterfall before him. Water fell from fifty feet above into a wide and deep pool before flowing downstream. At the edge of the pool, the water was not as choppy as other places on the river. He took Aspen to the water's edge and waded a few steps out into the pool. About a third of the way across, the water was splashing the bottoms of his shoes. He turned her around, and once on dry land, directed her around to the side of the hill leading up the falls.

At the top, he looked down at a spectacular view of the river below. From this height, he could see smoke from the camp downstream. Even when the river was lost from view because of a bend, he could still see its form in the break in the trees. He had a very strong desire to leap down into the pool below, though he knew that the idea would probably result in injury or death.

Who knows what lies beneath the surface? If there's a rock there, I'm a goner.

Above the falls, the water raced toward the precipice and was virtually uncrossable. After wrenching himself away from the cliff, Reith and Aspen carefully made their way down. He decided to attempt a full crossing himself. He left his bag, sword, bow, and arrows beside the pool and instructed Aspen to stay. On the other side of the river, there was a sturdy oak tree about fifteen feet beyond the water's edge. He steeled himself, then began to cross.

If I'm going to ask them to do it, I might as well try it first. If only I had a rope to tie to that tree to help with crossing.

The water was cold, colder even than the water of the Great River he had forded several days earlier. Reith's skin was on fire where the lapping river touched him. Where his clothes were wet, what little wind blew past chilled him to the bone. He clenched his fists, gritted his teeth, and forced himself forward.

The ground beneath him was smooth, with very few large rocks. He felt forward with his foot before committing to a step. About halfway across, the water was up to the middle of his chest. He managed to make it to the other side with no difficulty.

Once free of the water, the air brought out the worst of the chill. His teeth started chattering, and he immediately turned around to cross again. Back on dry ground, Reith took off his shirt and replaced it with the dry one from his pack. This helped a bit, as did mounting Aspen and feeling her warmth course through his legs.

Back at the camp, he sought out Heth.

"What did you find?" she asked him.

"The river is impassable downstream. A few miles down, it enters a canyon and there is nowhere to cross. About two miles upstream, there is a waterfall that empties into a large pool. At the edge of the pool, the water is gentle enough and shallow enough to cross." He held up his hand to his mid chest where the water had been when he had crossed.

"And how was the terrain? Can we make it up there?" Heth inquired.

"We should be able to get there in an hour or two."

"Okay, let's do it."

"Heth, the water is very cold," Reith warned.

"So be it. It's the only way. Will you allow your horse to be loaded down with supplies for this journey?"

"I will," he said, stroking Aspen's mane, "and she will too."

Heth walked to the upstream side of camp and called for attention.

"We have discovered an easier crossing about two miles upriver," she announced. "Everyone must try and carry what they can. The aged and very young may load their things on the horses or give them to someone stronger. Then, when we are ready, we will make our way to the crossing."

Reith helped an elderly man place his pack on Aspen. Two small children presented their packs as well and soon, Aspen was loaded down with several packs, and Reith found himself holding two beside his own."

Serve them, he thought, remembering the words of the voice at Erador.

With the added weight and being on foot, it seemed to Reith that it took several hours to reach the waterfall again. In reality, the sun had only moved a few degrees in the sky. The survivors of Suthrond were hardy folk. Living in the wilderness for a few weeks had shaped them into men, women, and children of action.

When they arrived, Reith volunteered to go first.

"I'll go first. I did it earlier. Do you have a rope?"

"What do you need a rope for?" Heth asked.

"I will tie one end to that tree over there," he said, pointing to the oak tree on the opposite bank he had seen earlier. "Then you can tie your end to a tree over here. It will give everyone something to hold as they cross."

"That's a good plan." Heth nodded. "Trigg!" she called.

Within seconds, he was at her side. "Yes?"

"Do we have rope? Reith wants to tie one end on that side and one on this side so we have a hand hold."

"I believe that we do. Hold on while I look."

In no time, he was back with a length of rope.

"Trigg," Reith said, "can you hold this end of the rope? Hold it all loosely so it can unspool as I cross. I don't really want it to drag in the water. Then, once I've tied my end, you can tie your end."

"Whatever you say," Trigg said.

"Be careful, Reith," Heth added.

"I always am, Heth." He grinned. "When I'm across, I'll call for Aspen. I'll try to meet her halfway if you are willing to lead her there for me."

With the plan established, Reith prepared for the cold trek across the river. He was not looking forward to the frigid water. He held the rope tightly in his right hand, and the rope sat on his shoulder. Then he plunged his foot in. Even though he was prepared for it, the icy waves made him gasp in shock. He paused for a few seconds, one foot on dry land, and the other losing feeling in the cold water. Then he forced himself to take the second step and third step.

He was soon halfway across. The rope was no longer tight on his shoulder, as it was sloping up toward Trigg. Finally, Reith stumbled onto dry land, teeth chattering from the cold. It was all he could do to not throw the rope down and hug himself for warmth as he headed over to the oak tree, sopping wet. He had kept his hands dry, so they were warm enough to maneuver the rope into a tight knot. He tugged it to make sure it would hold and then signaled to Trigg to tie his end.

When Trigg gave a tug, Reith began to inch his way back across with his hand on the rope. Heth came toward him with Aspen. They met in the middle, and

Reith took Aspen's reins. Then they carefully made their way across.

Once across, Reith set about making a fire. His teeth were still chattering, and it took him a few tries with his flint and tinder to get a small blaze going. When the fire was built, he joined Heth and Trigg to help people across. Hand after hand, he grabbed and pulled. Some of the children were crying because of the cold. These he carried to the fire to warm up.

Nearly all of the people had made it safely across. There were only a few left on the northern bank while several others plodded through the water. A boy, perhaps two or three years old, was screaming and squirming in his mother's arm. Her left hand was clinging to the rope, and her right arm was holding him up. She let go of the rope and held the boy in both hands to soothe him. But when she took another step, she fell face first into the water. The boy's howls were cut off.

"Janna!" someone from the shore screamed.

"Finn!" yelled another.

Heth, Trigg, and Reith jumped forward into the water. Neither the boy nor the woman resurfaced. Heth and Trigg reached the spot where she fell first.

"There's no sign of them," Trigg called out after plunging his arms and body in to look for them.

Reith began feeling around in the water for any sign of life or movement. The icy waves did not faze him because he was so intent upon his purpose.

Please, please, please let me find them.

A shout rang out from the bank, "Look!" Reith whirled around to see hands pointing downriver, where a dark shape was floating.

Reith leapt out of the river and stripped Aspen of her load. "Come on girl, let's save them!"

Chapter Eight

They couldn't gallop down river due to the rocky terrain, but Aspen quickly picked a path and they gained on the dark shape. After a minute, they were beside it.

"Keep going, Aspen," Reith urged. "We have to get ahead."

He looked back to see a few of the Suthronders following on foot about fifty yards behind. After Reith returned his gaze forward, his heart sank when he saw the terrain. The river was swiftly flowing, and rapids were present every hundred feet or so. There was no place to get in. Not if he wanted to ever get out again. *I've got to try.*

Reith finally found a spot where the river was not nearly as choppy and there were no rapids. He stepped in, oblivious to the cold, and waded nearly halfway. The dark shape was nearly upon him when he saw the tiny hand floating on the water. The current was pulling it away from him, toward the other bank. He lunged forward, and his hand closed on the shirt of the little boy. The force from the boy and the current pulled him off balance, and his head went under. Icy water pressed at his skull. He gasped at the shock as water flooded his lungs. He began sputtering under the water, all the while holding tight to the shirt in his hand.

His lungs screamed for air, and he flailed and kicked, trying to force his body to the surface. His feet kicked only water, and he soon lost sight of which way was up. His lungs felt as though they were shriveling up inside of him, and his chest felt tight. *This is it.*

Just then, strong arms grabbed him and pulled him up, and he pulled the little boy to himself. Water poured down his face and he coughed violently. The next thing he knew, he was on the shore on his hands and knees coughing up what seemed to be most of the water from the river. When his coughing fit was over, he collapsed and rolled over on his back, exhausted. He closed his eyes and rested for a minute.

Reith was startled when Aspen's nose brushed his face. He sat up and became aware of his surroundings. Heth, Trigg, and a few of the others were gathered around looking at something on the ground that he couldn't see. He slowly got to his feet and went over to them. In the middle of the group, the boy's body lay still. Heth saw him and stood up, grass and dirt still clinging to her knees.

"Thank you for jumping in, Reith," she said with the remnant of tear tracks down her face. "But he's gone."

Reith helped Trigg and two others dig a hole along the banks of the river. One of them was named Titus, and he was a boy of thirteen. His skin and hair were sandy colored. The other was named Kydar, and he was dark and Reith's own age.

The four of them took turns digging with the only shovel in the group's possession. One would dig, silent save only for the occasional grunt from the exertion. The others watched as the digger went down into the earth and the mound of dirt grew beside him.

The body of Janna, the mother, hadn't been found. Reith heard murmurs of speculation that she either got carried down river or else her leg got caught in the riverbed and her body was still floating somewhere in between here and the crossing point upriver. The thought of her dead body floating there, dragged to a diagonal from the current, was very unsettling to Reith.

When the hole was deep enough and Kydar had to be hoisted out by the other three, they laid the small body of Finn in. Someone had shut his eyes. They laid his hands across his chest so that he looked like he was sleeping.

The four grave diggers used the shovel and their hands to push the dirt over Finn, a blanket for his eternal sleep. Trigg and Kydar each picked up a large rock and gently placed them on dirt above Finn's lifeless form. Titus and Reith followed suit. Soon there was a mound of rocks in the rough shape of the body below.

The Suthronders had no more tears to shed. They had already grieved their fathers, husbands, brothers, sons, and friends. The dry-eyed sadness on every face was somehow more emotional than flowing tears.

Heth stepped forward to Finn's grave.

"I really don't know what to say," she said, her eyes fixed on the pile of stones before her. "He was so young."

A wave of assent washed over the mourners.

"He was too young," Heth began. "And Janna. She was too young too."

She hesitated, clearly not knowing what to say next.

"There's only one person to blame." The voice came

from a girl around Reith's own age who was standing next to Kydar. They had a strong resemblance, and Reith guessed them to be siblings.

"The Gray Man. He killed our families, destroyed our town, and chased us out into the wilderness. Our blood is on his hands."

They decided to camp there beside the river. Heth settled on a guard rotation, and Reith was thankful to be left off. So much had happened since he had arrived at the camp that afternoon. Still, he wished to be useful, so he helped Kydar, Trigg, and a few others light a few campfires. In the gathering twilight, Reith sat beside one of the fires. His hands were raw from the shovel and his muscles ached.

He stared at the flickering firelight, losing himself in his thoughts. The heat warmed his face and chest and the dusk pulled heat from his back. He felt like two people. The one facing the fire, warm. The other looking into night, cold.

Reith realized with a start that he had missed several minutes of the conversation around the fire. He looked around and found that he was seated to Kydar's right. The girl he thought was Kydar's sister was sitting on Kydar's left. The younger boy, Titus, who had helped dig the grave, was directly across the fire from Reith. Reith had a hard time seeing him past the bright firelight. A girl even younger than Titus was sitting between Reith and Titus.

During a lull in the conversation, Reith asked, "I've met Kydar, but what is your name?" He glanced at Kydar and then at the girl.

"I'm Dema," she said. She leaned forward, offering her

hand. He reached over to meet hers and they shook in front of Kydar's face.

"And you know Titus," Kydar added, gesturing to Titus, who looked at Reith with neither a smile nor a frown. "And this is his younger sister Tara."

The young girl looked at him sheepishly.

"Pleased to meet you," Reith said. "Though of course, I wish it were under better circumstances."

"Well, now that we all know each other," Dema replied with a smile, "tell me about the Gray Man."

Her statement caught him off guard. It was a demand, not a request. There was a glint of hunger in her eyes. In the corner of Reith's vision, he saw Titus and the younger girl lean forward to listen.

"He's insane," Reith began. He relayed to them his encounter with the Gray Man and how he survived.

"Who plays sick games with people's lives?" Dema asked, her eyes sparking like the fire.

Kydar added, "What does he want?"

"He's looking for something," Reith said, unsure if he should mention his sword.

"Suthrond didn't have anything special." Dema leaned back and contemplated the fire.

"I think he was looking for my master, Vereinen," Reith explained. "He's a chronicler. He studies the history of Terrasohnen, and he took me on as an apprentice a few years ago."

"So what does he want? Information? An artifact? A treasure map? What could a chronicler tell him?"

"I don't know," Reith lied. He didn't want to speculate about his sword, especially when he had no idea why it was important. He wanted to keep that piece of information to himself for the time being.

"What would be worth killing hundreds of people?" Kydar asked. No one had an answer for him.

There was silence around the fire for several minutes. Reith watched sparks ascend to the heavens, each one a temporary beacon in the dark before vanishing in a puff of smoke.

"I've been admiring your sword from afar since you showed up," Dema said after a few more sparks popped in the fire. "May I see it?"

Reith unsheathed it and passed it over to Dema.

Her eyes widened as the sword glinted in the firelight. "Wow."

"I have never seen its equal," Kydar admitted. "But then again, that's not saying much. I haven't seen too many swords. And the ones we had in Suthrond were very plain."

"This one looks like the sword of a king," Dema said, admiring the detail in the metalwork and holding it out to test its weight. "Where did you get it? Did you kill a king?"

Reith laughed. "No, I found it when I went to Erador. It was in a library."

"A sword in a library? With books?" Dema asked, incredulous. "Are you sure you haven't been carrying around a long and very ornate letter opener for a week?"

"Now that's a use I haven't put it to," Reith said, chuckling. "If I ever get a letter, I'll use this to open it."

"You're telling me," Dema said as she passed the sword to Kydar, who inspected it closely, "that you traveled all the way to Erador, the ruined city, and you went to the library?"

"Well, I guess it would be more accurate to say I was hiding and it just so happened that I found the library. The Gray Man was there, looking for whatever it is he wants."

Kydar remarked, "That's some lucky find. Do you know how to use it?"

"I haven't had to yet," Reith replied. "I prefer my bow."

"I wish I had a sword like this one," Kydar said longingly. "Shoot, I'd take any sword at this point."

He handed Reith his sword back and Reith sheathed it. There were a few moments of silence before Dema broke it again.

"I wanted to stay and fight when they attacked. But father said to go with Kydar and protect our people."

"It wouldn't have done any good," Kydar argued. "We would have been killed, just like everyone else."

"We're all going to die someday. Might as well die in a fight," she retorted. "One day, I'm going to go back. I'm going to go back and kill the Gray Man for what he did."

"I'll go with you," Reith said. "Once we get everyone to safety, that is."

"Well don't leave me out." Kydar reached out and put an arm around each of Dema and Reith. "We'll go together. No matter what, we will avenge our family and friends."

Warmth and affection filled Reith. For the first time in what seemed like forever, he had friends. He had a place to belong. He had a people to belong to. He hadn't realized until that moment how much he had missed that feeling. He lowered his head and turned away so that the others wouldn't see his eyes watering. He squeezed Kydar with his arm and felt Dema do the same.

"We're in this together," he said.

The morning sunbathed the world in shades of red, orange, yellow, and purple, illuminating the riverbank and casting shadows from the trees. Light reflected off the dew on the leaves and grass. The air was cool and crisp, like a fresh apple. To the west, the forest stretched out to the horizon. To the east, the land seemed to grow more open, with fewer trees and rocky ground. And here, at the river, the sun shone on the fresh pile of dirt hiding the body of a toddler.

Only one of the fires was lit, the one on the southern end of the makeshift camp. There, four guards talked in hushed voices, keeping watch over the camp with a wary eye south, where the elves lived.

Reith stretched and his muscles groaned. He was sore from the previous day's events. Around the camp, others were stirring as well, waking up to face the day. Reith stood and went over to the guard fire to warm his cold hands. Trigg was there, but he didn't know the other three.

"Good morning, Reith," Trigg said, somehow very chipper despite the early hour. "You look dead on your feet."

"I feel dead on my feet," Reith replied. "I feel old, Trigg."

That got a laugh out of the old man. "You don't know old."

"Then maybe you could teach me." Reith knelt by the fire and held his hands out toward it, occasionally rubbing them together. Slowly, the warmth worked its way into his bones. Across the camp, he saw Heth coming toward them.

"Any activity to report?" she asked the guard when she got near, though she looked only at Trigg.

"No ma'am," Trigg said. "No sign of anything in any direction. We're alone."

"But for how much longer?" Heth wondered aloud. "It

wouldn't surprise me if we have been seen. The smoke is visible for miles and the fires are beacons in the night."

"We want to be seen, don't we?" Reith asked, standing up. He crossed his arms and stuck his hands under them to warm them up more. "We're going to the elves, right?"

"Aye," Heth said.

"Then we should want to be seen," Reith continued. "The last thing we want is for the elves to think we're an army invading. An army would be stealthy, silent. They would try to remain hidden. If they thought us to be an army, we would all be killed in our sleep. But one look at us in the light, and they will know we pose no threat."

"The boy speaks wisely," Trigg said. "I'm not much for going to the elves, but if that is our course, I'd like to go about it in a way that doesn't end with arrows poking out of me or my throat slit."

"Well then, let us go and be seen."

In almost no time, the camp was completely packed up and ready to depart. Reith loaded Aspen down with bags, though she scarcely complained. Heth had Reith near the front of the procession, as he was one of the few who could be counted on in a skirmish.

As the sun rose to its mid-morning level, the survivors of Suthrond and Reith began the march south, further into the land of the elves. To their right, the forest seemed thick and impenetrable. Still, there were trees to contend with on their chosen route, and every so often, Reith had to guide Aspen around a tree.

For the sake of young and old alike, there were frequent breaks. At the first such break, Reith was giving Aspen some water when Kydar and Dema came over.

"I love your horse," Dema said, reaching out to stroke Aspen's mane. Aspen allowed this intrusion. "What's her name?"

"Aspen," Reith replied.

"How did you get her?" Kydar asked.

"I stole her from the Gray Man's men," Reith explained. "She was too noble to serve such masters."

"Well tell us the story then! Reith the horse thief, tell us your secrets."

Reith grinned and recounted how he had used the fruit to gain Aspen's trust on that rainy day that seemed to be years ago, though really it was barely a week ago.

"It's a good thing you got her," Dema said when he had finished. "For one, I hate to think of this precious creature serving such a cruel master. And second, if you didn't get her, you wouldn't have gotten to us in time." She visibly shuddered at the thought.

"Enough of that talk," Kydar said. "We wanted to ask you if you wanted to go hunting with us tomorrow morning. Heth told us to go and see what kind of fresh meat we can get. We'd like to take you along."

"I'm in," Reith answered. "I went hunting all the time back in Coeden. And then nearly nonstop since I left."

"Great!" Dema remarked. "We will get the guards to wake us an hour or two before dawn."

"Sounds like a plan," Reith said enthusiastically.

The rest of the day passed slowly for Reith. He was too excited about hunting and also frustrated with the slow pace and frequent stops taken by his fellow travelers.

"When it was just me," he told Aspen, "I could cover two or three times the distance we have today."

By mid-afternoon, the group was traveling slower than it had all day. The children looked worn out and many were getting cranky. The elders kept the resolve on their faces but had clearly used up their energy reserves. Heth reluctantly called for camp to be made earlier than she had hoped.

"I think we only got about ten miles today," Reith told her as he took bags off of Aspen.

"Well, that's ten miles closer to the elves," Heth replied, trying to see the good in the situation. Reith could see in her face and tone that she was frustrated by the lack of progress. She helped him with the last bag, saying, "I hear that you are going hunting tomorrow."

"Yes, with Kydar and Dema," he replied, not knowing where this conversation was going. He hoped she would let him go. "They invited me."

"Oh, I know. They told me," Heth said. "I think it's a great idea. But I want you all to go north to hunt. I don't want you going south and surprising the elves. You could get yourselves killed."

"You're right, I hadn't even thought about that."

"And when you go north," she added, her voice dropping so that only he could hear, "go as far as you can and see if we are being followed. I have a bad feeling that we are still not free from the Gray Man's arm. If he were to fall on us from the rear ..."

"Say no more," Reith said, picturing for himself the massacre that would result from such a catastrophe. "I will watch for him."

"Keep going north as far as you can each morning on your hunting trips as long as we continue to journey toward the elves. And tomorrow, when we move again, do not load up Aspen. I want you to ride on her as a rear guard. I want two on horseback trailing us to give us fair warning of attack."

"You can count on me," Reith promised.

Reith awoke with a start in the pre-dawn blackness. Someone was touching his arm. His heart raced until he realized it was Kydar bending over him, waking him up.

"Calm down, it's just me," he said. "You'll wake everyone if you're not careful."

Reith yawned, sat up, and rubbed the sleep from his eyes. His heart maintained an excited beat, and he quickly came to full wakefulness.

"Meet us at the north end of camp," Kydar told him before slipping off into the night.

Reith quickly packed his bag. He hung his sword at his side and his bow and quiver from his back. Then he silently picked his way through the camp to the north side.

The moon was high and nearly full, illuminating his path well. At the edge of the camp, Kydar and Dema waited for him.

"It's about time, sleepyhead," Dema teased.

Reith held back a smile. "Oh shut up."

"Let's go," Kydar said.

They went north, back over land they had traversed the day before, though in the moonlight, the world looked mysterious and foreign. They barely talked for fear of spooking any potential prey. It was unnecessary, though, as they saw nothing worth shooting.

Kydar and Dema carried matching bows of a dark color, with ends that curved back out. They were slightly shorter than Reith's bow, but they each looked plenty powerful.

After a while, the horizon on their left began to lighten ever so slowly. The darkness seemed less oppressive, and the world shifted from black, white, and gray to a full complement of colors.

Reith held up his hand to stop his companions. In the distance, he thought he could see movement. He put a finger to his lips and slowly crept forward, taking great care to avoid stepping on any fallen branches.

As they got closer, he could see it was a hog digging through the dirt with its snout. At about twenty-five yards, Reith stopped and notched an arrow. He sighted along the arrow, aiming for the neck.

He let the arrow fly. There was a squeal from the pig and then a thud as it fell.

"Good shot, Reith!" Kydar said.

They rushed forward to claim their prize. The hog was dead by the time they reached it. Reith removed the arrow from its neck and wiped it off on the ground.

"Let's get this thing ready to take back," Dema ordered, unsheathing her knife.

They found a branch about six feet long and tied the pig's feet to it so that two of them could carry the branch on their shoulders with the pig dangling between them. All three took turns under the heavy branch, and by the time they reached the camp, their shoulders were sore. They left the pig at the cooking fire. That morning, all feasted on the spoils of the hunt.

Chapter Nine

When they broke camp, Reith was on Aspen, pacing behind the crowd. Beside him was another man on a chestnut horse. This rider's name was Rangel. He was about Trigg's age, with a short white beard and wrinkles that made him look like the ripples on water when a stone was thrown in. Heth had explained to them that their job was to range to the north of the main body to make sure no pursuit was coming.

"I plan to go all the way back to the river, if that's fine with you," he told Rangel. Rangel, a quiet sort, nodded in reply. "Alright then, until later. Let's go, Aspen!"

Aspen trotted away from the Suthronders. Reith felt the wind on his face and his heart soared with pleasure. The miles melted away and soon they were standing on the bank of the river, near the grave of Finn. There was no sign of the Gray Man, for which he was glad.

"If he does come, he will follow the trail from Suthrond to the beach down river from here," he said aloud, mostly to himself. "Then he'll see that we traveled upriver to the crossing. Even a novice tracker would be able to find us."

He turned Aspen west, and they walked along the bank of the river, dodging the trees as they made their way the mile and a half or so back to the old Suthrond camp.

Even from the far side of the river, he could still see the remnants of the camp. The places where fires had burned were scarred, and the ground was agitated by feet.

"I wonder if the Gray Man would dare cross the river."

For several minutes he stared across, looking for a glimpse of movement in the trees. He contemplated crossing over, but decided against it. *The water is too cold, and what purpose would there be? Would I go all the way back to Suthrond?*

Finally, Reith decided that he should be headed back, so he turned Aspen upstream. He appreciated this newfound time to himself. He looked down at his sword, which was hanging at his side. He fingered the hilt, imagining drawing it out in some fierce battle charge.

But then his thoughts shifted to Vereinen. *Where is he?*

That question had been at the back of his mind ever since he had left Coeden.

Did he even make it to Erador?

He was puzzled by his master's disappearance. Vereinen prided himself with his punctuality. If he said he would be somewhere, he would be there at the agreed upon time. *He must have a good reason for not being there. Or else* …

He didn't even want to think about the Gray Man and what he might have done to Vereinen. His only hope at the moment was that Vereinen had gotten away from Coeden before the Gray Man had arrived.

He came upon Rangel about three miles north of their

previous night's camp. When asked if he had seen anything, Rangel replied, "Nothing."

The two rode in silence, side by side. Reith was content with the lack of conversation but kept looking at Rangel out of the corner of his eye. Rangel seemed perfectly happy to exist beside Reith in solitude.

They soon reached the previous camp and were now walking through foreign country. Without a word, Rangel prodded his horse into a trot and pulled ahead of Reith. Caught by surprise, Reith urged Aspen forward and they soon caught up.

The ground was littered with the obvious signs of a large party. Footprints were visible in the soft dirt. Grass was trampled down and crushed. He even saw several discarded pig's ribs which someone had evidently been snacking on during the journey.

Eventually Rangel found a place to stop and dismounted, and the two of them shared a silent meal. Once or twice, Reith tried to engage Rangel in conversation but was given only one- or two-word answers in response, so he soon gave up. The attempt wasn't completely in vain, however. He did learn that Rangel had been a cobbler in Suthrond, a maker of shoes.

At the end of the meal, Reith planted his apple core in the soft earth. It was one of his last fruits from Erador. After lunch, they continued at a trot until the Suthronders were in sight again. By now, Reith estimated that the group had traveled five miles since the morning.

I wonder how long until we reach the elves?

For the afternoon, he and Rangel alternated maintaining a half mile gap between them and the group while the other rode a few miles north to check for pursuit. After three such tradeoffs, it became clear that Heth had called for a halt for the day. They had gone perhaps ten miles again. Reith and Rangel trotted into camp.

"No sign of any pursuit, whether elven or the Gray Man," Reith told Heth for both he and Rangel.

"Well that's good," Heth said. "Let's hope it stays that way until we reach safety."

In the morning, Reith was again shaken awake by Kydar. He gathered his things and they met Dema at the north end of camp again.

"Let's go further left today, into the woods," Dema suggested. "I bet there is more living in there than out here."

Kydar and Reith agreed with this course of action. They made a diagonal path to the northwest and soon found themselves surrounded by more trees. The trees leaned in on them, looming over them. They seemed to be listening to the three humans. It gave Reith a foreboding feeling. A glance at the other two told him that they felt the same way.

They continued on their chosen path, none of them wanting to be the one to break the silence and admit their discomfort. Reith didn't know why, but this forest felt older than the one on the other side of the river.

After an hour of fruitless searching, they turned back to the east, back to where the trees thinned out again. Once free of the forest, they all breathed a sigh of relief.

"I'm sure glad to be out of there," Kydar said. "That place creeped me out."

"Tell me about it," Dema added. "It felt like there were a million eyes on us the whole time."

Reith nodded. "I'm glad I'm not the only one who felt it."

They continued roaming the land, but over the next hour, they saw nothing larger than a squirrel, so it was with great disappointment that they went back to the camp empty handed.

As they approached the camp, they saw that it was strangely quiet. They had anticipated that the Suthronders would be busy packing up and getting ready to move, but no one did. Most were standing around or sitting by the fires. As they reached the edge, Kydar asked one of the women, "What's happening?"

"There's an elf," she said.

Reith, Kydar, and Dema rushed into the camp, picked their way through between the tents and the people, and came to Trigg who was standing near the southern edge of the camp. A few feet beyond him was Heth. She was facing a tall figure who was perhaps thirty paces away from her.

The figure was tall, perhaps six feet, with an abnormally angular face. It seemed to Reith to have more lines than curves. He had on brown leather boots that came up to his knees along with a green cloak. A sword hung at his side, a quiver of arrows sat snug against his back, and a bow was in his hand, which he held down by his hip.

Heth displayed freely that she had no weapons and walked slowly toward the elf, who for his part laid his sword and bow on the ground and took a few steps closer to her. When they were ten paces from each other, each stopped. They began speaking, but Reith could not make out what was said.

"What has happened?" Dema whispered to Trigg.

"About five minutes ago, the guards raised the alarm of a figure coming up from the South," Trigg whispered back.

"It seemed like he was going to come into the camp, but then he stopped around where he is now. He came no further until Heth began walking toward him."

"I wonder who he is and where he's from," Kydar remarked.

"And how many more of them are around." Trigg added nervously.

"Well we are in elven country," Dema said, rolling her eyes. "I'm sure this isn't the only elf we'll ever meet."

"Hush, I'm trying to listen," Trigg scolded.

It was a futile effort, as both Heth and the elf maintained conversational tones. Every so often, Heth or the elf would gesture toward the assembled camp. Heth's back was to them, so they could not read her expression and determine how things were going. Of the elf's expression, they could glean nothing.

The talking continued until a half hour had gone by. Trigg had taken to pacing back and forth at the edge of the camp. Kydar and Dema remained on high alert, ready to fight if the need arose.

"Reith!" Heth's voice rang out in the silence. "Come here." She had turned around to look at him and her expression was tense.

He glanced over at Kydar and Dema. There was fear in their eyes. Trigg gave him a little push.

"Go on, now."

He turned to Heth and slowly began walking out. It felt like walking out into a lake. With each step, safety was a little further away.

Heth gestured for him to lay down his weapons, which he slowly did. He felt naked without his bow and his sword. But still he walked on.

The elf was sizing him up as he approached, and Reith returned the favor. Now that he was close, Reith could see that the elf had ears that were slightly pointed at the top. The elf had forest-green eyes, which looked at him with a level of ferocity that made Reith want to recoil.

"Yes, this is him," the elf said to Heth in a voice that was rich and musical. "This was one of them."

"Sorry, what's going on?" Reith said, incredibly confused by the conversation he had joined.

"The elves saw you, Kydar, and Dema this morning as you hunted."

"We were in the woods among the trees," the elf stated plainly.

Reith remembered the feeling that they were being watched and shuddered.

"Why did you not reveal yourselves to us then?" he asked, meeting the fierce green eyes of the elf.

"Such meetings must not come about by chance, human," the visitor said. "Long have our races lived separate lives. Should not the meeting of our two peoples be an occasion of formality and courtesy?"

"I have explained our story and why we are here," Heth told Reith. "And he is very interested to hear your part."

"Please, tell me your tale," the elf said, holding out a hand of welcome. "But before you start, allow me to introduce myself. I am Pallin, Captain of the Legion of Crain."

"It is a pleasure to make your acquaintance," Reith replied, stumbling over words that felt foreign and formal to him. He sounded like someone of old from one of Vereinen's stories.

Pallin stared back. "Tell me how you came to this place."

Reith began his story with his relationship to Vereinen and his hunt that fateful morning. He told of finding

Coeden burning and his run-in with the Gray Man. He told of his escape and journey to Erador and of the Gray Man there. The elf found great amusement in his story of the rescuing of Aspen.

"We came with haste to Suthrond to discover what had become of the survivors. I came upon their trail and found them on the bank of the Rammis River. We crossed the river that day. This is the third day since our crossing."

The elf was silent, pondering this tale. Reith could make nothing from his face. Finally, he spoke.

"The Shadow walks," Pallin said, mostly to himself. "These are troubled tidings indeed."

"Shadow? What shadow?" Reith asked.

The elf appeared to not hear him. Reith looked to Heth, who shrugged.

"I have a question," Pallin continued. "My scouts discovered an apple tree some miles north of here, between us and the river. It most certainly wasn't there before you humans came through. Do either of you know anything about it?"

"Oh, that would be me," Reith replied. "I did that." He told Pallin of the trees and the stream at Erador and how he had been planting fruit all along his journey.

"Streams in the wasteland? Ever-spring fruit? These are strange times, indeed." Pallin's brow furrowed.

"You mean you had magic fruit that you never told us about?" Heth asked curiously.

Reith flushed. "Sorry, it didn't seem as important as warning you about the Gray Man."

"There will be much time to discuss these matters later," Pallin said. "For now, we must decide what to do. I am afraid that your danger is not yet abated."

"You think the Gray Man will come and attack?" Heth asked.

The visitor shrugged. "Perhaps, but that is not the danger I had in mind. No, the danger I fear is from my own people. It has been many years since we interacted with any humans. And our memories are long. There are some who will not forget or forgive the sins of the past."

"It goes both ways," Heth retorted, and Reith knew she was thinking about Trigg and his deep-seated hatred of the elves.

"Now it does no good to argue about the wrongs committed by our ancestors and yours. I am simply warning you that your reception will not be warm."

"Anything is warmer than cold steel," Heth said.

"I'm afraid you are right. But you cannot go back while your doom still roams the earth. All that is left is moving forward."

"To where?" Heth asked.

"To Crain. I told you I am the Captain of the Legion of Crain. Crain is the name of our city and our province in the Kingdom of the Elves. To Crain we shall go. You will throw yourself upon the mercy of the Lord Gwandoeth. He is honest and true. He will provide for you. As for the rest of my people …" He sighed at the thought. "Well, I hope they have the same courtesy. But know that I am not optimistic. It will be hard for you among us. But I will advocate for you."

Heth nodded. "Thank you, Captain. Your generosity shall be told for generations among our people."

"You're very kind. Now Crain is but a half day's march from this place. Are your people able to make such a trip today?"

"We are old and we are young, Captain. As you already know, we cannot travel far in one day."

"Then perhaps we shall camp together this evening

after a day on our feet," Pallin said. "Please ready your people, Heth."

"We will be ready soon."

Heth and Reith turned to walk back to camp and gasped. Beyond the camp stood hundreds of elven soldiers, each clad similarly to Pallin. It seemed that no one in camp had noticed, as intent upon watching Heth and Reith as they were.

"What is this?" Heth asked furiously.

"It is no trap, if that is what you are thinking," Pallin said. "I simply commanded my legion to wait. They shall escort us to Crain. You have nothing to fear from any of them. I shall wait here until you return, ready to march."

Behind them, Heth and Reith could hear the camp starting to stir. Muttering rose like a beehive disturbed.

"They've seen the soldiers," Heth said grimly. They walked back to the camp, picking up their weapons as they went. Trigg, Kydar, and Dema rushed out to them. Titus followed them like a puppy.

"Shall we fight?" Trigg asked, a hand on his sword. He was frantic.

"Calm yourself, Trigg," Heth said, placing her hand over his sword hand. "They mean us no harm."

"No harm? No harm? There are hundreds of them. They'll kill us all."

"No they will not. Pallin is honorable," she said, gesturing back at Pallin, who was waiting patiently. "They will escort us to their city, Crain. There we will petition their Lord for mercy and safety. Now, go get everyone ready to march. Keep them calm. If someone gets anxious and shoots an arrow, we are all dead."

By now, the rest of the refugees were crowding around, wanting to know what was happening.

"Listen up," Heth called out. "The elves are not our

enemy. As you can see, they are making a wall between us and our real foe, the Gray Man."

That's a very shrewd way to put it, Reith thought.

"They are going to escort us to their city where we will ask their lord for mercy. You have nothing to fear. They are going to help us. Now, get ready to march."

The muttering between Suthronders continued, but they did turn and pack their meager belongings for the trip.

"What was the elf like?" Kydar asked Reith.

"He was hard to get a read on," Reith replied. "He's very intense, and his eyes see right through you. But I think he's good."

"What did you talk about?" Dema asked.

Reith gave them the synopsis of his encounter with Pallin.

"Of course, he can't know who the Gray Man is," Kydar said.

"Actually, he said something weird after I told him about the Gray Man. He said, 'The Shadow walks.' Does that mean anything to you?"

They both shook their heads.

"What a time to be alive, though," Titus said, officially joining the conversation after lurking. "Elves and humans meeting at last. After so many years."

Kydar nodded. "You're right, Titus."

"Strange times, indeed," Reith said, echoing Pallin's words for earlier.

Chapter Ten

I n a short time, the refugees of Suthrond were ready
to begin their march. Already half the day had gone
and the sun was high in the sky. It was warm and
would only grow warmer, especially on the march. Heth
and Reith walked out to meet Pallin.

"We are ready, Captain," Heth announced.

"Good." Pallin raised a fist into the air and
immediately his legion began to march forward. Those on
the edge of the line walked quicker to come along the sides
of the humans. The result was a large semicircle on the
northern side of the humans. Heth turned and beckoned
to Trigg, who announced the march.

Pallin set the pace and Heth and Reith fell in behind
him. Soon, several more of the elves joined Pallin at the
front. The rest maintained the semicircle around the
humans. Kydar and Dema walked quickly to catch up to
Reith and the three followed after Pallin toward their next
home.

Reith watched the elves with fascination. As he had
noticed earlier, they were all clad in a military uniform of

some sort. They also had the same pointed ears as Pallin, but other than that, there seemed to be quite a difference from one elf to the next. Some had dark hair, almost black. Others had hair so blonde it was nearly white, but not from age. Still others were red headed.

From what Reith could tell, nearly all of the elven legion were male, but he saw a few females among them. These, he noted with interest, had more graceful faces than their male counterparts. Not that the male elf face was not graceful; it was that the female face surpassed it.

They marched for several hours, with a break every hour or two. The humans kept their distance from the flanking elves, and the elves for their part seemed content to stay away from the humans. He didn't know if this was from commitment to their marching arrangement or that they simply did not want to be near them. Reith felt like the elves were taking it in turn to study him, but whenever he turned his head to see if he was being watched, the elves faced forward, focused on their march.

It was late afternoon when Pallin called Heth and Reith to him.

"It is late in the day, and we still have several miles to go. Perhaps it would be best to camp here and come upon the city in the morning light."

Heth agreed to this course of action. A halt was called and the humans began setting up their camp. The elves split into two camps, one in front and one behind the humans.

"It is for your protection," Pallin explained. "We want to keep you safe from all dangers."

Privately, Heth shared her idea of what that meant with Reith.

"I think he is concerned that elves from the city might come upon us at night."

"That would be catastrophic," Reith said.

Two large bonfires were set between the humans and each elf camp. At the southernmost one, Pallin invited Heth and Reith to join him and a few of his officers.

"This is Laneras, Drierden, and Baros," Pallin announced, introducing the three. "And this is Heth. She is the leader of these humans. This is Reith. He is the one that warned them of their danger."

The three elf officers nodded to the two humans. Laneras was fair haired, Drierden had dark hair, and Baros had a lighter brown complexion. Of the three, Drierden looked to be the oldest and Laneras the youngest, though Reith really had no idea how old they actually were.

"Tell us about your homeland," Laneras said, leaning forward to hear the reply.

Heth smiled politely. "I am from the town of Suthrond. It is but a few miles north of the river. There we farm, mostly. My father was a farmer, and I helped him tend to his land."

"What is it that you grow?" Laneras asked.

"Primarily wheat and corn," Heth replied. "Good for us and good for the animals."

"What about you, Reith?" Laneras continued, turning to him. "I understand that you are not from Suthrond."

Clearly he would be the one pushing the conversation. Drierden and Baros seemed less inclined to engage with the humans. While Laneras leaned forward, they sat back, so that their faces were veiled in shadow away from the fire.

"I am from Coeden, a town West of Suthrond. I am a chronicler's apprentice. Or at least I was."

"A chronicler's apprentice," Laneras repeated. "And what did your chronicler tell you of the elves?"

"Not much, and I wish he had told me more. But he

did tell me of Erador and how humans, elves, and dwarves used to live together. Of elves and their customs, we know little."

"It's a shame how destiny has divided us," Pallin said mournfully, and Laneras shared his stormy expression, but Drierden and Baros we're less sad looking. For a few moments, all was silent. Then Reith remembered something from his earlier conversation with Pallin.

"Captain," he said to Pallin, "earlier, when we first met, you said, 'The Shadow walks.' What did you mean by that?"

The faces of all the elves darkened, and for a second, Reith wondered if he had made a big mistake.

"Do you not know?" Pallin asked. "Has your study with the chronicler taught you nothing? You yourself brought us these tidings."

"I don't understand," Reith said, thoroughly confused.

"Have you not met someone who seems veiled in shadow? You have brought us word of great evil roaming our land, great evil indeed."

"You mean the Gray Man?" Reith asked, putting two and two together. "But he's just a man, isn't he?"

"I have not seen him with my own eyes, so I cannot say for certain. But our lore masters tell tales of Shadows that walk the earth bringing death and destruction to any in their path."

"Then how do you know he's a Shadow?" Reith asked. "He's just a man, I think."

"Our lore masters can tell you better than I can," Pallin replied. "But know this: There are those that forsake all light in this world. They cast off everything that is good, everything that is right, everything that is pure, and transform into something else. They embrace darkness and evil. They give up part of themselves and thus they become a Shadow. They even look like shadows."

"Why would they give up part of themselves?" Reith asked.

"Our legends tell of some who did it for power. Others for revenge. And others for pleasure. But the legends all agree: There is a dark power in and behind each Shadow. This means that your Gray Man is a far more dangerous enemy than you ever could have imagined."

───────

That night, Reith could not fall asleep. His mind was on the Gray Man and this idea of Shadows. The idea that the Gray Man had some sort of dark power was abhorrent to him.

Maybe it's just an elven myth, he thought to himself. *After all, they haven't seen the Gray Man yet. They don't know.*

But a different part of his mind saw the truth in their claims. Everything about the Gray Man had seemed off. He was insane, evil, and unpredictable. *He even looks like a shadow …*

He thought back to those haunting gray eyes, how the color had seemed to be drained from him. Thinking back, it did seem like the Gray Man was perpetually standing under a shadow, even in broad daylight.

If Shadows are real, why did Vereinen never tell me about them?

In the three years he had been with Vereinen, they had covered a lot of ground, but there was still so much left to learn.

Maybe he was waiting until I was older and knew more. I just wish we had known that we wouldn't have that much time.

Anguish over his missing master washed over Reith.

Tears came to his eyes as he lay in the dark. He was glad for the darkness at this moment. He could hide those tears.

By the time Reith finally drifted off to sleep, the fires in the camp had burned low, casting their own shadows.

He awoke with the sun already fully risen and the camp starting to stir. He yawned, stretched, and sat up, looking around. Kydar and Dema were nearby collecting their things.

"Good morning, sleepyhead," Dema said, giving him a smile. "I guess sleepyhead is your new nickname."

"G'morning," he replied groggily.

"How was your talk with the elves last night?" Kydar asked. By the time Reith and Heth had left the fire the night before, Kydar and Dema were asleep.

"It was interesting."

He told them about Shadows and his suspicions that Pallin was right. As he told them, he saddled and packed Aspen.

"They're reading into it too much," Dema said. "There's no such thing. If there were such a thing as Shadows, we would have heard about it."

"That's what I thought," Reith retorted. "But everything about the Gray Man lines up with what Pallin said about Shadows."

Kydar shook his head. "I don't know, Reith. Seems kind of far-fetched."

"When you see him, you won't be so sure."

"Well, Shadow or not, I'd like to stick my knife in his heart," Dema snapped.

At that moment, Trigg came around announcing it was time to leave. The march began in the same formation as the day before. Pallin explained to Heth and Reith that they were ten miles out from Crain.

"When we reach the city, I will leave you with a

number of my men. I and the rest will enter the city and seek an audience with Gwandoeth. You shall wait. If all goes well, he should come out to see you, or else bring a few of you in to see him. I imagine he would want to talk with both of you."

Shortly after the march began, Reith saw Laneras coming toward him.

"Good morning, Reith," Laneras said, smiling warmly. "I hope all of that talk of Shadows didn't keep you awake all night."

"Not all night, no." Reith grinned back. "Kydar, Dema, this is Laneras. He's one of the officers I was with last night."

For once, Kydar and Dema seemed at a loss for words. Then Reith remembered it was their first time speaking face to face with an elf.

"It is a pleasure to meet you," Laneras said, offering his hand, which both shook in turn.

"It's all mine," Dema said finally.

"Laneras was very curious about life in our homeland," Reith explained. This got the conversation rolling and soon Kydar and Dema were chatting with Laneras as if he were an old friend.

At the first break, the four of them sat together.

"Reith," Laneras said, "May I examine your sword?"

"Oh, uh, sure," Reith replied, putting down his water and unsheathing the weapon.

Laneras let out a low whistle when it was presented to him. "This sword is a wonder," he remarked. "Wherever did you get it?"

"I found it in the library of Erador."

"A curious thing to find in any library, let alone one in a city ruined by dragons. I wonder who it belonged to."

The sun caught the blade just right and blinded Reith for a second.

"Do you know much about sword play?" Laneras asked.

"No," Reith said. "I haven't actually ever used it. I prefer my bow right now."

"Once we get to Crain, I know there would be a few interested in training you in swordplay."

"I would love to learn, especially with such a deadly foe loose in the world."

The call was made to prepare to march, and Laneras gave Reith his sword back, which he sheathed.

"It was great meeting you two," Laneras said to Kydar and Dema. They told him that the feeling was mutual. "I will see you all around. And please know, no matter what happens at Crain, that you do have some allies among us. Pallin and myself, for instance."

"We are grateful," Reith told him.

As the day wore on, the trees became fewer and the terrain grew smoother. They saw evidence of fields plowed and sowed, and even a few shoots. They were near Crain. They also found that they were now walking on a dirt path between fields. The path joined another and a bit further on, it was paved with stones.

And then, rising above a grove of trees, Crain. Its wood and stone battlements soared a few dozen feet into the air. Even from a distance, Reith could see several figures pacing back and forth at the top.

"Here is where I leave you," Pallin said to Heth and Reith. "You shall find that the grove of trees over yonder will serve for a camp until you are more settled with us. I hope to be back with good tidings soon. In the meantime, I leave Laneras in charge. If you need anything, he is a most gracious host."

Pallin and a few other elves, including Drierden and Baros, departed.

"You should probably let everyone know what's going on," Reith told Heth.

"Good idea," she replied.

In a few minutes, everyone was assembled in the clearing.

"My people," Heth called out in a loud voice. "We come to the gates of Crain. Pallin, Captain of the Legion of Crain has gone to discuss our matter with the lord of the city. For now, we wait. We shall make our home in this clearing until a home can be found for us."

Reith unpacked Aspen, giving the bags and things he unloaded to their rightful owners. Then he unsaddled her and sat down on the ground with Kydar and Dema near the edge of the clearing. Through a gap in the trees they could still see the city battlements. Aspen grazed contentedly near them.

"Did you ever think you would be here?" Kydar asked Reith, a look of wonder in his eyes. "Here, at the gate of an elven city?"

"Never in my life. I had hoped to travel. But always within the realm of the humans. Galismoor, Kal-Epharion, those places. Never to the elves." For once, the trouble that lay behind did not worry these three humans.

Soon, elves from the city came to the clearing and presented Laneras with some loaves of bread and wineskins.

"From the larder of Captain Pallin for the guests," Reith overheard them tell Laneras. The elves had very strange expressions, a mixture of curiosity and horror at the sight of all the humans. One saw Reith looking at him and hastily looked away.

Heth took the food and drink from Laneras and

distributed it fairly among the refugees. The bread was thick and hearty. The wine was sweet and red and very strong. Of each, Reith only needed a little. He allowed Aspen to sip some of the wine. She seemed to enjoy it immensely.

Another hour passed by, and then another, and Reith started to get anxious.

"What do you think is taking so long?" he asked Kydar and Dema.

"I don't know," Dema said. "Maybe they're making a plan."

Kydar tilted his head curiously. "What sort of plan?"

"Well, I can't imagine they are just going to leave us here and keep sending us food," Dema said, rolling her eyes at Kydar. "We need places to live, jobs to do. That sort of thing."

He frowned. "Oh, that makes sense."

"Dema has the measure of it," Laneras remarked, as he had evidently overheard the conversation. He squatted down beside them. "There are many things to consider. Lord Gwandoeth is not one to make a hasty decision. He will think things out, make a plan."

"What do you think will happen?" Reith asked Laneras.

"Gwandoeth is fair and just. He will seek to keep you safe. I think he will give you jobs to make your way with us. He will feed you. The issue is shelter. We don't have empty houses you could move into. I don't know what his solution will be to that difficulty. It also depends on how long you will stay here. If you could go back in a month, that will lead to different plans than if you were to stay here for years."

"How long do you think we'll be here?" Kydar asked.

"Who is to say?" Laneras replied.

"The Gray Man still wants to kill us," Reith said. "Until we get word that he is killed or else otherwise engaged, we may have to stay here."

Just then, Pallin returned. He was alone.

"Laneras, can you fetch Heth, please."

Laneras hastened to obey.

"Reith," Pallin continued. "Lord Gwandoeth seeks to speak with you. You shall accompany me into the city. For your own safety, please leave your weapons here."

"He wants to speak to me?" Reith asked.

"Yes, you and Heth," Pallin replied. "Heth because she is the leader, and you because you bring strange tidings to our ears."

Reith unbuckled his sword and placed his bow and quiver on the ground near Kydar and Dema.

"Watch over these, please," he instructed. "And Aspen, too."

"Good luck, Reith," Kydar said.

"Be brave," Dema added.

Laneras returned with Heth.

"Good, thank you Laneras," Pallin told him. "Heth, you and Reith shall accompany me into the city to speak with the Lord Gwandoeth. If you are ready…"

"I am. Let's go." Heth's face grew stoic and cool. "I'll be fine," she said to Trigg, who was nearby looking anxious. "You're in charge while I am gone. Be strong."

Pallin led the way through the trees. Heth and Reith followed. They were soon on the road leading to the gates of Crain. The city loomed over them, its wall ten feet high and the battlements reaching higher. The gates were wooden and standing open. There were guards one either side. They let Pallin and the two humans through, but both humans were on the receiving end of stares. Reith pretended not to notice.

The gates opened up to a road paved with stones. Homes and shops, mostly made of wood with some stone, were built right to the edge of the street. Horses pulled carts loaded with produce and goods through the streets. Elves bustled to and fro, and elven children ran through the crowd.

The elves dressed primarily in green, red, orange, yellow, white, and brown, which gave Reith the odd impression of a forest in autumn. Smells of cooking meat, baking bread, animals, and elves mingled together into a rich and complex aroma. It smelled different than Coeden, but how Reith could not decide.

His eyes roamed all over, trying to take everything in. His head swiveled back and forth as he tried to catch glimpses into the buildings when a door would open. Every once in a while, his eyes would meet the eyes of an elf, who usually looked away in embarrassment of being caught staring. One set of eyes, however, did not look away. His eyes met the eyes of a younger female elf. She had long brown hair and eyes to match. Her expression was curious, and her gaze was fierce, like that of Pallin's. They looked at each other until Reith had to turn forward to avoid walking into anything.

Pallin led them on through the street. Occasionally, he would greet another elf on the road. As they went on, the houses and buildings grew taller. In the center of the city, a circular stone tower rose above even the tallest house. This tower was their final destination. On the top of the parapet, several elves patrolled, looking over the city. Two guards stood by the door at ground level. They let Pallin and the humans pass. Pallin pulled open the door and ushered the humans into a small, dark room. Several candles were lit and their flames flickered.

Around the edge of the room, a staircase rose up into

the ceiling. In the center of the room was a desk, and behind the desk sat an elf, older than Pallin and quite plump. When he caught sight of the humans, he nearly upset his ink bottle, which he had been using to write on a large piece of parchment.

Pallin announced, "I am back with the two humans, Pryderus. May we go up to see his lordship?"

"He is expecting you," Pryderus said. "Though why he would bother seeing such *things* is beyond me." The contempt in his voice made Reith understand Pallin's delay in returning.

"They are not things. They are humans," Pallin retorted, looking apologetically to Heth and Reith. "And they have been brought here to see his lordship at his lordship's command."

"Humph," Pryderus grunted, returning to his parchment. He pointed to the stairs without even looking up again.

Pallin paused to allow Heth to take the lead up the stairs, which she did. Reith fell in behind her, and Pallin brought up the rear. Out of the corner of his eye, Reith saw Pallin shoot a nasty look at Pryderus.

The staircase followed the wall and led up to a wooden door, which was shut. Pallin gestured for Heth to knock, which she did. The sound of the three blows reverberated around the stone room.

"Enter!" came the voice from the other side. Heth took a deep breath, pushed the door open, and the two humans entered the office of the elf Lord of Crain.

Chapter Eleven

The office was richly furnished. Wood panels covered the stone walls and created a welcoming environment. Rounded windows in the walls let in sunlight, the beams illuminating any dust particle in the air. Stairs continued up along the wall to the rampart above. Shelves lined the walls and were covered with books, scrolls, and loose parchment. A sturdy desk stood near the middle of the room. It was evidently carved by a master craftsman, as there were designs etched into the wood. Behind the desk sat a gray bearded elf with piercing blue eyes and short white hair. Around his neck hung a silver medallion.

As the humans and Pallin entered, the elf put down the book he was studying and rose to greet them. He towered above the others, well over six feet tall. Reith would have been greatly intimidated if not for the smile on the elf's lips. Still, Reith was daunted in his presence.

"Welcome to Crain," the elf said in a voice rich, deep, and strong. "My name is Gwandoeth, and I am pleased to welcome you, Heth and Reith, into our halls."

"The pleasure is all mine," Heth replied. "We humbly seek your mercy and your help."

"My help you shall have," Gwandoeth answered. "I spoke with Pallin earlier about your plight. He told me such an interesting and sorrowful tale. Heth, if you would, I would like to hear it from your lips."

"Certainly my lord," said Heth, and she began to explain. Reith, who had heard everything before, let his mind wander. He inspected the bookshelves beyond Gwandoeth, noticing some books titled *A Concise History of the Northern Provinces*, *The Tales of Bergond the Warrior,* and *The Magistrate.*

What I wouldn't give for a few days alone with these books, he thought to himself.

He turned his attention upon Gwandoeth, who was listening intently to Heth. His eyes were focused on hers and he nodded along with her story. He even supplied "Hmm's" and "Mmhmm's" when appropriate.

Not only is he a leader, but he is also a listener.

Heth finished her story and Gwandoeth turned his blue eyes on Reith.

"Now, young Reith, your tale. I am most interested in certain aspects of your story."

"Well, Lord Gwandoeth, my story begins in Coeden, which is some miles west of Suthrond. I am an orphan. When I was thirteen, I was taken into the service of a chronicler by name of Vereinen as his apprentice."

"And how old are you now?" Gwandoeth asked.

"I am sixteen, sir."

"Thank you, sorry for the interruption."

"It's fine. Not many days ago, I was out hunting, as I hunt three or four times a week. When I returned, Coeden was ablaze and my townsfolk were killed. I encountered a man who can only be described as gray. His skin, his eyes, his voices, all were gray. The Gray Man spared my life on a whim and I escaped. Before my encounter, I had discovered a note from my master instructing me to seek him in Erador, the ruined city. With nowhere else to go, I traveled west and crossed the river into Dragonscar. At Erador, I discovered two wonders and one dread. The first wonder was a stream and a grove of fruit trees in the middle of the desolation. The second wonder was a marvelous sword, which is back at our camp now. The dread was the Gray Man. He was looking for something."

At the mention of the Gray Man looking for something, Gwandoeth's brow furrowed and his eyes flashed with concern. It was gone as quickly as it came and Reith continued his tale.

"I overheard him and his men. He was looking for something that matched his ring. I don't remember what his ring looked like, though. He said they would search for a few days, and then go back and finish off the Suthronders. So I left Erador, stole a horse from the Gray Man's camp by the river, and traveled to Suthrond. I found the trail the Suthronders had left and discovered them on the northern bank of the Rammis River. I have been with them ever since."

Gwandoeth sat in silence for a few moments. His eyes were closed and his hands were clasped as if in prayer. Finally, he opened his eyes and looked across at Reith.

"You bring strange tidings, indeed. This Gray Man seems to be a fearsome enemy. His presence in our land does not bode well."

"Is he a Shadow?" Reith asked.

Gwandoeth peered at him suspiciously. "What do you know of Shadows?"

"Only what I have been told." He looked toward Pallin, who averted his eyes.

"Make no more mention of Shadows here," Gwandoeth ordered. "Your lives are at stake. If my people learn that you have been chased here because of a Shadow, they will shun you at best. At worst …" He trailed off, leaving it to their imagination.

"Please, sir," Reith urged, wanting Gwandoeth's opinion.

"No more," the lord said loudly. "I have said all I will. It would be better for everyone if we changed the subject."

"What is your plan for us, my lord?" Heth asked hastily, seeking to move the conversation past the sticking point.

"That, Heth, I do not know yet," Gwandoeth replied. "There are so many things to consider. Do you have any recommendations?"

"We have those who are old and those who are young. Many can be put to work. We would like to earn our place here as long as we stay. Let those who can be placed with elves work with them."

"That is an excellent idea, Heth. But it shall take great care and planning to implement. My people will be suspicious of you. It will be a difficult road to tread."

"No more difficult than losing our family and friends to the Gray Man's attack, crossing the river, and seeking refuge with your people," Heth replied, her tone firm.

"Of course, you are right," Gwandoeth conceded. "I did not mean to minimize your troubles and difficulty. I think my mind is clear on our way forward. Let Pallin and I spend the rest of the day determining where your people may fit in our city. In the morning, we shall announce what has happened and what will occur moving forward. Then we shall interview your people, one at a time, to determine their places here. After those interviews, we shall determine where you shall work and where you shall stay."

"That is greater kindness than we could have expected," Heth replied.

"Pallin," Gwandoeth said to the captain, "take our guests back to their camp. Then make haste to return so that we may discuss. Leave the humans in the care of Laneras for the time being."

Pallin led the way back down the stairs, through Pryderus's study, and out the door. Pryderus was busying writing and took no notice of them. Once out in the open, Pallin apologized for him.

"I am sorry for Pryderus and those who will be just like him. There are those who see difference as a reason to hate."

Back at the camp, Reith filled Kydar and Dema in on the developments. He told them of his experience in Crain, from the gates to the tower and Lord Gwandoeth's office. Laneras listened in with interest as well.

"So we will be interviewed one by one?" Dema asked nervously.

"Yes, so they can determine what we will do here," Reith answered.

"What do you think we will do, Laneras?" Kydar asked.

"Well, I imagine that farm work will be the most plentiful job you could do."

"Can I join the Legion?" Dema asked, her voice growing excited.

"Hmmm," Laneras said, thinking it over. "I hadn't thought of that as an option."

"It would make sense to train some of us humans to

guard ourselves. And even learn to fight so we can go back and kick the Gray Man's—"

"Yes, I think that may be a good idea," Laneras interjected. "I would have to run it by Pallin, and Gwandoeth would have to approve as well. But I personally see no reason why you couldn't train with us. Of course, you wouldn't be a full member of the Legion."

"Why not?" Dema asked.

"Well for one, you're not an elf. You're also not a citizen of Crain. Not yet. Plus, I think that many in the Legion would object to a human joining."

"I'd like to join the Legion too," Kydar said. "If I can, of course. Or at least train with them."

"What about you Reith?" Laneras asked. "Would you like to join the Legion's human corps?"

"It's tempting. I'd like to learn to use my sword. But I think I want to continue what I was doing in Coeden. Is there a chronicler here I could work with?"

"We have a lore master and cleric," Laneras said. "From what you have described, you would probably fit in well."

"I think I would like that. I saw Gwandoeth's library and it got me missing books."

That evening, more bread and wine was brought to the humans, as well as a bit of white cheese. Pallin came out with it and spoke to Heth privately, then he went back into the city.

"What was that about?" Kydar asked Reith and Dema.

"I don't know," Reith replied, "I hope everything is all right."

When Heth walked by later, Kydar asked her what was going on.

"Oh, it was nothing really," she said. "He just wanted

to tell me to have ten ready to enter the city tomorrow an hour after dawn for interviews. I shall go, and as shall the three of you. You're young and strong, and I'm sure they will put you to good use."

That evening around the fire, Reith, Dema, and Kydar asked Laneras questions about himself.

"How old are you?" Dema asked. This was something Reith was dying to know as well.

"I have gone about the sun four and twenty times," Laneras replied with a smile. "And how old might you three be?"

"I'm fifteen," Dema said. "Kydar is seventeen."

"And I am sixteen," Reith answered. "I honestly had no idea how old you were."

"I am young for my race," Laneras explained. "At twenty, we come of age. Though, of course, we pursue wisdom all our lives. Mature but always maturing is the saying among my people."

"We come of age at eighteen," Kydar said. "I am almost a man. I will be in the fall."

"That is good, but always remember to seek after wisdom."

"When did you join the Legion?" Reith asked.

"When I came of age. At that time, all elves are required to decide where they will go. Of course, not all who desire to join the Legion actually do so. There is a rigorous entrance examination. Perspectives are tested for physical fitness, mental ability, and ethical reasoning."

"That's really interesting," Reith remarked. "You desire your warriors to be smart and just as well as good with a weapon."

"Yes, we only take on the best."

"Did you grow up here in Crain?" Kydar asked.

"Yes, my father is a miller. I worked with him until I joined the Legion. But not everyone in the Legion of Crain is from here. Pallin, for instance, is from the capital city of Sardis. He was commissioned here."

"What do you do for fun?" Dema asked. "When you're not working, how do you spend your time?"

"I enjoy hunting and fishing," Laneras answered. "It's good to get away from the city by yourself. I enjoy the silence."

Their conversation continued until the fire burned low. Then Laneras excused himself.

"I must sleep. And so should you. You have important matters to attend to tomorrow."

"Good night, Laneras," Kydar said. "And thank you for taking time to talk to us."

"It was no trouble at all. I am interested in learning about humans, so you were doing me a service."

Reith awoke with the sun. Its beams pierced through the trees. Some other humans were already awake, clustered in small groups talking quietly with one another. Reith saw Titus and Tara across the camp with their mother, Lara.

He rustled through his bag and took out the last peach from Erador.

It's a miracle that it is still good, he thought. He ate the peach and then decided to plant it at the edge of the clearing. He judged where the best spot would be for sunlight and rainwater. There Reith dug a small hole and covered the peach pit with earth. He sprinkled a small amount of Erador water on it from his jug, which he had wanted to ration. He stepped back and saw, to his delight, that a green shoot was already poking through the soft earth.

In a few hours, there will be peaches here.

"So this is the result of your magic fruit," a voice said behind him. He turned to see Heth leaning against one of the trees. "It's already several inches high and you just planted it. It's a miracle."

Reith rubbed the dirt off of his hands and nodded, not entirely sure what to say.

"We had peaches," Heth continued, looking at him, though her eyes were seeing years past. "On our farm. My father grew them along with the wheat and corn."

Reith said nothing, knowing any interruption would be unwelcome.

"In a way, it's like having a bit of home here, once this peach tree comes up ..." She trailed off and the two were silent for a minute. "Will I ever go home, Reith? Or did the Gray Man take my home as well as my friends and family?"

"I don't know, Heth."

"I'm not very young, Reith."

He didn't know what to say to that.

"I may die here. Is it worth it, living somewhere that's not home?"

"It's worth it for living. You'd die if you stayed."

"Living, dying, neither seem to matter anymore." In that moment, it seemed to Reith that her face changed, so that now he was looking at Heth as she was years ago, as a little girl. But then the sensation passed just as quickly as it had come.

"Each breath we take matters," Reith said. "We all have the choice of what to do with our next one. Live here and help your people. Help them, serve them." He echoed the voice he had heard in Erador without even thinking about it.

"Promise me, Reith," Heth said, looking him in the eye. "Promise me that if I die here, you will bury my body north of the river. Bury me in Suthrond. If you can bury me by the peach trees, bury me there. Don't let my bones stay here. Let my bones go home."

"I promise."

"And promise me this, too," she continued, her eyes pleading, "don't let my people stay here forever. Take them home too. Do whatever it takes."

"I promise."

"Kill the Gray Man."

"Dema said she wants to."

"Promise me that you will kill him and take my people home."

"I promise."

"May this peach tree stand as a sign between you and me," Heth said, gesturing to the green shoot that was now a foot tall. "This preach tree, as long as it lives, will be a sign that we have made a promise. As often as you eat from this tree, remember your promise to me."

"On this tree and on my life, I will uphold my promises to you."

Heth nodded and turned away, leaving Reith alone with the budding peach tree.

———

Heth left Trigg in charge again. Reith, Kydar, Dema, Titus, Tara, Lara, Rangel, and two older women, Jepp and Flora, were all chosen to be the first interviewed. Pallin and several elves led them to the gates of Crain and through the city to Gwandoeth's tower. The humans received plenty of stairs this morning. Pallin had informed them that Gwandoeth had officially announced in the city square that humans had come to live among them.

Pryderus sat behind his desk working hard, or pretending to work hard, as it seemed to Reith. Every few seconds, Pryderus's eyes would jump from his parchment to the ten humans standing in his office. His dislike for the humans was on full display.

Pallin and Gwandoeth conducted the interviews together. They began with Heth, with the rest of the humans waiting in the room with Pryderus. After Heth went up the stairs and the door shut, there was silence downstairs except for the occasional scratching of Pryderus's pen on his parchment.

"What's going on, mom?" Tara asked. Pryderus stopped writing and looked up at her.

"We're waiting to find our place here in Crain," Lara said.

"I want to go home," she whined.

"I know, sweetie, I know. But hush now."

Pryderus started writing again, and the scratch of his quill was again the only sound in the room. Reith glanced at Kydar and Dema, who were looking at Pryderus with dislike.

Just then, they heard the door upstairs open and then Heth came down.

"What happened?" Dema asked.

"I will be assisting Gwandoeth on the human resettlement. So I will be conducting the interviews with him and Pallin and then making sure that everything goes smoothly."

"I'm glad you'll be in there with us," Kydar said.

"Reith, you're next," Heth said, and Reith stood and walked to the stairs. He ascended and entered Gwandoeth's office again. The lighting was different today, as the light was coming in from the windows on the other side of the room.

Gwandoeth sat behind the desk with Heth and Pallin seated on either side of him. Gwandoeth pointed Reith to the chair opposite him in front of the desk, which he sat in.

"Good morning, Reith," Gwandoeth said. "Let's get down to business. Where do you see yourself fitting into our society while you are here?"

"Well, sir," Reith began, "I hoped that I could do work similar to my work in Coeden with the chronicler Vereinen."

"A worthy goal, and one to which you seem to be well suited," Pallin replied.

"Is there anything like that here in Crain?" Reith asked.

"Why yes, I think we have just the place for you," Gwandoeth answered. "In Crain, we have a small temple. The cleric is also a lore master. I think you would get along just fine with her. If she is agreeable, you would also live in temple keeper's lodgings."

"I think it would be splendid for Reith to live and learn with your lore master," Heth said. "Remembering the past is crucial for moving toward the future." Reith's mind went to the promise he had made her by the peach tree.

"Is this arrangement agreeable to you, Reith?" Gwandoeth asked.

"I think so, sir," Reith replied. "Though I am not much for religion. Occasionally preachers would come to Coeden, but I did not care for them much."

"Don't consider it a religious endeavor. Consider it for its historical nature," Gwandoeth said. "I think you shall learn a lot and will even have much to teach us."

"Okay then, I will do it," Reith agreed.

"Good!" Gwandoeth said, smiling. "Pallin, could you write up a note for Pryderus to pass along. Invite her to come here this afternoon, right after lunch." Pallin dipped a quill and scrawled a quick note. When he was done, he folded it over and sealed it with wax and Gwandoeth's seal.

"Heth," Pallin said, "let us go down and get the next one. Reith, you may wait in Pryderus's office until you are summoned."

The three left the office and walked down the stairs. Heth took Lara, Titus, and Tara with her upstairs, and Pallin gave the sealed note to Pryderus and whispered instructions to him. Pryderus frowned, rose, and left the tower. Pallin followed the four humans up the stairs. With Pryderus gone, the atmosphere in the room was immediately better.

"What happened?" Dema asked. "What are you going to do?"

"It seems I will go to live and work with their lore master," Reith said. "Pryderus is taking a note to her now."

"A lore master? That sounds like the perfect place for you," Kydar remarked.

"I don't know. They said she is a cleric in a temple. I don't know about religion. In Coeden, we got the occasional traveling preacher. It seemed that they mostly cared about us giving them money so that we could save our souls."

Kydar frowned. "We had a few like that too. I didn't care much for them. As if the gods cared about this preacher's wallet."

"Still," Dema said, "it should be an interesting experience for you. You'll have so much you can learn!"

The interviews went fairly quickly, such that only the two older women, Jepp and Flora, were left by the time Pryderus had returned. Lara, Titus, and Tara had been approved to move to a farmhouse outside of Crain to work. Rangel would go to work with a cobbler in Crain. Kydar and Dema were approved by Pallin to undergo testing to train with the Legion. Dema in particular was excited about this possibility.

"It sure beats farming," she said.

"Tell me about it," Kydar agreed.

Just after Jepp ascended the stairs, Pryderus returned. He ignored the humans and resumed sitting behind his desk and making notes on the parchment. The talking died down in the presence of the grumpy elf.

After Jepp and Flora were assigned to vineyard work, Gwandoeth invited the humans up to his apartment, which was right above his office and below the parapet. Stairs led to a landing where there was a wooden door. Upon opening the door and going inside, Reith noticed Gwandoeth's apartment was furnished much like his office. Wood panels made the room feel inviting. He had a sturdy wooden table and several chairs, along with a small kitchen area. A door led to the next room, where Reith supposed he slept. There they had a lunch of bread and fish, with wine to wash it down. The conversation was cordial, with Gwandoeth inviting his guests to tell him more about their lives before coming to Crain.

After lunch, as they were continuing their conversation, there was a knock on the door.

"Come in," Gwandoeth called.

The door opened to reveal Pryderus.

"My Lord," he said, not even looking at any of the humans. "The lore master is here."

"Very good," Gwandoeth replied. "Reith, would you kindly go with Master Pryderus. Your new life awaits."

Chapter Twelve

Reith descended the stairs behind Pryderus. At the bottom stood a tall elven woman. She wore a long green robe that brushed the floor. Beneath the collar were seven silver stars. Her hair was golden, with a hint of red. She seemed older than Laneras, maybe Pallin's age, but he could not be sure.

"Hello Reith," she said, her voice light and musical. "I am Ellyn."

She held out a hand to him, which he shook.

"It is a pleasure to meet you, Ellyn," Reith said.

"Come, we have much to discuss."

They left the tower behind. Reith walked beside Ellyn as she glided through the streets of Crain. Everywhere they went, the elves nodded to her in respect. They scarcely seemed to notice Reith, and for that he was grateful.

She took him along a side street. He kept looking for a grand temple rising above the city but he did not see it until they were right at its front steps.

"Here we are," she said. "The Temple of Crain."

The temple was small, much smaller than Gwandoeth's

tower. It was made of white marble, seamless in its construction, as though carved out of a single block. Later, he found out that is indeed how it came to be. Large windows of stained glass shimmered in the sunlight, reflecting a rainbow of colors.

Ellyn pushed open the door and Reith found himself in a room about sixty feet long and thirty feet wide. At the far end of the room, three steps led up to the altar, on which sat several scrolls and candles. A large stained-glass window was behind the altar, and it depicted several elves and symbols, of which he knew nothing. Other than the altar, the rest of the room was bare, with no furniture or ornament. Two doors were in each of the far corners from where he stood.

Ellyn walked through the room toward the door on the left, which she pushed open to reveal a short hallway. There were three doors in addition to the one they had walked through and she took Reith through the first. Shelves lined the walls, floor to ceiling. They were covered with books and scrolls. In the center of the room were comfortable looking leather chairs.

"I see that you approve," Ellyn said, smiling at Reith's obvious delight. "Welcome to the Temple Library. Have a seat."

He sat in the nearest chair. The room smelled of paper, leather, and knowledge.

"Tell me about yourself, Reith." Ellyn sat down in a chair opposite him. "I hardly know anything, save for what I heard from Lord Gwandoeth this morning and what was in Pallin's note today. Do start from the beginning."

"Well," Reith began, "I am from Coeden; it's a human town across the river. My parents died of fever three years ago, and I went to live with a chronicler named Vereinen as his apprentice. I helped him with his research and writing, and I hunted for us."

"It sounds like you will do just fine here with me," she said. "Go on."

He continued his tale, like he had told Gwandoeth the previous day, when he had first met the lord of the city. He looked carefully for any sign of recognition in Ellyn's face whenever he mentioned the Gray Man, but she kept the same calm, thoughtful expression during his whole tale. Reith wondered if he should even mention the word Shadow. From Laneras, he knew that Ellyn, as lore master, knew about Shadows. But Gwandoeth's warning still rang in his mind.

When he finished his story, she looked at him carefully, studying his face and eyes.

"There is something else you wish to ask," she noted, sensing the conflict within him. "Something you have been warned to not ask."

"I am of two minds," Reith admitted. "I was told you have the answer. I have also been told not to speak of it."

"I think I can satisfy your curiosity and your honor," she said, the hint of a smile gracing her lips. "You have heard more about this Gray Man than you have shared. And you have been warned to keep that knowledge to yourself."

He nodded, hoping she would keep going.

"This temple, Reith, is a shelter, a sanctuary from whatever else is happening outside. Know that and live into it. That is my first lesson for you. Know that you are safe here. You are safe to ask questions."

He was dying to ask his questions.

"And now, my guess as to what your question is: You have heard that this Gray Man might be a Shadow. You want to know more. Is that it?"

"Yes, it is. How did you know?"

"Your eyes, Reith. The eyes always tell the truth. When you talked about the Gray Man, your eyes were searching mine for a hint of recognition. You did well to do this. Many people will give away their secrets if you would just look for them in their eyes. Unfortunately for you, I do not give away my secrets easily. Know that this is a sanctuary where you can ask any question. But know too that I cannot answer every question. Some are unanswerable and others the answers are too terrible for all to bear."

His face fell with disappointment. He tried to mask it, but Ellyn had already noticed.

"I intend to give you the information you seek when you are ready to hear it. But first, we must get to know each other, you and I."

Reith braced himself for more questions.

"Pick a book."

"What?" Reith asked.

"Pick a book. Pick any book in this room, whatever catches your interest. Then read it. At dinner, you and I will discuss what you have read."

"And that will help us to get to know one another?"

"Of course. Your choice of book will tell me much of your interests and desires. Your discussion with me later will tell me much of how your mind works, how you think. Yes, this is a great way to get to know one another. I'll be in the next room if you need me. Otherwise, I will see you when it is time for dinner."

Reith looked around at the books and a big smile came to his face. Here he was, a human, placed in an elven library and told to read whatever he wanted. *It's a dream come true! If only Vereinen could see me now.*

But then his heart sank at the thought of his master. It had been so long since he had seen him and he had never gotten a chance to say goodbye. *No. I'll see him again,* he chided himself.

He figured he had several hours until dinner. Reith took fifteen minutes to make his book selection. There were all sorts of books here. From their spines and covers, he saw that many were history, some were myths, some were philosophy, others were theology, and some were about science. He was looking for any book that may hold the secrets of Shadows.

He settled at last upon a medium sized volume called *An Inquiry of Light* by Lyle Bergondson. He did not think he could finish it before dinner, but he figured he would give it a start.

He settled down in one of the leather chairs and lost himself in the book. It was part history, part theology, and part mythology. Many of the names and places were foreign to him, but he was able to make good progress. Reith lost himself in the book, as he had so many times at Vereinen's house in what seemed like the distant past.

Finally, he heard the door open and Ellyn came back in. She wheeled in a small cart with food and drink laid out on top. There were grapes, chicken, corn, and several dishes he did not know.

"How did your study go?" she asked, helping herself to a small plate on which she scooped some of the food.

"This book is fascinating," Reith said, putting down *An Inquiry of Light.*

"An interesting choice indeed," Ellyn replied, eyeing the book. "That is one of my favorites and one of the most important books of our faith. It is a wonder you should pick it." She gestured to the food. "Please, help yourself."

Reith grabbed a plate and loaded it up with food. He chose mostly that with which he was familiar but was polite and took some of the foreign food as well. He found that he liked all of it.

Between bites, he asked, "What do you know about me based upon my choice of book?"

"Well," she said, contemplating him. "You are inquisitive and curious. You seek answers to your questions, and you lack the patience to wait for me to give them."

Reith opened his mouth to protest, but Ellyn continued.

"There is nothing wrong with curiosity," she said. "Curiosity is good. In this case, I gave you no limits. Your search for truth is admirable."

"What else?"

"I also know that you are intelligent. A lesser scholar may have chosen a shorter book. You chose a book you knew you couldn't finish in the time allotted because you thought it to be the best use of your time. You also were efficient with your time, as you only took a few minutes to make your selection. That means you are decisive. Some can take hours to choose in this place."

"It was a temptation."

"And one that you handled. How am I doing so far? Am I hitting the mark?"

"Bullseye," he replied.

"And now for the second half of my inquiry. What is this book about?"

"Well light, I supposed."

"Yes, Reith, light, very good," she said sarcastically. "More."

"Lyle is very concerned with light. He thinks that in light we find the divine. He calls your deity the God of Light. This god is the light source, the thing that illuminates all and gives purpose and meaning."

"That is a better summary than most elves could give,"

Ellyn said. "And what do you think of all of that? Do you agree with Lyle?"

"Well, I don't know about a god or even multiple gods, but I do think Lyle is onto something. We see everything by the light. We want to bring truth to light."

"And what of darkness?" Ellyn asked. "Where does darkness come in?"

"Lyle says darkness is absence of light, which makes sense. You cannot light a darkness candle in a well-lit room. It's nonsensical."

"Good!" Ellyn said with a smile. "You are grasping the argument. Now, I will tell you that of all the books in this room, the one you chose is the one that would answer your questions."

He reached for it eagerly, but she reached quicker and snatched it from his grasp.

"Oh no, no easy answers. You are getting the argument. Now, let's see if you can reason your way to the solution." She leaned forward, a hungry look in her eye, like an animal seeking its prey.

"Well a shadow, in the ordinary sense, is what happens when something comes between the light and the observer. We all cast a shadow when we stand before the sun."

Reith closed his eyes and pictured a tree's shadow, then he pictured the Gray Man, gray and terrible.

"Is a Shadow then someone who blocks the light?" he asked.

"You used the correct words, but I don't think you understand. Not yet. What does Lyle believe about Light itself?"

"He believes that light comes from the God of Light."

"Exactly. And therefore a Shadow is …"

"Someone who blocks the God of Light."

"Yes! That is fundamentally what a shadow is."

He thought about it for a moment, his brow furrowed in concentration.

"But how do you know the Gray Man is a Shadow?"

"I am very certain. Everything you have told me points to it. His insanity, his disregard for the lives the God of Light made, and of course his shadowy complexion. There is no doubt in my mind that is what he is."

"Then if he is a Shadow, that means that all of this is real."

Ellyn sat there, letting him ponder the implications of it all.

"The existence of a Shadow proves the existence of the Light," he said slowly. It was a lot to take in.

"And now you know why we have this temple here, our temple to the God of Light."

Ellyn and Reith walked through the streets of Crain toward the gate, as Reith needed to get his things from the camp. Along the way, he noticed again the deferential way that the elves of Crain treated Ellyn.

She waited at the gate while he went to the camp. She had promised that he could keep Aspen in a small barn out back of the temple where she kept some chickens.

Trigg was the only one he knew well in the camp. Heth was still in the city, though she had sent word to Trigg that she would be back later that night. Kydar and Dema were not around.

"What will they have you doing?" Trigg asked.

"I will go live in their temple," he said. "I will study with their lore master."

"Sounds like you have landed on your feet then. I don't

know where they'd stick an old fellow like me. I don't really trust them, if you know what I mean."

"Lord Gwandoeth and Pallin are good, and they will take care of you. Plus, Heth is here and she will fight for you if need be."

"Well you take care, Reith. I reckon I will see you around sometime."

"I hope so," Reith replied. "Though I hope even more that someday we go home."

"Home, home." Trigg's voice filled with longing. "If only. You keep hoping."

"I will."

He retrieved his pack and sword and went to have a look at the peach tree, which was now three feet tall and laden with several large, juicy peaches. He picked four of these and placed them in his bag. Then he saddled Aspen and rode her to the gate.

Once there, he dismounted. Ellyn reached forward and gave Aspen a pat on the nose, earning an appreciative neigh.

"I think she likes you," Reith said, and Ellyn smiled.

They walked through the city, back to the temple. Behind the temple was a small barn. There was hay for bedding and Ellyn had even gotten some oaks for Aspen, which she enjoyed.

"Good night, girl," Reith told the horse, stroking its mane. "I'll be back in the morning."

Inside, Ellyn showed Reith where he would stay. There was a small room two doors down from the library that contained a bed, a small dresser, and a bedside table.

"Sleep well, Reith," Ellyn called. "In the morning, I will show you your temple duties."

"Good night, Ellyn," Reith said. "I will sleep well

tonight. I haven't had a real bed in forever. And thank you so much for taking me in. I really appreciate it."

"It is good to have someone to help around here." With that, she left the room.

Reith looked around his new room. Like every other room in the temple, the walls were marble. The dresser was empty except for a robe similar to the one Ellyn wore. He decided he would not put it on unless she told him to. He didn't want to be disrespectful to his gracious host.

On his bedside table, he saw that Ellyn had left *An Inquiry of Light*.

Some late night reading, Reith thought to himself. He settled into bed, pulling the covers over himself, and instantly felt tired. The bed was soft and warm. He leaned over and blew out his candle. Moonlight fell through his window, giving the room a cool, blue air. And then he slept as he hadn't slept in weeks.

———

When he awoke, sun gleamed into the room, warming Reith's cheeks. Judging by the angle of the rays, it was mid-morning. He sat up and stretched, feeling rested and energized as he hadn't for so long. He rose, put on his shoes, and walked down the hall toward the library. There he found Ellyn sitting in a chair, reading.

"Good morning," she said as he walked in. "You slept late."

He smiled. "That bed was so comfortable."

"Let's go into the sanctuary."

They entered and the light from the stained glass caused the room to have a golden glow. She led him to the altar, where seven candles were lit.

"One of our most important tasks is keeping these

candles lit. There are seven, the number of completeness. I keep spare oil in the closet on the other side of your bedroom. Every morning, I want you to check these candles and fill them with oil. You will do this again each evening."

Reith nodded. "Easy enough."

"As you slept in, I already did them this morning. I keep the sanctuary open for prayer as long as the sun is up. At dawn, I unlock the door and at sunset, I lock it again. We will share this task. I can unlock the door in the morning if you lock it at night."

"What else would you have me do during the day?" he asked.

"In the mornings, see to your horse and the chickens out back. We will spend part of the morning cleaning our temple. If you finish your morning tasks, the rest of the morning is yours to spend how you wish. In the afternoons, you will study. I will give you books to read, assignments to write, and we will have conversations. I wish to learn from you as much as you wish to learn from me. In the evenings, you are free to do whatever your hand finds to do, except be back at sunset to lock the sanctuary."

"Thank you, Ellyn," Reith said. "This sounds like a wonderful opportunity."

The corners of her lips curved into a small smile. "I pray it is so. One other thing. You may have noticed a robe like mine in the closet in your room. You may wear it while performing temple duties. It should fit you just fine. It's a way to dress reverently while in temple service. Though, if you are uncomfortable, you may pass."

"I did see it," Reith said. "I didn't want to assume anything about it. I will wear it tomorrow."

"I look forward to it."

The next few days passed in a blur of newness for Reith. He was learning all sorts of things about elves and their history from Ellyn. He even got a chance to read two of the books he had spied in Gwandoeth's office his first day here, *A Concise History of the Northern Provinces* and *The Tales of Bergond the Warrior.* Mostly, he learned that the elves were an old and proud people. They valued honor and loyalty above all else.

A few times, Kydar and Dema visited him in the temple. They were awestruck by the beauty of the temple but not nearly as excited as he was about the learning and the books. Kydar gave him a hard time about the green robe at first but had to admit that it looked quite comfortable. The first few times he saw them, they were weary.

"Pallin is running us ragged," Kydar said a few days after their arrival. "There is running, obstacle courses, and weapons training. And then there is the study of ethics and learning in general. It wearies the body and mind."

"Laneras said we are doing really well, for human children," Dema added, rolling her eyes.

"Are you learning to fight with swords?" Reith asked.

"Wooden so far," Kydar said. "And it's very painful when you get struck."

"Well, you need to get better at blocking the blow," Dema remarked, and she lightly punched Kydar in the arm. He yelped and grabbed the spot, rubbing it and muttering at her under his breath. "What was that?" Dema asked, smiling at her brother.

"I said I'll get you back the next time we spar."

"I doubt that, O brother. You're not quick enough."

She struck him lightly on the other arm and then jumped back from his retaliatory blow.

In addition to the visits from Kydar and Dema, Laneras came by the temple a few times as well and confirmed that Kydar and Dema were indeed doing well.

"They're strong and smart," he said. "If they were elves, they would have a chance at becoming an officer in a few years. How is it going for you here?"

"I'm enjoying the work and learning a lot."

Laneras nodded. "Ellyn is a great teacher. I learned a lot from her."

———

A week into their stay in Crain, Heth came by to visit Reith.

"How goes the work of resettlement?" he asked her.

"We have placed everyone in our company. Many of the elves are distrustful of us, but the work goes well. There have been no major incidents yet."

"Is Trigg playing nice?" he asked.

"Oh, you know Trigg. He's gruff and slow to warm, but once he does, he is as loyal a man as you'll find."

"So he's not doing well, then," Reith replied flatly.

"You have read between the lines, Reith. He is slow to trust, and the elves for their part are slow to trust him. Still, there is some progress."

"Now that we are all settled, what will you do?"

"Oh, a bit of this, a bit of that," she said. "If any needs arise among the humans, I will be called upon. My next task is to determine whether or not we should go home. Pallin has scouts near the river at all times. Three days ago, the scouts saw a company of men at the beach where our camp was originally. The scouts remained hidden in the trees and could not see if it was the Gray Man or not. But the assumption is that it was him."

"Did the scouts attack?"

"No, they were outnumbered ten to one. But the good news is the Gray Man did not make a crossing attempt. Instead, they turned back to Suthrond and it has been quiet on the riverfront ever since."

"I wonder what his plan is," Reith said.

"At the moment, it is no concern of ours. We are not strong enough to regain our homeland. He could strike at any time if we went back. Perhaps in a month or two we shall send someone to Galismoor. Maybe the king can help us."

The next day, Reith entered the sanctuary to check on the candles. He was surprised to find that he was not the only one in there. A woman with long brown hair was kneeling in prayer. She glanced up when he walked in, and their eyes met. Hers were brown like her hair. Pointed ears poked out from her wavy tresses.

"Uh," he said, caught off guard by the presence of an elf. "Good morning."

"Good morning," she said. Her voice was bouncy, as if each syllable was a spring to the next.

Then he remembered. "I saw you the other day, when I first came into Crain."

She looked at him, not saying a word.

"Oh, I am so sorry, you're here praying," he said, his face flushing red. "I will leave you alone."

She continued to look at him. Then she burst out laughing. Her laugh was musical and reverberated around the stone room.

"You should see your face," she replied, the laugh still on her tongue. "It's as red as a tomato." She gracefully stood up and extended her hand. "My name is Ellamora."

"Reith," he said, shaking it.

"It is nice to finally meet you, Reith. You are right, you did see me the other day. I was fascinated by the idea of humans in our city."

He shrugged. "I'm honored to be here."

"You are more honored than you know," Ellamora remarked. "This is a sacred place and you have been given a sacred duty. I come here to pray often, as do many of my people."

"I am eager to learn more about the customs and beliefs of the elves."

"And I of the humans," Ellamora replied. "I met a few of the others with Laneras. He's my friend. He told me you had ended up here."

"So if you're not here praying, what are you doing here?" he asked.

"Why meeting you, duh." She gave him a wry look "I came here in friendship. But I also come with a warning."

"A warning?"

"This is the calm before the storm, Reith," she said, her smile leaving her face. "There are some who hate that humans are living here. And all it takes is one spark to ignite an inferno."

"What do you mean?" Reith asked. "I thought you came in friendship?"

"I do, and I want to be friends. But there are powerful people who do not want humans in Crain. They will take the first opportunity to make you leave."

"Who? What people?" Reith asked.

"When the spark ignites, know that I am on your side. Trust me."

"I will, if you truly desire to be my friend."

"No matter what you hear, you have to promise to trust me."

"I promise."

"I don't think you understand." Ellamora sighed, looking torn. "Someday, maybe soon, you will hear something about me that will cause you to doubt. Know that I am a human friend, no matter what."

"Okay," Reith said. "But you can't tell me what that thing is?"

"I can't. If word came back to ... Well, if word got around, that we had talked, I'd be in trouble."

She turned and walked to the door. But then she slowed, as if unsure. She looked back at Reith.

"Reith?"

"Yes?"

"Family isn't everything."

And with that, she left, leaving Reith confused. As he filled the candles with oil, he wondered about Ellamora.

She seems alright. I'll have to ask Laneras about her the next time I see him.

Later that day, Ellyn invited him into the sanctuary. As they walked in, he saw three elves praying silently. When the elves saw the new arrivals, they stood up, bowed toward the altar, and left.

"What was that about?" Reith asked.

"Some who have not let their love for the God of Light touch their darkened souls," she said simply. "Those who love the God of Light love those who are created by the God of Light."

"They left because I am a human?"

"Unfortunately, yes," Ellyn said, looking at him sadly. "There are some who believe that the presence of a non-elf is defiling."

"Why do they believe that?"

"They have been taught all their lives that elves are the pinnacle of the God of Light's creation."

"And are they? Are you, I mean?

"No, not according to our sacred texts. But you can see how it has crept into our thinking over hundreds of years of isolation from the humans and dwarves. Now on to other matters. I would like to teach you our most sacred prayer."

"I would like to learn," Reith said.

"Very good. Here is how it goes."

God of Light, forever our guide, lead us on paths of peace. Shine on us so we may shine on your world. Illuminate our hearts with truth. May it be.

Ellyn said it a few times until Reith had it down.

"Many elves begin and end their prayers with this simple prayer."

"I like that it is short," Reith said.

"The God of Light does not care for quantity of words, only quality."

Ellamora came by twice over the next few days to pray. Reith stayed out of her way during her prayers but made sure to be near the door when she was about to leave. He was curious about this elf.

"Why do you come here to pray?" Reith asked her.

"Because it gives me hope, hope that I will see my father and mother again."

"I'm sorry for your loss. I lost my parents, too."

"In that, we share a bond of sadness," Ellamora replied. "I believe my parents are with the God of Light, and that is where I want to be too."

"When you say with the God of Light, what do you mean?"

"Death is not the end." She shook her head. "The God of Light did not make us to be a candle which burns down and is no more."

"You believe that there is something after death?"

"I do, and so do all who worship the God of Light. We will exist beyond our death."

"Why not die now then, to join them?"

"Because, Reith," Ellamora said, smiling at him, "whether we live or die, we are in the presence of the God of Light. This world is full of his wonders. If I'm alive, I can explore all that he has made."

"Even with all of the suffering that happens here?"

"Even with all of the suffering." Ellamora nodded. "That is where hope comes in."

"You have given me a lot to think about," Reith said.

Chapter Thirteen

The next morning, Ellyn gave Reith a few silver coins to go to the market to get some supplies for them and the temple. He dressed in his ordinary things, as the clerical robe drew too much attention.

The stares from the elves had grown less since the beginning of his time in Crain, but the stares that remained were the hostile ones. These he ignored to the best of his ability. The market was located near the middle of the city, by Gwandoeth's tower. He planned on stepping in and seeing Heth and Gwandoeth before heading back to the temple.

On his way, he heard shouts. The crowd started moving toward them like a river flowing downhill. He quickened his pace. *Whatever that is cannot be good.*

The crowd formed into a large circle around the commotion. He moved sideways through the throng to get a better angle to see what all the fuss was. When he saw the source, his heart sank.

Trigg was fighting an elf in the center of the circle. They were wrestling and punching, each trying to gain the upper hand. They grunted with each swing of the fist and each landed blow. Without thinking, Reith pushed through the onlookers to the center. He jumped on Trigg and pulled him away. Blood was flowing from a cut near Trigg's eye. The elf remained on the ground, cradling his arm.

"He broke my arm!" the elf cried out, and a stir went through the crowd.

"Trigg, we have to get you out of here," Reith said. He looked around for any sort of break in the crowd, but there was none. Everywhere he looked were angry elven faces, an impenetrable wall of hostility.

"What is the meaning of all of this?"

Gwandoeth's loud, booming voice came from beyond the crowd, and soon he had pushed his way to the center. His eyes quickly surveyed Reith, Trigg, and the wounded elf on the ground.

"What happened here?" he asked, quietly so that only those closest to him could hear.

"He broke my arm!" the elf on the ground cried out again. Whispers went through the crowd like wind on a wheat field.

"He started it!" Trigg said angrily through gritted teeth. The adrenaline was wearing off and Reith could tell he was starting to feel the pain. "I was trying to buy bread and he was giving me a hard time. He pushed me, so I pushed him."

Gwandoeth sighed. He looked around at the angry faces around the circle.

"Go back to your business, every one of you," he called out.

"No!" a voice yelled from the direction of the tower. The crowd parted to let someone walk through. Pryderus stepped into the center of the circle.

"Our business is here," Pryderus said with a sneer. "This is our city and this is our business."

"Away with you, Pryderus," Gwandoeth warned.

"I don't think so. You want us to go away so you can let this *human* off for his crimes. And we will not have it."

Murmurs of assent swept through the crowd.

"You brought these *humans* into our city without our consent. And we don't like it." The murmurs grew louder. "People of Crain," he shouted. "Do you want humans here, uninvited?"

"No!" called a few of the crowd members.

"Do you want them eating our food?"

"No!" a few more yelled. The mood was shifting.

"Do you think we have been shown poor leadership by those tasked with protecting our rights?"

More yells came, "Yes!"

"This human has broken one of our arms! Should he pay?"

"Yes!" was the answering roar.

"Well then, people of Crain, what are we to do? Will we sit idly by while our leader makes bad decisions that put us in harm's way?"

"No!" nearly everyone was yelling now. Reith looked at Trigg and found fear in his eyes.

"And there is more," Pryderus added. He was clearly enjoying this. "Not only has Gwandoeth allowed humans into our city, but these humans are hunted by a Shadow." At the mention of a shadow, the throng rose into a frenzy. Everyone was screaming, and Reith was worried that the mob would assault him and Trigg in their madness. Pryderus held up a hand to quiet the crowd, but he had a massive smile on his face. After several minutes of frenzied yelling, the crowd settled down.

"We are all in grave danger! You know the stories:

Shadows lay waste to cities and destroy all in their way! This danger was brought here by these humans and allowed to take root by Gwandoeth. The elves should be for the elves!"

The crowd roared in approval.

"For the elves! For the elves" they chanted.

When their volume dwindled, Pryderus bellowed over them.

"I move that we remove Gwandoeth from office!" he yelled.

"Yes!" Everyone was in a frenzy now. Reith felt a pull at the back of his shirt. He turned to find Laneras there.

"Come quickly," he said. "You're in danger."

Laneras pushed through the crowd, using the threat of his sword to persuade any who did not want the humans to pass. Luckily for Reith and Trigg, most of the elves were focused on Pryderus.

"We need to get Heth," Trigg said weakly. His cut was losing a lot of blood.

"Reith," Laneras began, "take Trigg to the clearing outside of town where you stayed when you first got here. I will get Heth. Hurry now. Don't stop for anything. If you see any humans, take them with you. Stay there until I return. This is going to get messy and I don't want you caught in the middle of it."

Reith and Trigg walked along the mostly deserted street, the latter leaning on the former. Reith tore off a piece of fabric from his shirt and gave it to Trigg.

"Put this on your cut," he ordered, and Trigg obeyed.

As they neared the gate, Pallin nearly ran into them.

"What happened?" he asked.

"Pryderus is trying to remove Gwandoeth."

Pallin swore, then said, "Go to the clearing."

"Laneras told us to."

"Good. I was afraid something like this would happen. I will set some of my trusted guards outside your camp, but stay there. Where is Laneras now?"

"He is getting Heth."

"I or Laneras will come to you later. Now go."

Reith and Trigg passed the threshold of the gate and made their way to clearing. There they waited, all alone.

What will happen to Gwandoeth? What will happen to us?

Over the next few hours, humans came to the clearing in groups of two or three. Laneras arrived with Heth, but he quickly went back into the city. Kydar and Dema came shortly after. Everyone wanted to know what was happening. After Reith explained as best he could, Heth said, "Gwandoeth and I were afraid of this."

"What will happen to us?" Kydar asked.

"I don't know," Heth admitted. "There is nowhere to run. We can't run even if we wanted to." Her face fell.

There was not much to do except wait. The day dragged on. Pallin returned shortly after noon with a dozen armed elves and left them to guard the humans. Laneras was one of them.

"It's for your protection," he explained to Heth. "I trust all of these. On your safety, they answer only to me and Laneras."

Heth sighed. "Thank you."

"I must get back," Pallin said grimly.

When he left, Dema turned to Laneras. "What's going on?"

"Gwandoeth was able to calm the crowd, but it won't do a lot of good. Now it's a political process. Pryderus has proposed removing Gwandoeth, and there was enough support to bring it to a vote. They both will make speeches, and then each citizen will cast a vote. But I think it's clear that Pryderus has the popular support. He's been waiting for a moment like this since you arrived."

"How did he know about the Shadow?" Reith asked.

"Please, don't talk about Shadows," Laneras said. "I assume he was listening at the door during your interviews with Gwandoeth."

Dema groaned. "That sneaky son of a ..."

Reith frowned. "What will happen to us?"

"Well, even Pryderus won't be so cruel as to send you back, not with a ... well, you know, hunting you. He used it as a political strategy, but I don't think he means to send you back. Instead, I think he will probably propose that all humans leave the city and camp here. Those who work in the city will most likely be reassigned. And he will target your food too."

"Does he hate us that much?" Kydar asked.

"It's hard to say." Laneras shrugged. "I think he is genuinely distrustful of humans. But more than that, I think he has had his eye on Gwandoeth's job for years. He was secretly gleeful when Gwandoeth allowed humans in. It was his big shot at becoming the lord of the city."

The sun began to set, and the reality of the situation began to set in. The humans helplessly waited for word of their fate. Every once in a while, a roar would rise up in the city and the humans would look around expectantly, but no news came of it.

As night was falling, dozens of elves with torches came out of Crain. Laneras and the guards readied their weapons, fearing the worst. When the crowd was closer, they saw that Pryderus was at its head.

"Peace, Laneras," he said, holding up a hand. The firelight glinted off of the silver medallion around his neck.

"Humans, I come with tidings," he sneered. "Today has been a momentous day, one that will be remembered for centuries. Today, I have replaced Gwandoeth as Lord of Crain."

"No!" Heth cried. Some of the other humans began whispering, and Reith looked at Kydar and Dema with concern.

"Silence!" Pryderus bellowed. When the clearing was quiet again, he continued. "It is our right to protect ourselves and our families. Therefore, from this moment, no human is allowed to pass through the gates of Crain unbidden by myself. This is for our safety as well as your own. Now, I know that you're worried that I will send you back to your homeland, where you face certain death. But know, humans, that Lord Pryderus is merciful. I am not so cruel. Those who wish to go back may do so freely. Those who wish to stay will be assigned work in the fields.

"I put before you life and death. Choose wisely. Anyone wishing to leave may step forward to submit their names. Tomorrow, they will be given supplies and sent north to the river. Those wishing to leave may line up to give their names to my daughter, Ellamora."

Ellamora stepped out from the shadows behind Pryderus. Reith's mouth fell open.

"She's Pryderus's daughter?" he asked incredulously so that only Kydar and Dema could hear. His eyes sought to meet hers, but she avoided his.

"You know her?" Dema asked.

"She came to the temple. She said to trust her." He felt anger rising inside of himself. But then Pryderus began to speak again.

"So we have no takers on the offer of supplies to leave? Very well. I shall have food sent to you all. Good night."

The crowd of elves with torches parted to let him pass.

Ellamora followed him with not a glance back at the humans.

The food promised by Pryderus ended up being stale bread, of which Reith ate little. *Just when things were finally starting to go right …*

He thought of Aspen, still in the city by the temple. *Ellyn is good. She will care for her.*

But then he thought of his sword and bow still in the temple. *Who will care for me?*

At dawn, Reith and the others were awakened by yelling.

"Wake up! It's time for work!" Reith looked around to see that it was Drierden.

The humans began getting up, slowly and sleepily.

"Faster, faster!" Drierden called, looking quite happy to be ordering the humans around. A company of elf soldiers were hanging around the clearing. Reith did not see Pallin or Laneras.

They were herded down the road, away from the city and out toward the fields.

"Where are we going?" Trigg asked. Reith saw that he didn't look so good. The cut on his face had scabbed over in the night, giving him a rather alarming disposition.

"You're going to work," Drierden said.

Several of the humans were sent off to the field. Others were sent to a barn. Reith and some of the others, including Kydar, Dema, Titus, Tara, Trigg, and Rangel, were all handed shovels.

"There needs to be a trench from here"—Drierden pointed at a partial trench a few feet away—"down to that pond." Then he pointed out a pond about 100 paces away. "Make sure it slopes."

"Why?" Dema asked, and in return she received a backhanded blow across her face that sent her staggering. She kept her feet, though barely. Kydar jumped forward, but Reith grabbed his collar and yanked him back. A dribble of blood was on Dema's lip, and she wiped it off with the back of her hand, giving Drierden a hate filled look.

"That'll teach you to ask questions," Drierden spat. "The lord wants you to work, and this is work that needs doing. So start digging."

Angrily, they all obeyed, even Tara, whose shovel was nearly as tall as she was. Drierden and a few other elves kept watch over them to make sure they were working. Soon, sweat started to drip down Reith's face. When he stopped to wipe his face off, one of the elves snapped a whip menacingly.

"Don't stop!"

They kept digging and Reith's arms began to burn due to the strain. Whenever he dared, he snuck a look at his taskmasters. Drierden looked quite pleased with himself.

The digging was tough physically, but it left Reith's mind free to wander. *Where are Pallin and Laneras? What happened to Gwandoeth? And who is Ellamora? She said to trust her, but look at the mess we are in.*

The trench slowly took shape. As the sun reached its peak, they were still many paces from the water's edge. The day grew ever warmer and more and more sweat fell from Reith's brow. His hands were red and raw from the coarse wood of the shovel.

What I wouldn't give for some gloves.

At midafternoon, Trigg fell to one knee in exhaustion. The whip cracked and he groaned as it struck him in the calf.

"Stop!" Tara cried out. For a second, it looked like

Drierden would strike her too, but at the last second, he changed his mind.

"Five minute break," he declared. Shovels were thrown down and everyone wearily walked down to the pond. They took turns drinking and splashing their heads in the water to cool down. The water felt good on his hands.

"Break's over!" Drierden called after what only felt like a minute. "Back to work!"

Reith's hands felt even worse now holding the shovel. He removed his shirt and wrapped it around his right hand. His left remained uncovered and raw. They worked hard the rest of the day. An hour before sundown, Drierden called for a break and they all walked back to their clearing. More elves were on guard there, and again, Pallin and Laneras were nowhere to be seen.

Reith's hands burned. Blisters were forming on each, though it was worse on his left one. He groaned as he sat down in the grass. Kydar and Dema soon sat beside him.

"I feel like I'm going to die," Kydar said.

"That's nothing," Dema retorted. She looked the worst of them all. Her lip was bruised and swollen.

"That was just the first day." Reith shook his head. "How long can we keep this up?"

Kydar sighed. "I don't know. Fighting the Gray Man seems like a better idea now than it did last night."

Stale bread was again brought out, but this time, Reith devoured it hungrily.

When his bread was gone, Reith laid down in the grass and the next thing he knew, it was morning. He didn't even remember falling asleep. His back was so stiff and every muscle in his body ached like he had been punched repeatedly. His hands felt marginally better, but a few minutes of digging would make them hurt all the more.

It was stale bread for breakfast. Several elves were

walking around with baskets, handing out the loaves. One elf handed Reith his loaf without even looking at him. Their hands brushed in the exchange and Reith felt something other than bread enter his hand. By feel he knew it was a piece of paper. He made no sign of recognition, and the elf didn't pause to look at him. Reith looked around and when the coast was clear, he stuck the piece of paper in his lap. He unfolded it and then held it against his loaf of bread. He took several bites to avoid notice, but in between bites, he read:

Working on a plan. Three days. Stay tough, stay strong. P & L.

He memorized the note and then crumpled the paper up in his hand so no one would see it. *P & L has to be Pallin and Laneras,* he thought. *What plan are they working on? What will happen in three days?*

Reith wondered if this was something he should share with Kydar and Dema or if he should keep it to himself for now. Kydar looked completely defeated and Dema's lip had swollen more overnight. *They need hope.*

From then on, he sought a chance to share the note with them. He folded it up and stuck it in his shoe for safe keeping. Drierden came around again, ordering them back to their worksites.

In the mass of humanity, Reith slid in behind Kydar and whispered in his ear, "Plan in the works. Three days."

Kydar looked at him questioningly. Reith shook his head and Kydar looked away.

When they arrived at the trench, they were instructed to grab their shovels. Reith again took his shirt off and wrapped it around his right hand. *I need one hand free from blisters.*

His left hand indeed bore the brunt of the work. Within an hour, several of his blisters and popped. When he showed any sign of pain and slowing down, one of the elves raised his whip hand. He gritted his teeth and got back to work. *Three days.*

At their midday water break, he knelt beside Dema at the pond and whispered the same message to her that he had whispered to Kydar in the morning.

"How?" she whispered back.

"Pallin," he said simply before standing up.

Blood trickled down his shovel as he dug away under the afternoon sun. He had never been in so much pain in his life. Looking around, everyone else was in the same misery that he was in. Poor Tara had tears in her eyes. She could barely lift her shovel anymore, and Reith could see her hands were bloody as well.

Three days.

A piece of paper again came with Reith's bread in the morning. *Tomorrow night.*

He managed to slip the paper to Kydar before they left and he saw Kydar slip it to Dema. They both looked at him with questions in their eyes but he had no idea of what was going on any more than they did.

The trench was nearly finished when they began their work. Reith's hands were on fire with pain, but it was somehow less today than yesterday. He did not bleed. His skin must have been toughening.

Poor Tara could hardly pick up a shovel. She dropped it like it was on fire and one of the elves raised his hand to whip her for her insolence. But before he did, he was knocked to the ground by a blow to the side by Titus's shovel. Luckily for the elf, the flat of the shovel hit him, so while it must have hurt tremendously, his skin was unbroken. Titus stood there, fire in his eyes, ready to take on the whole world for his sister.

"You little…" the elf yelled, jumping to his feet. The other elves around came to their comrade's defense. Reith, Kydar, and Dema all dropped their shovels and jumped forward to Titus's defense. Unfortunately, they didn't get there in time to help.

The whip struck Reith on the arm and then again across the back. He yelled in surprise and fell to his knees in agony. Another blow fell on his back and then his neck. He held his head to block the blows and laid there until it was over. He groaned or yelled out with each crack of the whip. When the blows stopped, he carefully looked up to see that three elves were taking turns whipping Titus, who was prone on the ground. He yelled with every strike of the whip. An elf stood over Reith with a whip.

"If you so much as look at him, I'll whip you again," the elf growled. Elves were standing over Kydar and Dema as well.

Titus's screams eventually died out, and the elves gave him a few more cracks of the whip just to be sure. When they were done, they allowed Kydar and Reith to attend to him. Several of the lashes had broken the skin. Titus had passed out from the pain.

"He needs help," Reith said to the elves. "He needs a healer."

The elves stood there, saying nothing.

"Please!"

"Take him back to your camp and leave him there," Drierden snapped.

Kydar and Reith picked Titus up. Reith had him by the feet and Kydar had him under the arms.

"Be quick about it!" Drierden barked. "If you aren't back soon, you'll get the same."

Reith and Kydar walked quickly with Titus between them. When they were out of earshot from Drierden, Kydar asked, "We're not just going to leave him, are we?"

"I don't know," Reith said. "I'm afraid if we leave him, he will get worse. Maybe someone will see us and help."

After several minutes, the arrived back at the camp. There was no one around.

"Let's take him to the edge of the clearing. Maybe someone from the city will see." They moved Titus to the edge and set him down, propping his limp form against a tree. Then they got some water and poured it over his wounds. The water ran red off of him, but presently the bleeding stopped. They heard footsteps behind them.

"What happened?" Ellyn asked. "I saw you from the gate."

"Ellyn!" Reith said. "Thank goodness you're here!"

Together, Reith and Kydar told her the story of what had happened.

Ellyn's face fell and she became angry.

"That's no way to treat guests," she said.

"I don't think we're guests anymore," Reith said. "What's happening in the city? Where are Pallin and Laneras? What happened to Gwandoeth?"

"I don't have much time, and neither do you. Gwandoeth has been locked in the tower. Pryderus has been preaching in the city center each day about the evils of humans and the superiority of elves."

"That's horrible," Reith said, disgusted that anyone could say that.

"Yes, yes it is. Unfortunately, many believe him."

"And what about Pallin and Laneras?" Reith asked.

"I haven't seen them much. They are laying low."

Reith decided he shouldn't mention the notes. *The less people who know, the better.*

"Let me go get some supplies from a healer," Ellyn said. "I can help Titus. I'll be right back."

She hurried away back into the city and Reith watched her go.

"What can we do for Titus?" Kydar asked.

"Nothing much right now. Ellyn can help him."

"I hope she hurries or we will look like him soon," Kydar said, his eyes wide with fear.

"We need to hold on for just a bit longer."

After about ten minutes, Ellyn returned carrying a bag.

"You had better get back," she said. "I will care for him. Don't worry."

She knelt to the ground and opened the pack. Inside, Reith could see linen bandages and some small jars of herbs.

"Go," she urged. "I don't want to have to mend you too."

———

Near sundown, they were finally allowed to stop their work. The trench was finally finished.

"I wonder what fresh hell they will have for us tomorrow," Dema said.

Wearily, they walked back to camp. They found Titus awake and sitting up. Bandages covered the worst of his injuries, but Reith could still see some of the marks where the whips had dug into his flesh. He managed a weak grin at Tara, who sobbed and tried to hug him. At her touch, he groaned.

"How are you feeling?" Kydar asked him.

"Ugh," Titus replied. "I feel like I fell off the roof."

Just then, Lara came back into the camp from where she had been working that day. At the sight of her son, she burst into angry tears.

"What happened?" she demanded.

"Titus saved me," Tara said, who was wiping tears from her own eyes.

"They were going to whip her," Kydar explained to Lara. "But he swung his shovel and hit the elf. Then several of them whipped him."

"Oh my boy!" Lara cried out, inspecting his visible wounds. "Who did all of this?" she asked, pointing to the bandages.

"A kind elf," Titus said. "She was here when I awoke and she bandaged me up with ointment and herbs."

"It was Ellyn," Reith explained. "I worked with her in the temple when we first got here."

Others in the camp were coming over to see Titus now. When Heth saw him, she was livid.

"Let's wait," Reith said, attempting to diffuse her anger. He didn't want to tell her too much for fear of raising her hopes. "Titus couldn't even travel if we left today. Give it a few days and we will see if our lot has changed."

"I hope it does," Heth retorted hotly. "We cannot live like this for long."

Chapter Fourteen

Instead of bread, Reith was brought a burlap bag. He looked questioningly at the elf who brought it. This elf was a different one than had brought the two notes with the bread. This elf glared at him as if daring him to ask about food. Before Reith could open the bag, the elf turned and walked back to the city.

The bag was surprisingly heavy, perhaps ten pounds or so. Reith opened the bag and looked inside. His stomach rolling, he instantly dropped it and turned. Sickness overcame him, making bile rise in his throat.

"What is it?" Kydar asked, alarmed.

Reith tried to control his heavy breathing and get a hold on his stomach. The sight and stench were overwhelming. All eyes in the refugee camp were on him.

"Don't," he choked out, but as he said it, Dema had already picked up the bag and turned it upside down. With a sickening thunk that echoed through the clearing, the head of Gwandoeth fell to the ground.

Dema ran from the clearing and Kydar actually did throw up. Reith doubled over, looking anywhere but at the

head of the dismembered former Lord of Crain. Yells of
sickened outrage rang out in the camp. He could hear
Trigg fuming. Heth managed to restore some of the calm
by throwing the bag back over the head.

With the head out of sight, Reith was able to stand up
and take stock of the situation. Several of the women had
passed out and nearly all of the children were crying. The
only ones not crying were the ones who had missed the
spectacle. Reith looked around, trying to wrap his mind
around such a senseless act of violence. He looked toward
the city. There, on the battlements overlooking the camp,
were dozens of elven soldiers. He could make out Pryderus
at their head.

White hot rage boiled up in him, making his jaw set so
hard he thought he might break it altogether. He went
tense all over. It was all he could do to keep a scream
inside.

Why would you kill Gwandoeth? What purpose does this serve?

Reith knew who was behind it as clear as he knew
anything. But was this a threat? A warning? A simple show
of force?

He did not want to be in the sight of Pryderus and the
city, so he marched off into the trees, where he could be
somewhat alone. He found himself at the peach tree, now
six feet high and laden with fruit. The fragrance of the tree
drove the stench of the head from his mind.

He closed his eyes and breathed deeply, lost in thought.
*Am I next? What about Laneras and Pallin? We aren't safe here, but
where can we go?*

Behind him, he heard soft footsteps. He turned to see
Ellamora.

"You!" he said sharply.

"Shhhh!" she hissed, holding a finger to her lips.

He sneered. "Don't. How dare you?"

"Stop, right now. Your life depends on it."

"And I'm supposed to believe you?"

"What did I tell you that first time we met?" she asked.

"You said trust you. But how can I trust you? You're Pryderus's daughter, and if you didn't know, he just sent me the severed head of Gwandoeth, so again, how am I supposed to believe you?"

"I said something else," she said, softly.

"Something about family."

"Family isn't everything."

"So?"

"Reith, I hate Pryderus more than you do."

"What? How?"

"He's not my father. He married my mother a few years back. I can't stand him. I never understood what my mother saw in him."

"And I'm just supposed to take your word for that?" he asked hotly. "For all I know, you could kill me, right now."

"I won't kill you." At that moment, Reith realized she had a pack on her back. She swung it around and placed it on the ground. There was his bag, bow, quiver, and sword, still in its sheath. "Here, these are yours."

"How did you get these?"

"Ellyn," she said simply. "She also gave me this" She handed Reith a letter, sealed with red wax with the temple seal stamped on it. "Read it."

He broke the seal and read:

Dear Reith,

You can trust Ellamora. She is for you and for your people. May the blessing of the God of Light be on you. I will look after Aspen until you return.

May it be.

Ellyn

He looked up from the letter. It was Ellyn's handwriting alright.

"Let's say I have begrudgingly chosen to trust you. What now?"

"You know the plan that's in the works?" she asked.

"You mean the one I have received no information about other than two notes which are seriously lacking in details?"

"Yeah, that plan." She allowed a slight grin. "Here is the plan. "You and me, plus Kydar and Dema, if they are inclined to join us, will leave immediately for Sardis. That's our capital city. We will go there and petition the king to help us."

"What about everyone else?"

"Leave that to us," Pallin said, striding out of the trees. Laneras was beside him.

"Pallin! Laneras! Thank goodness you are alive!"

"Yes, that's all well and good, but we need to stay focused," Laneras told him.

"As I was saying," Pallin continued. "As you know, we have been scouting the river. Actually, we've done a bit more. We followed the trail of the Gray Man. He's leaving the area and traveling north. We don't know how far, but we think he's going a long way. This allows for all of the remaining humans to travel north today and cross the river, then set up camp or rebuild Suthrond. We will maintain a garrison of troops near the river while we continue to scout. Pryderus will think this is for us to prevent humans from crossing over again, but in reality, we will be there to fight the Gray Man if he comes back."

"Meanwhile," Ellamora took over, "we will be going to

Sardis. We will hopefully win the king's favor and return with more troops. He will not like that Gwandoeth was slain. He will seek vengeance on Pryderus."

"So this is what you have been working on these past few days?" Reith asked.

Pallin nodded. "Secretly."

"It's a good plan," Reith told him, "but why did Pryderus kill Gwandoeth?"

"Gwandoeth was plotting against him," Pallin said. "Pryderus found letters Gwandoeth had written."

"Who was he writing to?" Reith asked.

"Lords of nearby cities, the king."

He raised a brow. "Even so, why give me his head?"

"Why do mad people do anything?" Pallin replied. "I think he wanted to scare you and show you he was in charge. But mostly, I think he wanted to scare you all off."

"Well he succeeded."

"It's not safe for you here, Reith," Laneras said, a pleading look in his eyes. "This plan will work and give you all the best chance of survival."

"You don't have to convince me anymore. I'm in," Reith answered with determination.

"Good!" Pallin let out a relieved breath. "Let's tell Heth, Kydar, and Dema. Would you bring them back here?"

In a few minutes, they were all assembled. The plan was quickly explained to the three newcomers, who all agreed to it.

"Kydar and Dema, your path is freely chosen," Palling said. "Would you accompany Ellamora and Reith or would you go with Heth and the rest?"

"I'm going to Sardis," Dema answered quickly.

"Me too," Kydar added.

"It's settled then." Pallin clapped his hands together.

"Heth, prepare your people. Ellamora, Reith, Kydar, and Dema, ready yourselves. You must leave as soon as possible, though take care to avoid being seen by any from the city. They must think that all the humans travel north."

By the peach tree, Reith looked to Heth.

"You're going home, Heth."

"Home, yes, but not yet settled. Make haste on your errand and return quickly."

"Take some peaches with you," Reith told her. "Plant the pits in Suthrond. Make the land fruitful again."

"And you take some as well. Plant them along your path. Then follow them back home."

Reith piled as many peaches as he could into his bag. Then he hoisted it to his shoulder. Kydar, Dema, and Ellamora were all ready as well. They embraced Heth as if saying farewell to a mother. Heth's eyes brimmed with tears.

"Take care," Heth said.

"We will be back soon," Kydar promised.

Pallin shook hands all around and gave Ellamora a quick hug. "Farewell."

"We shall see each other again soon," Laneras said before doing the same, though he held Ellamora longer.

"Let's go," Ellamora ordered. "To Sardis!"

The four companions traveled north out of the camp and went a mile or so in that direction before turning east for several miles. During this first part of the journey, they talked little, afraid of encountering an elf who would give them away.

"If Pryderus finds we have gone south, he will send

assassins to pursue us and we will die with arrows in our backs," Ellamora muttered.

The trees were old and tall, and most of the time the trees covered the travelers in shadow. The leaves were green and full. Whatever sunlight made it through were small, individual beams of light illuminating a shaft down from the sky. It was quiet in the woods, but one could not see for more than a score of paces before a tree would block the view in that direction. Reith was simultaneously relieved they had cover and apprehensive that someone could approach them without being seen.

After two hours of marching, Ellamora called for a halt. The four sat down and drank eagerly from their jugs. Reith pulled out his map of Terrasohnen, the one he had taken from Vereinen's, and spread it out on a rock. The land of the elves was mostly blank, while the land of the humans had many details.

"Ellamora, help me with this map," Reith said. She slid over and knelt beside him. "I reckon we are here," he began, pointing to a spot just south of the Rammis River. Vereinen had drawn some trees here. "I know Sardis is on the Great River." He pointed again to the map, identifying where the elven capital was. "How do you plan on getting there? My master had little knowledge of your land."

"Between here and the Great River, hardly any of my people live," Ellamora explained. "There are some small towns and villages, but no cities. The elves mostly live along the coast or at the edge of the forest and the plain. I propose that we travel through the forest to the river and follow the river down to Sardis. That way we avoid detection and notice. I believe it is in our best interests to remain unseen. If my people knew there were humans about in the land, well, they would act just like Pryderus. It does us no good to be seen."

"How long do you think this journey will take?" Kydar asked.

"About a week, perhaps," Ellamora answered. "Maybe more if the Dark Powers have any say over it. It's hard to say. Every time I traveled from Crain to Sardis, I went by the main road that goes south from Crain, along the edge of the forest, usually on horseback. That typically took five days."

"Dark Powers? Dema's eyes widened. "What are they?"

"The dark powers," Ellamora explained, "are the powers that hold the keys to the kingdoms of Terrasohnen. I was taught when I was young that before time began, the God of Light wrote the story of Terrasohnen into being. He wrote the world and the Guardians into existence. He ruled the world with justice and righteousness and his Guardians looked after the upkeep of the world. But then he wanted to write elves, humans, and dwarves into the story as his children and there was a great war among the Guardians. Some of them did not want these three races to rule the world and some wanted to follow the God of Light on this next adventure in the story.

"The ones opposed to the God of Light became the Dark Powers. In the great war, they were all banished to the spirit realm by the God of Light, and the elves, dwarves, and humans were all written into the story as the new caretakers of the world. Ever since, the Dark Powers try to exert their influence to bring about the end of the three races and the Guardians of Light try to thwart them."

"That's a load of rubbish," Dema said incredulously. "There is no such thing as Powers and Guardians and the God of Light. This is a kid's story."

"How do you know it's a kid's story?" Ellamora challenged.

"Because that is what it is!" Dema sputtered. "It's a story to tell children to get them to obey. 'Watch out or the Dark Powers will come and get you.'"

"If there is no Maker," Ellamora reasoned, "then where do right and wrong, love, beauty, and justice come from?"

"They just exist," Dema replied. "I don't know, some things just are."

"All things have a beginning," Ellamora shot back.

"Guys, calm down," Reith said. "Let's talk about something else."

The little tiff was soon banished from memory as the companions began to march again. They walked among the trees, and the only guide they had were the sun's rays, which were now coming from high in the sky above them. The day grew warm, and there was little breeze in the forest to ease their heat.

Each patch of ground looked like every previous patch of ground, even to Reith and his finely honed hunting eye. Still, Ellamora was confident in their direction and they pressed on.

With each step, they were further and further away from Crain and their troubles behind. As such, their mood lightened considerably and they began to laugh and joke.

"Shortly after my mom married Pryderus," Ellamora said with a wicked grin, "he made me mad for some reason or another, so I put bugs in his soup. He ate the whole bowl!"

This brought on raucous laughter from the three humans.

"How old were you?" Kydar asked once his laughter had called down.

"I was seven," Ellamora said. "But wait until you hear this next one. When I was nine, I started moving his possessions around. A pen a few inches here, a shirt to the floor when it had been on the bed, that sort of thing. He started getting angry about it. He would walk into a room and stop and stare for a moment. I could see the wheels turning in his head! 'That wasn't there before.' But he never said anything about it; he thought he was going mad!"

Reith, Kydar, and Dema were howling with laughter now.

"This next one is more recent," Ellamora added, continuing her tales. "I shrunk a pair of his pants. I let them sit in boiling water for a while. Then I set the pants really close to the fire."

"What happened then?" Dema asked.

"He put them on and they were several inches too short. But then he bent down to put his shoe on and the pants ripped, right down the seam!" They had to stop for a few minutes because they were laughing so hard.

The travelers were in high spirits when they stopped for the evening. Ellamora was very prepared. She had a small hatchet that she used to make firewood and they soon had a sizable blaze going. She produced some bread and dried meat from her pack and they all ate heartily.

"At some point, we will need to hunt," she said.

"Well luckily for you, I'm the best hunter in all of Terrasohnen," Kydar boasted. Dema and Reith rolled their eyes, but Ellamora laughed.

"Hey Reith, let me see your sword," she told him. He unsheathed it and passed it to her, earning a whistle. "It's beautiful." She turned it over in her hand and inspected the metal work on the hilt. "Do you know how to use it?" she asked.

"No, I've never used it," he admitted. She hopped up to her feet.

"Well, get up then." She grabbed two of the longer sticks that she had procured earlier. "These will do."

Reith stood up and she tossed him one of the sticks. It was about as wide as the grip on his sword and just as long.

"Kydar, Dema, step aside," Ellamora ordered, her eyes narrowing into fierce slits. The siblings scrambled out of the way to the far side of the fire and sat watching the proceedings. "Now, the first step of sword fighting is to size up your opponent. Determine who they are and how they will try to attack you."

"I think you're going to try to make me look silly," Reith complained.

"Quite right," she replied. "And now we fight!"

She lunged forward and aimed a blow at his left shoulder. He managed to get his stick up just in time to block her attack. Quick as lightning, she whirled about and came at him from his right side with a backhanded slash. Reith stuck his stick out and down to receive the blow, but her slash kept rising, up, up, past his hand. He howled in pain and dropped his stick as she made contact with his right shoulder.

"What did you do that for?" he demanded, rubbing his shoulder with his left hand.

"Teaching," she said simply, pointing her own stick at Reith's throat. "And you're dead."

"I feel like I'm dying," he said. His shoulder was aching.

"You'll be fine." She rolled her eyes. "Now class, what was Reith's blunder?"

"He got hit," Dema said with great sarcasm. Kydar shoved her and Ellamora smiled.

"Exactly. He was off balance and he was not anticipating. He was reacting."

"What, I'm not supposed to react?" Reith asked.

"Yes and no," she said. "You need to size up your opponent and anticipate where the next blow will come from. Then you can strategize how to meet that attack and counter it with your own. If you simply try to block every swing, you will never win. It's only a matter of how long you can stay alive. A real sword fight in battle is a zero sum game. One winner, one loser. It's a game of life and death."

"My turn," Dema chimed, picking up Reith's dropped stick. She assumed her position with confidence. "Laneras taught me a few things."

"Oh really?" Ellamora said, determination etched on her face.

Both fighters moved at the same time. Their forehand blows met in between them with a clash. Dema tried a backhand cut toward Ellamora's neck, but Ellamora ducked and the blow went over her head. The lack of contact caused Dema to take a step forward to steady herself, and Ellamora took the opportunity to smack her shin.

"Ow!" Dema yelped, hopping around on one foot.

"Laneras may have taught you a few things, but he taught me everything he knows," Ellamora said, a look of satisfaction on her face. "You did do better than Reith, though. Reith, why don't you try again?"

His shoulder was still sore, but he took the stick from Dema and swung it in front of him a couple of times. He looked at Ellamora and sized her up. Her body language appeared more defensive this time, less aggressive. *She expects me to attack immediately.*

"And ... go!" Ellamora hollered.

Reith lunged forward and took a big step toward her. She held her ground, challenging him. But instead of the fierce attack, he feinted for her head, then swung low for her knees. She just managed to block this surprise blow, and he sent a vicious backhand swipe toward her waist. She blocked this one, too, but took a step back to do so. Reith pressed and swung straight down at the top of her head. She again blocked this and gave another step. He began raining blows on her from the left, right, top. She dodged every one of them but fell back several steps in the process. On the last of these, her foot hit a root and she stumbled to the ground, dropping her stick. Reith stepped forward and held his stick to her neck.

"I yield!" she said. He lowered his stick and stood there, panting. She stood up and dusted off her hands and pants. "Excellent work, Reith!"

"I sized you up," he told her, flashing a sly smile.

"That you did, and quite excellently as well!"

They took turns sparring that evening until all were too exhausted to continue. Reith drew first watch that night. He patrolled their makeshift camp, holding his sword. He practiced swinging it about, testing its weight.

If it comes to a fight, I need to be ready to wield this weapon and not a stick.

After a few hours, he woke Kydar for his shift and laid down. His shoulder didn't hurt so much anymore.

Chapter Fifteen

R eith awoke to a few drops of water dripping on his body from above. The trees were doing a great job of shielding them from most of the rain, but here and there, droplets came through. They pressed on through the rain that morning, existing in an uncomfortable constant state of semi-dampness. Their conversations and tempers were short that day. Dema yelled at Kydar at one point for breaking too many sticks with his feet as they walked.

By early afternoon, the rain let up and the sun came out. The temperature rose and combined with the humidity in the air, caused the four companions to sweat profusely.

They picked a place to camp and even managed a fire, despite the general wetness of the area. There was enough brush and wood under the thickest of trees. Ellamora had brought their practice sticks, and the four of them took turns sparring that evening. When they were all too bruised and exhausted to continue, they sat down around the fire.

"You're all fast learners," Ellamora observed, nursing

some of her bruises. While she won most of her matches, all three humans were beginning to get a feel for the game and did very well.

"We have a good teacher," Kydar said.

Ellamora flushed, waving him off. "Oh stop it."

"I just hope I'm good enough to face the Gray Man," Dema said with determination.

"Maybe someday," Ellamora remarked. "But for now, hope against hope that you do not meet a Shadow in open combat."

They sat in silence, each of the party lost in their own thoughts.

Kydar spoke again after several minutes. "What do we do when we get to Sardis?"

Now that he was confronted by this question, Reith realized that he had been planning on walking right into the king's palace and speaking to him. He realized now that this was a childish dream.

"When we get there, I will go to the king, alone at first," Ellamora replied after thinking it over. "We will find you a safe place outside of the city to wait. If the king listens and is sympathetic, I will then bring you in to speak to them."

The three humans all protested at the idea of staying outside the city, but Ellamora shouted them down. "This is for the best. Imagine if they have a reaction like Pryderus's. At best you could expect to be shunned in the city and sent back. At worst, you could be imprisoned, or worse."

"That makes sense," Reith said, and Kydar and Dema nodded in agreement.

Ellamora took the first watch that night, and while Kydar and Dema went to sleep, Reith decided to stay up and talk with this elf girl. For all he knew about her and her world, there was still so much he did not.

"After this, what will you do?" he asked. "I can't imagine your step-father will be eagerly awaiting your return to Crain."

"He might be anxious to have me whipped for my insolence," she replied sourly. "Maybe I'll stay in Sardis. I have an uncle there. Or maybe I will travel to the sea and live on the coast."

"What will you do? How will you spend your time?"

"I think I might study with the healers," Ellamora said. "Or join the clerics, like Ellyn."

Reith nodded slowly. "I think you would be good at either of those things."

"I want to help people," Ellamora replied. "I want to heal their bodies and souls."

"A worthy goal," Reith answered.

"I always enjoyed studying with Ellyn in the temple."

"I did too, for my short time there. But I still have so many questions."

Ellamora looked at him. "Well go on, ask away. I don't think I have all the answers but I can help you."

"You said earlier that the Dark Powers were banished to the spirit realm," he said. "What is that?"

"You and I are body and soul, together," Ellamora explained. "With our body we touch the physical world." She plucked a blade of grass and held it up. "And with our souls, we touch the spirit realm." She let the blade of grass fall, and a soft breeze carried it away. "The Dark Powers lost their connection to the physical world when they rebelled against the God of Light's good ways. And so they were banished."

"Does that mean that the Guardians are still around? Physically, I mean."

"The Guardians do take physical form and can appear to us as we appear to one another. They say sometimes a stranger on the road could be a Guardian in disguise."

"So that's why there are Shadows," Reith said, thinking through the implications. "For the Dark Powers to influence things physically, they need a body. They need a person."

"Exactly," Ellamora said, smiling encouragingly to him. "Dark Powers need a willing host. A Shadow is someone who has opened themselves up to be used by the Dark Powers in this way. It is a great and unnatural evil."

"I think the Gray Man must be a Shadow then," Reith said.

"I think so too," Ellamora replied.

"How do you kill a Shadow?" Reith asked.

"No one really knows. Some say that if you kill the body, the Dark Power inhabiting it is destroyed as well. Some think only a strike to the heart can kill the Shadow."

"What do you think?" Reith asked.

"I think that if I ever come across a Shadow, I will make sure it is good and dead before I turn my back on it."

Reith thought about the Gray Man, and then he had a strange thought. *I wonder if the Gray Man ever thinks about me?* He shuddered at the idea that somewhere, the Gray Man was thinking about him, No One.

That's just what I am in this mess, No One. Who am I to go against the Gray Man? Who am I to challenge the Dark Powers?

As if Ellamora could read his thoughts, she said, "Hope is not lost, Reith. We have a terrible and formidable enemy, but light is always stronger than darkness. The God of Light will erase all Shadows."

"How can you be sure?"

"I am as sure as I know that the sun will rise again in

the morning. The God of Light promised and so shall it be."

The fire was burning lower now, so Ellamora threw some more wood on it.

"It just seems like the darkness is winning. There is a Shadow. There is death. There is pain."

"I know this darkness well," Ellamora replied, a look of sorrow passing over her face.

"Tell me about your mother, Ellamora." Reith hoped the request was not too imposing.

She looked a long way off in the distance, as if peering back through time itself.

Finally, she spoke again, "My mother was music come alive. She was melody and rhythm, harmony and rhyme. In everything she did, she would sing, hum, or whistle. Sometimes it even seemed that she was dancing to some song in her head, even while doing chores or cooking. She was beautiful, loving, and kind. And then she married *him*. I don't really know why. I supposed that the death of my father caused a great emptiness inside of her. But then she got sick, and within a day, she was gone."

"I am so sorry to hear that," Reith said, sympathetically. "My parents are gone too."

"Do you think of them much?"

"No," Reith admitted, guilt stirring within him at his admission. If he were honest with himself, he had buried their memories deep inside so that the pain wouldn't consume him. All of a sudden, grief over his missing master burst inside him. "I think about Vereinen more. He was my master back home. He took me in when they died."

"It's a lonely world," Ellamora said softly.

They sat in silence for a long minute. Sparks were flying out of the fire, aimed skyward, yet they always fizzled out a few feet above the flames. Out of the corner of his eye, Reith saw the firelight reflected in tears on Ellamora's face. He gently patted her arm. She looked up at him, and her eyes conveyed her gratefulness at the touch of another. He reached over and pulled her closer to him.

In that moment, an understanding passed between them. They were orphans alone in the world. But at least they had each other. And for now, in the light of the fire in the forest, it was enough to chase away the darkness.

When he went to bed, Reith fell asleep almost immediately. The next thing Reith knew was that he was being poked and prodded by Dema as she tried to wake him up for guard duty. He had the very last shift of the evening, in the darkness before dawn.

He walked around their makeshift camp a few times, looking for a sign that anything was amiss. In their remote part of the world, he highly doubted they would be intruded upon by an elf. He eventually settled in a tree, like he did when he was hunting. He liked being up in the air. The leaves gave him plenty of cover to see but not be seen.

He sat in the tree in a crook in one of its branches about eight feet in the air, letting his feet dangle below him. Reith watched and waited, alone with his thoughts.

There was little breeze that evening, but what breeze there was sent the smoke from their fire directly into his face. It was just a small amount of smoke, so he didn't really consider moving. It was a minor nuisance at the moment. Finally the breeze turned and he took a deep breath of the refreshing clean air. And then he smelled something different, something musky. His hunter's instincts kicked in and he found that he had an arrow on his bow string before he even realized what was going on.

He sat there, still as a statue and watched the trees upwind, waiting for the animal to show itself. He heard a low growl and saw a figure rising up onto giant hind legs. *A bear.*

Reith had no time to think. He shot his arrow at the giant beast's heart and jumped down from the tree. He landed hard, and his right ankle twisted, sending him to the ground with a startled cry of pain. He twisted into a sitting position and notched another arrow.

The bear was already recovering from the first arrow. He shot at it again, then pushed through the pain and stood up, ignoring the throbbing that coursed up his leg. He pulled another arrow and notched it. All of this had taken only a few seconds, and the bear was angry now, staggering toward him with rage.

He let loose another arrow and this one, too, found its mark. He could see the fury in the bear's wild eyes as it roared. In seconds, he sent another arrow straight into the bear's chest. The animal was too close now to shoot, so Reith drew his sword.

Then three things happened at the same time. The bear raised its gigantic left forepaw, claws gleaming in the moonlight, Reith raised his sword and stabbed it at the bear's throat, and three arrows came out of the gloom to hit the bear, one in the chest, one in the throat, and another in its wide-open mouth.

Reith felt pain and tasted blood. The bear howled and the next thing Reith knew, he was on the ground next to a very large mass of fur. His whole body was on fire and he felt his consciousness leave him.

He was walking along a path under the light of the moon. The light was reflecting off towering walls of white, a hundred feet high on either side. It was cold, and the night air forced him to wrap his cloak tight about him.

"Save them. Serve them. Fight for them. Then find me."

These words echoed in his mind. It was the same voice he had heard at Erador among the fruit trees.

At the thought of Erador, the landscape melted away and he found himself in Erador, but not the one he remembered. This was the Erador of old, the Erador of power. Human, elven, and dwarven soldiers ran to and fro on the battlements of the Citadel, yelling and pointing at dragons.

In the air, dozens of serpent-like creatures with wings were flying about, breathing fire and roaring. And yet Reith felt no fear. He looked around and saw fear in the eyes of all those around him, but it was as if he were invisible to all of them. He watched the dragons flying. Some were as big as a house. They were all different colors, some black, some white, some blue, some red, some orange, some green. The fire from their mouths was orange, yellow, and red.

All of a sudden, he felt the ground lurch beneath his feet and the Citadel was falling. He descended through the empty air into nothingness.

And just before all went dark, he heard the voice again, "Save them. Serve them. Fight for them. Then find me."

When Reith awoke, he was lying on what seemed to be a soft bed, but he soon realized it was just a pile of clothes nested around him. All memory of the dream had been pushed to the very corners of his mind, forgotten for the moment. It was soft and warm, but as he tried to sit up, his pain came back to him. His left arm was in a sling held close to his body. Beneath the sling were more bandages on his left arm, from shoulder to elbow. Any movement sent pain shooting up his arm. His forehead felt wet, so he gingerly used his right hand to reach up and feel what was on his face. His brow was drenched in sweat. He also found bandages all down the left side of his face from near his eye to his chin.

He let out a groan, laid back, and closed his eyes again. He heard someone move closer to him, so he opened his eyes and saw the concerned face of Ellamora.

"How do you feel?" she asked.

"Like I just survived a bear attack," he retorted, grimacing as the talking caused the wounds on his face to stretch.

"You've been out for a day and a half, Reith." Her eyes were wide and her face was pale with worry. She mopped his forehead with a cloth.

His brows shot up in surprise. "A day and a half? Wow."

"You took the bear's claws full in your face and arm. Luckily, the cuts were not very deep and the bear missed anything important like your eyes. I cleaned and bandaged your wounds and we thought you would be okay. But then you got a fever and we were scared we would lose you. Thank the God of Light your fever broke."

She was close to tears now.

"It's okay," Reith said. "The bear is dead and I'm all right." He grimaced again from the pain of talking. "Or at least as all right as I can be, given the circumstances."

"Praise the Light," Ellamora said.

He looked around. "Where are Kydar and Dema?"

"They are out getting water from a nearby stream."

Reith nodded, then asked, "Is there anything to eat? I'm starving. I haven't eaten in two days. It's hard work, vanquishing a bear."

Ellamora couldn't stop her grin from showing through her concern. "How does bear stew sound?" she suggested, walking over to the fire and the pot that was sitting near it.

"Bear stew for the bear vanquisher. I like the sound of that."

He ate the stew as best he could. His left arm was useless, so it was a good thing he was right-handed. Either way, he was unable to hold the bowl, so he had to prop the bowl in his lap and scoop from there to his mouth.

Before he had finished eating, Kydar and Dema came back with the water. They were relieved to see 'the bear vanquisher,' as Ellamora had called him.

"Oh, thank goodness, Reith," Dema said. She tried to give him a hug but he screamed bloody murder when she touched his left arm. She apologized profusely.

Reith was in no fit state to stand up for a few days, let alone move forward toward Sardis. In addition to his cuts, his ankle was sprained. It was purple and swollen and he could not put any weight on it.

The four of them settled down in that camp, enjoying the bear meat while it lasted. Kydar had even skinned the creature and used its fur to make a blanket, which Reith commandeered for his sleeping arrangement once it had dried out. Twice a day, Ellamora changed Reith's bandages and put a salve made from herbs on his wounds. He was getting better and stronger each day, and after three days, he was good enough to get up and walk around and help with some of the chores. The next day, his bandages were gone, but Ellamora swore she would put them back on if she saw him scratching the scabs.

On the fifth day after the bear attack, Reith judged himself ready for travel. His ankle was mostly good as new, though it was a bit stiff and sore. They went slowly that day and by the time they stopped that evening, Reith was exhausted and sore all over. But he did not complain.

They decided it would be best to have two guards on duty at all times. Mostly this was for Reith's benefit, as he could hardly be counted on in a fight at the moment, if it came to that. That night, Kydar and Dema took the first watch. Reith gratefully collapsed onto the bear fur blanket and was out like a light.

Kydar and Dema woke Reith and Ellamora in the middle of the night for their shift on guard duty. Reith took a few laps of the camp to stretch out his legs. His ankle was stiff and sore but quickly loosened up from the exertion. Ellamora sat near the fire, looking away from it into the darkness of the trees. He came and sat near her.

"How are you feeling?" she asked Reith.

"I'm all right," he replied. "My ankle was stiff and I needed to walk it out."

"That's good to hear."

"If we're attacked, it's on you tonight," he teased, "I won't be much good with this." He held up his sword which was lying by his side.

She smiled. "My sword is good enough for the both of us."

"You said Laneras taught you?" he asked.

Ellamora nodded. "Yes, he did. Of course, Pryderus didn't approve. He thought I should be spending my time becoming a lady and wooing suitors. Bleh."

"I'm sure Laneras is a great teacher," Reith replied.

"The best. When my mother died, he sort of took me in as his little sister. He taught me how to fight, how to shoot. How did you learn to shoot?"

He told her of the long hours at the practice range in Coeden and of the competition from which he won his bow.

"We need to have a shooting contest soon, all four of us."

"I'll kick your butt!"

"I'd like to see you try!"

The rest of their guard shift went by uneventfully. Nothing stirred in the forest. The sky began to grow ever so slightly lighter on the eastern horizon. It was then that a buck happened to walk near their camp. Reith and Ellamora each hit it with arrows and it fell. As the sun rose, Kydar and Dema awoke to the smell of fresh deer sizzling over the fire.

"Breakfast!" Kydar chimed happily when he spied what was making the wonderful aroma.

They all ate heartily, better than they had in a while. When it was time to leave, all four were uncomfortably full. They packed their meager belongings and headed out on a southwesterly course.

"I think we may hit the river today," Ellamora said.

By late morning, they noticed that the trees were more spaced out here. They also began to notice well-worn paths through the forest. Reith pointed out that these were man made, or rather, elf made paths.

"We're close to a town," Ellamora told them. "Pull your cloaks up. I don't want anyone to see that you are humans from a distance."

The forest soon opened up into a wide lane. In the distance, they could see smoke rising over the town.

"I will go in alone," Ellamora explained. "I can buy whatever supplies we need. I think this may be a town on the river. Go hide on the south side of the town, and I will be back soon. Stay hidden."

And with that, she walked down the wide lane and was soon out of sight.

"Come on," Reith urged the others, "before we're seen."

The three humans walked into the trees and cautiously made a wide circle to the south. They encountered no one and soon could hear the dull roar of the rushing of the river. They discreetly crossed a path and came, almost without warning, to the edge of the wood. The forest then opened up on the river below them. Several small fishing boats floated up and down the river. From the looks of them, they appeared to be fishing boats, as the elves on them were mending and casting nets into the water.

Directly up river was a small fishing village. It was built right on the edge of the river, with several docks jutting out into the flow. The river was wide and calm right here. All of the structures were made of wood and there was a faint smell of fish, even where the humans were standing, several hundred paces away from the town. It was unwalled, though Reith doubted that this place was ever in any danger of invasion, it was so out of the way.

The humans settled in among the trees and waited for Ellamora, careful to avoid being seen from either the river or the town. The minutes slipped by slowly and they grew drowsy.

After about an hour, they saw her leave the town and walk along the path toward them.

"Psst," Kydar whispered as Ellamora drew near. She heard them and simply gestured for them to follow her.

Dema moved to step out on the path, but Ellamora waved her hand as if to say, "Stay in the trees!"

Ellamora continued walking, and for anyone watching her from the town, it looked as if she were alone. The humans did their best to keep up in the trees but soon were a dozen paces behind her. She seemed to pay them no mind but kept walking at her deliberate pace.

After a mile and several twists and turns in the path, she stopped.

"I think we're safe here," she called out, and the three humans stepped out onto the path. "I wanted to make sure no one saw you."

"Well, tell us about it," Dema said.

"There's not much to tell. It's a small fishing village. I bought a few things, but the woman at the shop was very talkative. She wanted to know who I was and where I was going."

"What did you tell her?" Reith asked.

"Bits and pieces of the truth. Told her I was from eastern province and was heading toward Sardis. She asked if I got lost, and I told her I wasn't lost; I wanted to go this way because I had heard about the village and their amazing fish. Well that got her going for a few minutes talking about how they have the best fish in the whole kingdom. So naturally, I had to buy some."

She pulled out a package that was wet with grease and opened it up. The aroma of fried fish wafted through the air, making Reith's mouth water.

"It would have been suspicious if I had bought four servings, but I did want to share."

She broke the fish into pieces and handed it out to the humans. It was delicious, crispy, oily, and salty. Reith loved every bite, of which there were too few.

"I bought you a new shirt, Reith," she added, tossing him a small bundle.

He had been down to one shirt as the bear had torn the other. He still had it, just in case. Reith unrolled the bundle to find a new green shirt. He held it up and saw that it would fit nicely. He tucked it into his pack with a word of thanks.

"And I bought these for all of us." Ellamora pulled two

short swords from her bag that appeared old and a little rusted. "We can use them for sparring practice. Real swords, no more sticks. And Kydar and Dema, you can wear these during the day."

"Thanks Ellamora,' Kydar and Dema said together excitedly.

"Now we all have swords!" Kydar said.

They stayed on the path the rest of that day, taking great care around bends in the road so that no one would see them. In the late afternoon, they left the path and went inland, away from the river.

Kydar and Dema couldn't wait to try out their new swords, and they sparred for a few minutes at a somewhat less than full effort to avoid killing each other. The clang of metal on metal rang out with each blow and soon they were both tired from the effort.

"Are you up for it tonight, Reith?" Ellamora asked.

He wanted to say yes, but he was still sore from the bear attack.

"Maybe tomorrow night."

"Tomorrow might well be your last chance before Sardis," she told him. "The woman in the village said that the journey on foot from there was about a two days walk, if you walk fast. I think we will be able to camp tomorrow night, and then we shall be within a half day's walk of Sardis."

That night, as Reith was trying to fall asleep, his mind went back to all the people and places he had left behind.

He thought of Coeden and all those who had died there. The image of their dead bodies still haunted him, and he shook the memory away. He next thought of Vereinen.

Where is he now? Is he safe?

Reith's mind drifted over to Suthrond and the refugees

he knew must be back there. Heth would have planted her peaches. Trigg would be working hard to restore the place. Lara would be hoping to carve out a life for herself. Titus and Tara would be doing their best to have a normal life.

He thought of Ellyn in Crain and his time spent in the temple with her. He thought of his horse, Aspen, whom he'd also left behind. He thought of Laneras and Pallin and wondered how they were getting on.

So many goodbyes, both said and unsaid, he thought. And then the words came back to him: *"Save them. Serve them. Fight for them. Then find me."*

Chapter Sixteen

T hey avoided the path the next day, wary because they were nearing Sardis. They made sure to stay well to the inland side of the path to avoid being seen by anyone.

"What is Sardis like?" Reith asked Ellamora as they picked their way through the trees.

"Sardis is a wonderful city. While Crain is made of wood and dark gray stone, Sardis is made mostly from white marble. It shines like a beacon in the night. At its center is the grand palace of the king, and next to that is the great Cathedral of Sardis, where elves from all over come to worship, especially on the high holy days."

"Have you worshiped there?" Reith asked.

"Of course, though not for a long time," Ellamora replied. "But I do remember the one time I was there. The priest told the creation story."

"I don't know that one," Reith admitted.

"Let me try to remember how it goes," Ellamora said, screwing up her face in concentration. "In the still of the eternal night, before the clocks of time started ticking, the

God of Light took his pen and began writing the story of Terrasohnen. By his words, Terrasohnen was crafted. The trees were scribbled into being and rivers of ink became rivers of water. The animals were sketched to life. Guardians were appointed to keep this land happy and safe.

"But after a time, the God of Light wished to put a bit of himself into the story. 'I will put my patience, my cunning, and my love of story in the elf,' he said. And as he wrote, the elves were born."

"'I wish to be more present in the story,' he said. 'I will put my determination, my wit, and my love of the earth in the dwarf.' And as he wrote, the dwarves were born.

"'Cannot a rope of three strands hold fast?' he asked. 'I will put my courage, my justice, and my love of beauty in the human.' And as he wrote, the humans were born.

"Now some of the Guardians were none too pleased at this turn. Others still held fast to the God of Light and welcomed his new creatures into the story. But some were selfish and devious. They sought to destroy the elves, dwarves, and humans.

"The God of Light took this as an assault on his very self, and war was waged. These cunning and vile Guardians were cast from the God of Light's presence. And now they prowl Terrasohnen, seeking to destroy the elves, dwarves, and humans and reclaim their place of honor."

Ellamora finished the story and its ending hung in the air before them.

"That's a beautiful story," Kydar said. "I've never heard it before. It makes me want to know more."

Dema snorted. "Oh, it's rubbish."

"If Shadows are real, then why can't it be true?" Reith asked.

They walked on in silence for several minutes, and Reith used this time to process this new piece of information. It fit within his understanding of the world, which he realized was rapidly changing from his previous understanding before this journey.

If only Vereinen could see me now, embracing this elven lore.

"What is the rest of the city like?" Kydar asked some minutes later.

"Well, there is a great stone wall around it. On the inside are houses and markets, where they sell the most wonderful things. They have food of all sorts, fine clothes from every corner of the kingdom, and goods and jewelry. The traders are busy."

"It sounds like a marvelous place," Dema said. "It's a shame we won't be welcomed." There was an edge to her voice.

"At least not right away," Ellamora said, almost apologetically. "But after I speak with the king ..."

"I hope we can go in," Reith sighed.

They kept traveling until the forest began to thin.

"Sardis is located at the meeting of the river and the forest," Ellamora began. "We should stop here. We can camp for the night and then first thing in the morning, I shall depart for the city."

They did not risk a fire that night, as they were too near danger to risk it. Ellamora also thought it best to skip the sword fighting, even with sticks. Reith still had a few peaches which they gladly ate. They planted the pits around their small clearing so that they may have breakfast in the morning.

As they sat around eating, they discussed their plan.

"I think we are about a three hour walk from the city," Ellamora said. "I will leave at dawn. I hope to meet with the king on either the second or the third day. I will say I am on an urgent quest from the Lord of Crain."

"How will you get them to believe that?" Dema asked.

"With this." Ellamora pulled out a sealed parchment. On it was a red seal. "I used Pryderus's seal," she explained. "And I am pretty good at forging his signature and script."

Dema flashed a wicked smile. "Excellent."

"As I said, I think the king should meet with me on the second or third day. If by midday on the fourth day I have not returned, you need to go back to your people, as secretly and as quickly as possible."

"It shouldn't come to that," Reith said.

"But if it should," Ellamora argued, "don't come after me."

The three humans promised not to stage a rescue mission for her.

The weather was warm, so they did not miss the fire. The moon and stars were bright, so they were able to see, which was helpful for guard duty. Reith even convinced Ellamora to allow him to take their joint shift alone so she could sleep and get ready for her trip to the city.

"After all," he said, "we will be able to sleep here all day waiting for you."

She was grateful for the sleep, and Reith spent his quiet shift contemplating the stars and the moon. The stars seemed different here, the constellations were slightly out of place.

It shows how far I have come, he thought, *In a few short weeks I went from chronicler's apprentice in Coeden to a human on the outskirts of the elven capital.*

He realized this was the first time he had been truly alone with his thoughts since the bear attack. He tried to look forward and see the future, but it was cloudy. So much could happen within the next few days. So much was still up in the air.

I asked Ellamora what she would do after this, but what do I want to do? I can't go back to Coeden, that's for sure. I could join Suthrond, but the Gray Man is still out there. Could I live among the elves? Would I be happy? And where is Vereinen?

Vereinen's absence was still a scab he kept picking at. Yet each time he picked, the absence of his master and mentor hurt as a physical pain, an ache in his chest, a hollowness in his stomach. Reith cared so much about the man who took him in when he had nowhere else to go.

Oh, I would give anything to have you back.

With no other home to turn to, Vereinen was his home. He could wander the world, but every day he was with Vereinen, he was truly home.

Maybe I'll go to Galismoor. If the elven king won't help, maybe King Calmon will.

At dawn, Kydar and Dema awoke Reith and Ellamora. She packed her belongings but left anything of which they may have need, such as her hatchet.

"I'll be back soon," she assured them. "Remember, by midday on the fourth day."

"You be safe," Kydar promised, giving Ellamora a hug.

"Go win over the king," Dema said, tugging her into her arms. She let go, and Ellamora turned to Reith.

"Take care, Ellamora," he said quietly before embracing her. In such a short time he had come to care so deeply for this elven girl that the thought of any harm coming to her was sickening.

"I'll be back," she swore. And with that, she turned and walked through the trees toward the road.

"What do we do now?" Kydar asked.

"Nothing!" Dema replied, lying down on the ground.

Reith sat down near her and inspected the peach trees that had sprung up overnight. There were four, one for each of them. They were already a foot and a half high and flowering, and they would likely have fruit by late afternoon.

The first day passed quickly, especially after Dema suggested target practice with their bows. They spent most of the morning shooting. In the afternoon, they took turns napping and standing guard. In the evening, the peaches had grown, so they each had one and planted the pits.

The second day found the humans rather restless. Dema just wanted something to happen and anxiously paced around their camp. Kydar tried to sleep. Reith spent most of the morning studying his maps but soon grew tired of looking at the same places over and over again. In the afternoon, he drew his sword and pretended to battle invisible foes. This was fun until he caught sight of Dema snickering at him.

"What?" he asked.

"You look like you're dancing."

He scoffed. "So? Battle is a dance."

It rained that night, and no one got any sleep. There was even the occasional flash of lightning and roll of thunder, which started them awake if they had drifted off.

The third day was the worst yet. The ground was wet and all three humans were damp and miserable. They spoke little and their tempers were short. At one point, Dema simply stormed off. The two boys let her go, not wanting to deal with it.

A few minutes later she was back.

"Come quick," she whisper-shouted to them when she was close enough.

"What?" Kydar asked. He was lying on the ground looking up at the sky with his hands behind his head.

"I said come on!" she insisted.

Kydar sat up and shrugged to Reith, and then the two of them stood up and followed her. She beckoned furiously, so they started walking faster. She walked through the trees toward the path. As they drew near, Reith could see movement ahead.

"What?"

"Shh!" Dema hissed.

All three hid behind trees and peered around the side, hoping for a better view. In the stillness, Reith heard the sound of many marching feet. He caught glimpses of metal shining in the sunlight. Several times, the light struck the metal just right and sent a blinding white beam directly into his eyes.

"Is that ..." he trailed off, looking questioningly at Dema.

"Yes," she whispered back. "Elven soldiers."

"Where are they going?" he asked.

"North," she said.

"But why?"

They watched for several minutes. Reith had no idea how many elves were marching north. Several hundred at the least, but a few thousand was also possible.

Where are so many elven soldiers going?

He pondered on this as they watched. When the soldiers had passed, Dema gestured for them to head back to the camp, where they could talk.

"What was that all about?" Kydar asked.

"It can't be good," Reith said.

"No," Dema agreed. "I wonder if this is the result of Ellamora's visit to Sardis."

They were wary the rest of the day. At the slightest

noise, they jumped. They decided to keep a guard night and day, and so Reith found himself on guard duty that afternoon. He kept a wide perimeter of their camp, ranging a couple hundred paces away to the south. He even dared to walk near the path, but he didn't hear or see anything. He decided to walk away from the path to see what he could see in that direction.

The undergrowth tugged at his feet as he walked and scraped at his legs. He was grateful for his pants. It was slow going, but he was able to pick a path through. About a quarter mile on, he found the ground began to slope steadily upwards. He looked up the slope and saw that it went up about fifty paces, and then he could see the sky beyond it.

I wonder what I can see from up there.

The trees were spread out more on the slope and the undergrowth wasn't nearly as thick, but he was still winded when he reached the top. His ankle protested the exertion, but he ignored the ache.

Below him, the valley of Sardis was rolled out like one of his maps. He was at the high point in the area. Away to the north, the forest spread out, covering the world in green growth. Looking east, he could see a wide road. Even from a distance, he saw that there were people on it, traveling to and from Sardis.

To the south, the sunlight caught the city of Sardis just right. Its marble walls and buildings shone as a beacon. The walls were so bright that his eyes hurt from staring at it. To the west, the Great River flowed slowly, wider here than it was to the north where Reith had crossed it to get to Erador. On the other side of the river, the fertile plain stretched out, seemingly endless.

Reith shifted his attention back to the city. It seemed to be carved out of the white marble. The outer walls of the city were high and strong. There was a main gate on the eastern side of the city that led to the main road along the edge of the forest. On the northern side of the city, the one closest to him, was a smaller gate leading to the road by their camp. On the river side of the city, he could see tall masts of ships rising over the walls of the city.

In the center of Sardis was a tall tower, blindingly white like all the rest. It soared above the rest of the city and came to a point several feet in the air. From where Reith stood, its highest point seemed to be level with him.

He noticed movement at the eastern gate. Sunlight glinted off of spears and helmets. An elven host was setting forth, marching east along the road. From what Ellamora said, if the elven host continued along this road, they would end up in Crain, as the road followed the edge of the forest to the east and north. From his vantage point, it looked as though an ant hill had been disturbed and ants were pouring out of the city.

Reith had no idea how many elves were in the host marching below, but he could tell it was more than had walked by them on the road. *Where are they going? Crain? And how many are there? Five thousand? Ten thousand?*

He watched this army march off until they were hidden from view by the trees below him. Then he decided to go back to Kydar and Dema to inform them of his sightings.

"Where are they going?" Dema asked when he had finished telling them.

"Ellamora said that the road goes to Crain," he replied.

"But why send an army there?" Kydar asked.

"I don't know, maybe to take care of Pryderus," he guessed.

"I hope so," Dema said. "That would mean that

Ellamora was successful and we will be welcomed into the city soon."

"I'd hate to think of the alternative," Kydar muttered.

Reith gave him a worried glance. "What's the alternative?"

"Maybe they're going to kill Heth and the others."

"Don't say stuff like that," Dema snapped. "It's bad enough knowing they're in danger from the Gray Man. We don't need to be inventing more danger for them."

"You asked, I answered," Kydar huffed.

"I'm going to have a look from the top of that hill," Dema said, and she walked off into the trees.

Kydar turned to Reith. "What do you think? Is she right?"

"I hope not," he retorted.

"I just want to go home." Kydar's voice grew wistful. "I'm tired, Reith. I'm tired of running, tired of camping, I'm just tired."

"I'm tired too," Reith replied. "Let's think of something happier. When this is all over, what will you do?"

"You mean after the Gray Man is gone for good? I want to settle down and start a farm. In Suthrond, hopefully. I'd like to meet a nice girl and settle down, have a family. That would be nice."

"It sounds wonderful," Reith said.

"I love the feeling of accomplishment when the crops come in. It's the most satisfying thing in the world, taking a small seed and reaping a harvest from it. I love the feeling of a hard day's work and the good sleep that comes after it."

"Seems like you were made for the ground," Reith observed.

"I suppose so. How about you? What do you want to do?" Kydar asked.

"I don't know, Kydar. I don't know."

"Come on, there's got to be something you really want to do."

Reith looked at his friend. In such a short time, he had grown very close to this boy from Suthrond who, like him, had suffered so much loss and faced it with bravery. So he took a chance.

"I think there is something I have to do," Reith said. "Now, don't laugh at what I'm going to tell you."

"I won't laugh," Kydar said. "I swear."

"When I was in Erador, I heard a voice tell me something. Like a voice in my head. But it wasn't my voice, you know?"

Kydar nodded, and to his great credit, he did not look at Reith as though he thought Reith was crazy. *He's probably just good at hiding that expression. You have to be if you grew up with Dema.*

"The voice said, 'Save them. Serve them. Fight for them. Then find me.'"

"What do you think that means?" Kydar asked, appearing genuinely interested.

"Honestly, I think the first part is about you. Well, you and the rest of Suthrond."

"So, you were supposed to save us? Hm, I suppose you did. You warned us about the Gray Man."

"But the ending is the part that I don't understand yet," Reith admitted. "Who am I supposed to find? And how?"

"I think it will be made clear to you when you need to know," Kydar told him. "If there is a voice telling you to do something, then I think that voice must know what's going on and will tell you what you need to know when you need to know it."

"You said, 'if.'"

"I did, but the more I listen to Ellamora's stories and think about this Gray Man, the more I see the truth in it all."

Reith let out a deep breath. "Me too."

"Strange, two humans getting into elven religion."

"I think that's not quite right. If it's true, it's not elven at all. It's deeper than that."

"True, true," Kydar said with a nod. "Still, who'd have ever thought that three humans would make it this far and learn so much?"

"Probably the voice inside my head," Reith said, and Kydar laughed.

Ellamora did not return that day. All three of them had gotten their hopes up that they would be able to sleep in actual beds that night, so they were all grumpy when nightfall came with no Ellamora. Perhaps it was the disappointment which led to even worse sleep than normal.

"You look terrible," Dema told Reith when he woke up.

"You're not one to talk," he said.

Hanging over all of them was the fact that this was the fourth day. At midday, their instructions were to leave if Ellamora didn't return. Reith didn't want to think about that.

All three spent the morning on guard duty, anxiously waiting for any sort of sound signaling Ellamora's arrival to take them into the city. As the hours ticked by, Reith began to attach sinister purposes to the armies they had seen marching yesterday.

They're going to destroy New Suthrond and kill Heth, Trigg, Titus, and Tara and the others.

The sun rose high in the sky and the heat of the day was oppressive. Still, they waited. The shadows grew shorter.

"Should we pack up?" Kydar asked. "Just in case?"

Dema shook her head and Reith said nothing.

It's all gone wrong. The armies are marching and Ellamora is in danger.

He stood up and began pacing. Every second, his shadow was shrinking, shrinking, until it was nothing but the ground beneath his feet.

Just then, they heard someone walking through the underbrush. A figure in a white dress appeared. It was not the Ellamora who had left them a few days earlier. This Ellamora had been cleaned of all the grime of the road and dressed in all the niceties of Sardis.

"Come on! The king wishes to see you!'

Chapter Seventeen

They were soon on the road to Sardis. Reith felt nervous on the path, and he could tell Kydar and Dema were too. They were jumpy and kept turning their heads to see around them. Ellamora noticed and reassured them.

"You don't have to worry about being seen," she explained. "The king wants to see you." She held up an official looking scroll as proof. It had a red wax seal with a crowned wolf's head crest.

"You still haven't told us everything that happened," Dema complained.

"Oh, so much happened," Ellamora said. "When I left you, I walked down this road into the city. The gates were open, and I composed myself as an ambassador. The guards didn't bother to stop me, and why should they? I entered the city and was momentarily confused. It had been so long since I had been there that I didn't remember my way exactly. But I knew I must make for the palace, so I pushed deeper into the heart of the city.

"I kept the tower in front of me because I knew the

palace to be next to the cathedral tower. After a while, I finally arrived. There was a sign labeled 'Business and Visitors' so I went and found a line of people, perhaps a hundred long. I got into line and waited. I felt like I was there all day, waiting. One by one, each person stepped forward to make their case to the magistrate who would decide their fate. Only a handful gained access to the palace, and everyone else left. The person in front of me wanted to speak to the king about chickens, and the one behind me wanted to enlist in the army. The one right after him had a tax debt to settle and was admitted almost immediately.

"Finally, it was my turn. The magistrate looked me over and asked my name and business. 'Ellamora Pryderus-kin, and my business is that I am an ambassador for Pryderus, Lord of Crain. I seek the king's justice on a matter of great importance.'

"'Delegates and representatives from the outlying provinces may come on the second or fourth Thursday of the month between the hours of one and three in the afternoon,' was what he said to me. Well, he recited it to me.

"'Please, sir,' I'd said, 'this is a matter of great importance.' I held up the letter that I had forged from my step-father, but he wouldn't even look at it.

"'It may be to you, but the king has loftier definitions of what is important. You may come back next Thursday.'

"Well at that point, I was ready to punch the magistrate."

"You should have punched the magistrate," Dema interrupted. "I would have."

"What happened then?" Reith asked. "This is still early on the first day, and you didn't come back to us until the fourth."

"I was getting there," Ellamora said. "I stormed off, just wanting to get away from the magistrate, I was so mad. I couldn't wait until next Thursday. I wandered around the palace complex and found myself standing in front of the great cathedral. Just wait until you see it up close; it is the most marvelous building, so tall and grand. Anyway, I was at the front of the cathedral about to go up the steps when someone tapped my shoulder. I turned around and found that it was my Uncle Cassius.

"He asked, 'Ellamora, you are a long way from home, aren't you?'

"Cassius is Pryderus's older brother. He is a healer and has lived in Sardis most of his life. I met him when my mother married Pryderus. I visited Sardis and saw him one other time, and he visited Crain once. I was very happy to see a familiar face, as I had no idea what my next step was.

"I went to Cassius's house, and we caught up and talked on the way. But once we were safe inside his house, his tone and expression changed.

"'Where are those humans you escaped with?' he had asked me. I was taken aback and thought of denying it straight away, but he held up an envelope with his name written in Pryderus's handwriting. Pryderus didn't know exactly where we had gone, but he had written to his brother to be on the lookout for me.

"He told me, 'I am on your side. My brother has taken a hardline of fanaticism against the humans, but I am all for helping them, and helping my favorite niece.'

"So I told him everything about all three of you, where you're from, about the Gray Man, about your time in Crain, and our trip here. The whole story was quite long and the day was nearing its end when I finished. Finally, I asked, 'Is there anything you can do to grant me an audience with the king? I cannot wait until next Thursday.'

"'There may be, but it is a longshot,' Cassius said. 'You see, I am actually expected up at the palace tomorrow. The king's chief servant is ill and I have been his physician. I would be stepping out of line asking for King Koinas to see you, but desperate times call for desperate measures.'

"The next day, I waited at my uncle's house while he went to the palace. He succeeded in helping the king's servant, so the king was happy to arrange a meeting with me. The meeting was set to be the next day after lunch, the third day after I had left you. My uncle took me to the market and bought me a nice dress so that I could appear before the king well dressed.

"The next day after lunch, my uncle brought me back to the palace. We did not go by way of the magistrate; we went in a smaller gate. The guards let us in with no trouble. The palace was splendid, with tapestries, paintings, and statues everywhere. I can't wait for you to see it."

"Tell us about the king," Dema said impatiently.

"I was getting there," Ellamora snapped. "Don't interrupt. As I was saying, we were led through the palace to the throne room. There on the throne was the king. He is tall and graceful, with long brown hair. He wore a red robe and a thin golden crown. Beside him stood his personal guards.

"When we reached his throne, I curtsied and my uncle introduced me to King Koinas. He rose from his throne and kissed my hand, and we retired to a side chamber with comfortable chairs and pillows. There, the king asked me to recount all that has befallen us since you came to Crain. Like I had with my uncle, I told him of the fate of Suthrond, the Gray Man, and my step-father's ascension to the Lordship of Crain."

"How did he take all of this?" Reith asked. "What was his mood?"

"It's hard to say," Ellamora admitted. "He certainly pondered what I said closely. Anyway, I told how I had traveled here to plead the cause of the humans. I was very careful in my words up to that point, and I made it sound like I had traveled alone. I didn't want to endanger you if my words were not taken well."

"Thank you, Ellamora," Reith said. "But obviously we came up, and that's why we are walking into Sardis."

"Right you are, Reith," Ellamora replied. "The king asked if no one was in my company for the journey. He did not seem angry or hostile, just curious and sympathetic, so I told him that I had made the journey with three humans."

"What did he say to that?" Dema asked.

"He nodded and said, 'I would very much like to see them.' Then it was all arranged. I was given this official summons, which will get us through the gate. We will go to my uncle's house and tomorrow you shall go before King Koinas."

"What do you think of him?" Reith asked.

"He seems fair and just. I do not believe you have any reason to fear."

"Well that's good," Kydar said.

"Do you know anything about troops leaving Sardis?" Reith pressed. He told her about the two companies they had seen leaving the city going north and east.

"No, nothing," she said, looking puzzled. "That's quite peculiar."

They were coming close to the city gates. The wall stretched up over them, gleaming white in the afternoon sun. Guards were stationed about the gate, eyeing each traveler with suspicion. Ellamora took the lead and handed one of the guards her summons. The guard read it, then looked up curiously at the three humans.

"Alright, come on in. Don't cause any trouble now."

"Oh, we'll be no trouble," Ellamora told him. The four of them walked through the gates into Sardis. Each guard gave them an inquisitive look as they walked by. Some seemed to give hostile looks.

"I'm pulling my cloak up," Reith whispered. "I hate being stared at."

"Agreed," Kydar said, and the two boys pulled their cloaks up around their faces, so that they were hidden in shadow. Dema, defiant as ever, did not. She reveled in the attention.

They walked along a busy street which led up into the heart of the city. Along the street was a market, with merchants selling food, wine, fabric, medicine, leather goods, and a plethora of other things out of little carts and store fronts. The colors were bright, the smells were exotic and interesting, and the noises were foreign to his ear. While he heard his own tongue, the accent was strange, somehow more formal and elongated.

Ellamora stopped at one of the food stalls and purchased four of a hot, flaky roll with a whole sausage inside of it. She passed these out to the humans, who eagerly devoured this elven food. The bread was warm, light, and flaky and the sausage was plump and juicy. It was the best thing Reith had tasted in weeks.

"These sausage rolls are a specialty in Sardis," Ellamora said. "They make them elsewhere, but the best ones are here in Sardis."

They continued along the street until they reached a large, marble fountain that spit water into the air a dozen feet above the street. Here, Ellamora turned and took them down a side street.

This street was quiet, with no one buying or selling. Reith rightly supposed it was a residential area. The houses here were tall and narrow. They were each two stories tall, carved out of white marble. The thing that set each apart were the doors. Each house had a door painted in a bright color, which stood out all the more against the white backdrop. He saw doors of red, blue, green, yellow, purple, orange, and every shade in between. It was like walking through a rainbow.

Ellamora eventually stopped in front of a house with a forest green door. She knocked, and without waiting for a reply, opened the latch and walked in. A staircase leading up the second floor was immediately in front of them. To their left was a dining room and a kitchen and to the right was a study richly furnished with a wooden desk, fine couches, and an elegant rug of emerald and violet fabric.

Behind the desk was an elf the spitting image of Pryderus. He was slightly older and thinner, but the resemblance was easy to see. When they entered, he rose to greet them.

"Welcome to my home, weary travelers," he said warmly. His voice was fuller than Pryderus's and moreover, looked at the humans with joy, not dislike, which made all the difference in Reith's mind. *Here is someone who we can trust.*

Ellamora introduced the humans to her uncle and he invited all of them to sit down. When they were all seated, Cassius spoke.

"Ellamora has told me much of your adventures, but I would like to hear from you as well. Reith, you seem to have traveled the farthest of your company. Why don't you go first?"

He was used to telling his story by now, and he effortlessly told Cassius of how the Gray Man had killed all of Coeden and spared No One. He spoke of his trip to and from Erador and his journey to find the survivors from Suthrond. When he reached the part when he had met up with them, Dema continued the story, supplying the details of how the Gray Man had similarly decimated Suthrond. Kydar supplied additional details.

"I am so sorry to hear of all of your troubles," Cassius said. "I pray they are soon at an end. You have an audience with the king tomorrow. Now, this Gray Man concerns me deeply. If Shadows walk ..." he trailed off into silence.

"If Shadows walk, it's better to be on the side of a king with an army!" Dema replied.

That night, Reith took the first real bath he had had since leaving Crain. The water was hot and he soon turned it brown from all of the grime of the road. After he felt refreshed. He even slept in a real bed that night. He had to share with Kydar, but the two of them did not mind in the least.

"Just don't touch me," Kydar snapped. "Keep your feet to yourself."

"You keep your feet to yourself."

It seemed he fell asleep as soon as his head hit the pillow. When he woke up, sunlight was streaming through the window. Kydar was gone, but the smell of breakfast was drifting up from the kitchen.

Reith rose and descended the stairs and found Kydar, Ellamora, and Cassius in the kitchen.

"Dema is still asleep," Ellamora explained.

Cassius had fried up some bacon and eggs for them, and the scent was the most heavenly thing he had ever smelled. There was a hot, dark liquid to drink, which Cassius said was coffee.

"Try it black, and if it's too strong for you, I have cream and sugar."

Reith sipped it. The flavor was rich, almost chocolaty, but incredibly bitter. He made a face.

"Cream and sugar it is," Cassius said, smiling at his expression. Reith found the taste much improved by the additives and even had a second cup.

After a scrumptious breakfast, Ellamora left for the market to buy the humans nicer clothes for their meeting with the king.

"We can't have you going dressed like you were out hunting," Cassius said.

With Ellamora gone, the humans spent the morning with Cassius. He was a marvelous host and completely opposite his brother. He allowed the humans to peruse his personal library, which consisted primarily of books about healing. He had a few that Reith recognized from Ellyn's library at the temple.

"What does it take to be a healer?" Reith asked curiously.

"It takes many years of study," Cassius said. "I began as an apprentice at age thirteen. I spent seven years studying and working with master healers here in Sardis. Then I spent two years traveling the kingdom treating any who came across my path. Healers are instructed to charge no payment but receive with thanksgiving that which those we help can provide. Those were two of the best years of my life."

Ellamora returned with new outfits for each of the humans. For Kydar, she had gray trousers and a navy blue shirt. For Reith, she had the same gray trousers and a green shirt. And for Dema, black leggings and a purple tunic. Ellamora had a good eye for their sizes and all fit comfortably.

After a light lunch of salad and fruit, it was time to leave and go to the palace. Cassius went first, with the three humans trailing behind and Ellamora in the rear. In this formation, they walked through the city toward the temple tower. On the walk, the elves they encountered tended to not pay much attention to the humans. Many would greet Cassius but would not look closely at the humans behind him. Some did notice, and gave them all very inquisitive looks.

The cathedral steeple rose higher in the sky the closer they got to the center of the city. It towered above everything else around them. They rounded a corner, and the entire structure came into view. Like most of the city, it was made of marble. Reith counted seven gigantic columns, a hundred feet high, lining the front of the cathedral. Behind the columns was a shaded area and two huge wooden doors were set in the wall. Reith wished that he could take a look in there. Ellamora noticed his interest.

"We can go in after we meet the king," she said. "It's splendid there."

"I will hold you to it," he replied with a smile.

They were stopped at a gate leading into the palace. Ellamora supplied the summons, and guards inspected her and the three humans for weapons. They had left them all behind at Cassius's house.

"This is where I leave you," Cassius said. "Ellamora, you know the way back, correct?"

"Yes I do, Uncle. I will see you soon."

Cassius turned to walk back the way they had come and the guard let Reith and the others into the palace. They found themselves in a well-lit wide hall. Light was streaming down from high windows. Columns lined the walls, and between the columns, Reith could see doors leading to other halls and rooms. At the end of the wide hall were two large wooden doors, ornately carved with runes and images. At their entrance, a steward came toward them.

"Welcome to the palace of King Koinas," he said in a dry, stuffy voice. "Please follow me, sirs and madams."

He led them through the wide hall toward the wooden doors. At their approach, two guards pushed them open and let them inside.

The room beyond had a tall ceiling, twice as high as the preceding room. The floor was black and white checkered tiles. This room was also lined with columns, but there were no doors between them as far as Reith could see. At the other end of the grand hall was an elevated platform with a large throne that appeared to be of solid gold.

The steward led them through the hall, and as they approached the throne, Reith saw that King Koinas had long brown hair and was wearing a thin golden crown, which rested gracefully on his head. Each hand had several rings of gold or silver with large gemstones. His clothes were nearly all black, with gold trim on them. He wore a calculating expression. When they were near, he made eye contact with Reith before looking to Kydar and then Dema.

Reith noticed there were others beside the throne. One younger elf had a band of silver balanced on top of his head. *Maybe a prince?* Reith thought. The others bore no mark of royalty, though one of them, an older elf, wore a long white robe that matched what was left of his hair. He had a large bald patch on top of his head.

"My lord," the steward said, "May I present the Lady Ellamora and the humans, Reith, Kydar, and Dema."

The king studied them from his throne. Then he spoke.

"It is well met again, Lady Ellamora. Thank you for

bringing your friends here today. I am most grateful to you for that service." He nodded his head to her, and she gave a small curtsy. "I have heard some of your tales from Ellamora, but I wish to hear more from you. Let us hear from Kydar, Dema, and Reith in turn, then we may judge what may be the best course of action." He gestured to Kydar to begin.

Kydar told his story to the king, of how Suthrond had been warned of attack and then was attacked. He continued, and Reith studied the listening elves with interest. During Kydar's tale, he studied the king. Koinas rested his left elbow on the arm of his throne and his chin in his hand. His gaze never left Kydar during his whole tale. He had a slight frown crease on his forehead.

I wonder what he's thinking, Reith wondered, unable to read the expression.

Next, Dema gave her account of her experience, and Reith turned his attention to the other listeners. The younger elf with silver hair was looking back and forth between Dema and the king. He looked nervous. The older elf, the one clothed in white, seemed to be listening, though he was staring off into space, so Reith could not tell. The other elves around appeared to be mere servants, listening intently while looking like they weren't listening.

"You did not witness the attack?" King Koinas asked, looking from Dema to Kydar and back when she told them about the destruction of Suthrond.

"No, Your Highness," she answered. Kydar shook his head no as well.

"Interesting," the king said. "You may continue."

When Dema finished her story, it was finally Reith's turn to speak. Koinas' dark eyes found his and stayed on them. He wanted more than anything to look away, but he held the king's gaze. He told of all that had befallen him since he had gone hunting that fateful morning in Coeden, of his travels to Erador, Suthrond, Crain, and Sardis, and even his encounter with the bear in the wilderness. In his mentions of the Gray Man, he tried to communicate just how vile and evil that man was. He told the story of how the Gray Man had spared No One's life. *Our hopes may rest in those details, or else the king might not see our danger.*

He finished his story and waited for the king to respond. The Koinas pondered for several seconds after Reith had finished. After, he straightened up and looked to the older elf in white quickly before looking back to the humans.

"Your stories tug at the heart of this king," he said, slowly. "I feel your pain, your sorrow, and your trouble, and your stories make me want to help."

Reith's hopes rose. The king continued.

"Perhaps your stories did this too well," he said, clasping his hands in front of him and looking from human to human. Reith snuck a glance at the older elf and the younger elf standing beside the throne and saw looks of concern on their faces. "Your stories seem almost too good to be true. They seem rehearsed, polished. It makes me wonder if you are being truthful."

"Please, Your Highness," Ellamora pleaded, bravely speaking up, but the king held up a finger to silence her.

"Unfortunately for you, I know better," he said, and Reith's heart dropped to his stomach.

Where is he going with this? How does he know better?

"I know better because I have heard a different story, one that contradicts your well-rehearsed story on several points." The king stood up and turned to the steward, who was standing near the throne. "Steward, please fetch the storyteller."

The steward turned and walked to a side door.

"You humans must be incredibly brave to come before a king and lie to his face. Brave or very, very stupid."

"We're not lying!" Dema cried.

"Oh, yes you are," the king sneered.

The steward came back at that moment with a cloaked figure behind him. The face of the newcomer was hidden in shadow.

"I find your description of events to be lacking," King Koinas said. "Storyteller, what say you?"

Reith turned to look at the storyteller, who raised a gray hand to pull down his cloak to reveal his gray face and eyes. There in the palace of King Koinas of the elves was the Gray Man himself. Reith felt as if icy water had been dumped over him. The Gray Man flashed a wicked grin at Reith.

Horrified, Reith had to turn his face away from the sinister gray eyes. Ellamora's mouth hung open in terror in a wordless scream. Dema and Kydar looked bewildered and fearful. The king was smiling at the Gray Man and the young elf and the old elf were looking at each other with dismay.

"Your Highness, what is the meaning of all of this?" the older elf asked.

"A few days ago," the king began, "this storyteller came to me with certain tales worth my while. He told me of unrest among the humans, of a mysterious attacker wiping out entire villagers. He warned me that humans may try to cross into my lands and that they may even try to invade our land."

"I thought it best to warn our good king of the danger facing him and his people," the Gray Man said in his terrible, colorless voice. "I simply did my duty."

"It's not true!" Reith said, pleading to the king. "He's the one! He did it!"

"Well of course you would say that, stupid boy," King Koinas said, shaking his head. "Is that all the defense you have? He even told me one calling himself No One was burning human villages and killing their inhabitants and was bent on crossing over to do the same in the elven land. And you, Reith, have been kind enough to identify yourself for us, verifying the story."

"Oh, No One," the Gray Man said, his gray smile growing yet wider. "You knew trouble would catch up to you eventually, and here it is."

Reith felt rage bubble up inside him at the injustice of it all that he bellowed, "I didn't do it, you've got to believe me!"

"Guards!" the king called out, and several came running. "Arrest these four. Take them to the dungeon. Then we shall decide what fate shall await them."

"No!" Ellamora said, "Unhand me!" she said as a guard grabbed her arm.

"Let go!" Dema yelled as she was similarly apprehended. A guard slapped her hard across the face, which only made her yell all the more.

"You can't do this!" Reith spat at the Gray Man.

"Sire, we must take care now," the older elf said. "Be reasonable. You can't throw these humans and Lady Ellamora in jail."

"I'm the king, I can do whatever I please. Take them away!"

Reith and the others were dragged from the hall, struggling the whole way. But the more they fought, the more their captors fought them. Reith received several painful blows before going limp in resignation and letting them drag him away. White hot tears came to his eyes at how unfair it all was. He wanted to scream and run and hit something and cry all at once.

As they were pulled from the hall, he saw the young elf storm off and the Gray Man ascend the stairs to the top of the platform to stand beside the king's right hand.

The prison was below the palace. There were no windows and the only light came from the occasional flickering torch. The floor was made of large, gray paving stones.

They were dragged by several cells, most of them ajar and empty. Dema was still struggling, and it took three guards to subdue her through blows and holding her tight. Eventually a blow knocked her out and she was still and quiet.

Reith was unceremoniously tossed into a cell, and he landed hard on his back on the stone. It drove the wind from his lungs and he felt like he couldn't breathe. His breaths were rattling gasps and he felt as though he was drowning. By the time he recovered, his cell had been locked and the guards were walking back up the passage.

His cell contained a bed, which was really just a slab of rock, and a bucket that appeared to have not been emptied from the previous occupant's time in the cell. The smell was revolting, making his stomach turn.

He gingerly stood up and walked to the door. Looking out, he saw only empty cells across from him.

Where did the others go?

"Hello?" he called out.

"I'm here," came the voice of Kydar somewhere off to his right.

"Kydar?" came the faint voice of Ellamora even further to his right.

"Where's Dema?" Kydar asked.

"I think she's still unconscious," Ellamora said. "She might be next to me, but there's no way to know."

"Can any of you see anything helpful?" Reith asked. Before any of them could answer, a different voice called out in the semi-darkness.

"Reith? Is that you?" It was the last voice in the world he had expected to hear but the one he had been wanting to hear for so long.

"Vereinen?" he asked. He couldn't believe his ears.

Chapter Eighteen

"Oh joy in the midst of sorrow!" Vereinen said. "I thought our paths would never cross again!"

"How in the world did you get here?" Reith asked, completely stunned by the turn of events.

"Who is it, Reith?" Ellamora asked.

"It's my master, Vereinen!" he said. "I can't believe you're here. I thought you were dead."

Vereinen replied, "Not dead, but not helpful to you in this cell, either, I'm afraid. I despaired for my life."

"Tell me how you got here," Reith demanded. "How did you escape from Coeden? Why weren't you at Erador when I arrived? Why did you come to Sardis? And how did you get imprisoned?" The questions poured as liquid from his mouth. After all this time, he would finally receive answers to the questions that had haunted him for so long.

"It's a long story, Reith, though I suppose we have nothing but time at the moment." Reith heard a sigh for the next door cell as his master resigned himself to that fact. "Where to begin, where to begin? Well I suppose the very beginning should suffice."

"From the time I left Coeden to go hunting on the day when …" Reith trailed off.

"Oh no, oh no, long before that. That part is the middle of the story. No, I mean to go back to the very beginning. Remember that I told you I traveled to Kal-Epharion in my youth on the king's business?"

"Yes I remember," Reith replied. He recalled thinking about that story as he studied Vereinen's maps when he had first left Coeden for Erador.

"Well, let me refresh your memory. And I'm sure your friends won't mind the details."

"Thank you, sir," came the voice of Kydar.

"As you know, I grew up in Galismoor, the human capital city. I was studying to be a chronicler and the king knew it was my wish to go to Kal-Epharion and study. So I was commissioned by the king to travel with a group of soldiers and traders who were on the king's business. We traveled there and I enjoyed my time with a local scholar. When it was time to go back to Galismoor, our company was increased by two. A boy a few years younger than myself at the time and his mother were to accompany us back to the palace."

"I don't see how this has anything to do with us in a cell in Sardis," Reith said flatly.

"It has everything to do with our current situation, Reith," Vereinen retorted.

Reith noticed a note of something strange in his master's voice.

Is it sorrow? Regret?

"Now please, allow me to continue. As I was saying, we brought back a boy and his mother. The boy's name was Solzar. Solzar and his mother—I think her name was Mina —came back with us. Solzar and I became fast friends. Long journeys will do that to boys about the same age. We talked the whole way back, with him telling me of life in Kal-Epharion and me telling him about my work as a chronicler.

"Our friendship continued when we were back in Galismoor. I continued my studies, and Solzar worked in the palace as a page, but I think he found great joy in studying vicariously through me. He was very bright, Solzar was. Very bright, very curious, and very daring. He pushed the bounds of what was socially acceptable for one of his position. He would speak to the nobles—which was unheard of, a page speaking to nobility. But he got away with it. He was charming.

"His mother was consort to the king. For three years they lived among us in the palace until one day Mina displeased the king and she was banished. They both were sent back to Kal-Epharion. I received a letter from him a month after he had left telling me that his mother was dead. I could tell he had cried over that letter, as there was evidence of dried tear stains. His sorrow gushed forth and I felt it in my own soul as well.

"I was sad, of course. Women in the prime of life don't usually die. But it was a long trip to Kal-Epharion, and I was in the midst of my studies. So I wrote back, giving him my condolences. But I stayed in Galismoor."

"It's a long way, as you said," Reith piped in, trying to connect the dots between this story and his own. He could not see the connection.

"Ah, but no distance is too far to travel for a grieving friend. I let him down, Reith. He was counting on me to return."

Vereinen paused a moment, then took a deep breath and continued.

"It is the greatest regret of my life that I did not go to him at that time. It might have made all the difference. But

I stayed, finished my studies, and within a year I was a fully qualified chronicler. It was my dream. But the memory of the boy who had been my friend haunted my mind and haunts it to this day."

"I still don't see—"

Vereinen interrupted, "Let me get through this, Reith. I have kept this secret in my soul for many years, and it is time for it see the light, or whatever light is in the dungeon."

Reith heard another sigh from the cell beside him, and he knew whatever was coming next was going to cost Vereinen a lot to get out.

"After that letter, I never heard from Solzar again. I wrote to him with my condolences, of course, but that letter received no reply. I didn't know if he lived or died or simply just didn't care to communicate with me. Perhaps the memory of his time in Galismoor brought him pain, due to his mother. So I did not press.

"Still, in that period of time, there were whispers of a darkness spreading in Kal-Epharion. There were unexplained disappearances, robbers on the road, and chaos in the streets. Winter lasted longer and fall began sooner. Each story told of a feeling of unease they had within the city itself. I tried to push them off as gossip and superstition. But still the rumors persisted, and from several sources, all confirming the darkness. They said even the sun was not rising as high. All who came to Galismoor from Kal-Epharion brought word of a darkness taking root in that region. Each whisper was a knife to my soul, a reminder of the wrong I did. Eventually, I moved to Coeden to be away from even the whispers of the darkness in Kal-Epharion. I did not know what was happening there, but I knew that I should stay far, far away."

"But why should the rumors of darkness affect you?" Reith asked, puzzled.

"It was not the darkness but that which was *behind* the darkness," his master replied.

"Powers? Dark Powers?"

Vereinen gasped. "How do you know about Dark Powers?" he asked.

"I learned of them in my travels. ," Reith replied. "I'll tell you soon. Please, finish your story. I want to know why I am in this cell."

Vereinen continued, "I settled into life in Coeden, as you well know. I came with my books and my memories. Eventually I took you in, Reith, and I thought that Solzar was behind me at last. But in our last month, Reith, I felt a growing unease. I thought something was coming to us, something dark, but I didn't know what. I also didn't know if I was simply being paranoid.

"The morning you left, the oddest thing happened to me. I was sitting at our table drinking tea when the strangest thought came to my head, unbidden. 'The key that was lost is in Erador.' It was a strange thought. It sounded like my own voice in my head, but it was nothing of which I had any knowledge. I put the thought aside and went about my day.

"That day I was reading an old book about the Dragon War. I read something like this: 'The restoration of Terrasohnen is locked away, yet the key has been lost.' Now this was a strange turn. I put two and two together and deduced that I needed to travel to Erador and find this key. And I had the strangest feeling that I ought to go immediately. So I scribbled a note for you, hid it where only you might find it, and left. I borrowed a horse and rode. I had no second thought about it, as it seemed the thing to do. You would get my note and follow me.

"I traveled through the forest, crossed the river, traveled through Dragonscar, and came at last to Erador. I searched for seven days. In all my searching, I found no key. Each day I expected you to turn up, but you never did. I began to worry for you.

"When the week was up, I despaired at what to do. Should I continue waiting? My supplies were almost gone and I had to leave Dragonscar. So I did one of the hardest things I have done, and I left. But where to go? I knew this key must be important, so I decided to travel south to Sardis. The elves are marvelous record keepers, and I knew that the Hall of Records in Sardis may hold the key, pun intended, to my search" Vereinen chuckled darkly at his own joke. "In a pinch, I was able to disguise myself as a passable elf, and I traveled down river to the first elven town I could. From there I traveled by boat to Sardis itself.

"By asking around, I found the Hall of Records and spent several days searching through the records to find out anything I could about this lost key. Unfortunately, my search was interrupted. As I was walking through the city one day, I was apprehended. A hood was thrown over my head and I was put into some sort of cart. When the hood was lifted, I was here."

There was a long pause from the other cell, and Reith wondered what the holdup was. Finally, Vereinen continued.

"There before me was a face out of a nightmare. It was familiar and foreign. It was friend and foe. It was Solzar and it was not. It was a Shadow."

Reith guessed exactly what face Vereinen was picturing in his mind. The cold gray eyes and the shadowy gray skin was seared into his own memory.

"Every hint of darkness, every rumor of a Shadow growing in Kal-Epharion, it was all true and I beheld it with my own eyes," Vereinen said. "The thing I had been running from for so long came at last to me." The despair in his voice was palpable, like a mist floating through the air of the prison.

"Solzar is the Gray Man?" Reith asked.

"I am afraid so," Vereinen said. "My old friend became the most despicable thing to roam Terrasohnen."

"But you didn't have anything to do with what he became," Reith attempted to reassure him. "He made his own choices. He let the Dark Powers in, not you."

"Reith, promise me that you will forgive me for what I am about to say."

"I promise," Reith said, confused.

"No matter what I say, promise me that you won't hold it against me," Vereinen pleaded.

His stomach churned with unease at the man's words, but he replied simply, "I promise, Master."

"I am afraid that while Solzar made his own choices to step through the door toward who he was becoming, I am the one …" He paused, clearly not wanting to say anything else. Reith heard a dull thud and imagined Vereinen striking the bars of his cell with a closed fist in anguish, tears running down his face.

"Go on," Reith said quietly. "You need to clear your conscience. The first step is admitting what you did."

There was another thud, this one louder. *He's fighting himself. It must be a great struggle in his soul.*

"Oh, Reith, forgive me for my folly. I … I am the one … I am the one who opened the door to his choices."

"What do you mean?" Reith asked.

"When we lived together in Galismoor, I was studying the Dragon War. I read about powerful beings called Shadows. I learned that Shadows are creatures which open up their souls to the Dark Powers to be their tools. It was fascinating to me—on an intellectual level, of course. Solzar was so inquisitive, so thirsty for knowledge, that I passed on what I knew about them without a thought as to why he wanted that information. But deep down, in my very soul, I knew. My friend was not content. He was a page in the palace, but he wanted more. I told you earlier he charmed the nobles, but I think it was all an act. He despised them and how that stood above him in the world. He wanted power. And so he craved whatever could make him powerful. And I saw this in him. I saw it and I gave the information over to him. It is I that made Solzar into the Shadow that he is today."

There was a gasp from the other direction, and Reith knew it to be Ellamora.

"It was all you!" Ellamora cried out, and Reith silently agreed with her, seething inside.

"I don't deny it," Vereinen said, with melancholy plentifully present in his voice.

"Why, though?" Reith asked, trying to get to the bottom of it all. "If you saw it, why did you give him the information?"

"Because for the first time in my life, I had a best friend," Vereinen explained. "I would have done anything for him, Reith." There was pleading in his voice. "He and I were closer than brothers."

Reith pictured a young Vereinen laughing with a youth his own age and his heart broke for his master.

"Why didn't you ever tell me any of this?" Reith asked tenderly.

"An old man's folly." Vereinen sighed. "We think the sins of the past stay there. But no, the sins of the past work through bread like yeast, like a dam bursting under the weight of a swollen river, and a fire that begins with a spark and eventually engulfs a forest. Oh, I see clearly now what he was and who he was to become. But in my youth, in my thirst for companionship, I overlooked it, to the peril of us all."

"You can't blame yourself," Reith said. "He made his own decisions. He's responsible for that, not you."

"If only, if only," Vereinen despaired beside him. "We don't blame a child for touching a hot pot, we blame the parent who carelessly let the child get too near."

"He wasn't a child," Reith argued. "You have nothing to be ashamed of, Vereinen!"

"And yet I handed the man who became our greatest foe the roadmap to who he is now. It was I who told him the way to his heart's desire."

There was silence save for the occasional sniffle coming from Vereinen's cell.

What can I say to him?

Reith sat down on his stone slab bed and pulled up his feet. He folded his arms across his knees and put his head down. *What are we going to do?* In the darkness, despair overwhelmed him. Here he was, thrown into a cell in the elven city. *I should have escaped to Galismoor.*

But then he remembered the voice and his task.

"Save them. Serve them. Fight for them. Then find me."

I tried. I tried to save them from the Gray Man and we ran into him anyway. How can I save them? I can't even save myself. I am locked here, I will never find you.

The tears came quickly and flowed down his face onto his arms and wetted his pants. Reith stayed like that for several minutes. He imagined the others sitting just like he was. There was nothing to say and nothing to do except wait. There was no window to let in light or to shine the hope of escape. There was only the darkness, the cell, the bucket, and the stone bed.

It was Dema that broke the silence.

"Hello?" she called groggily. She evidently had just woken up. Her voice was soft and faint.

"We're here, Dema," Ellamora replied. Reith could feel the bitterness in her voice as she said it. "All of us, and Reith's master, Vereinen."

"What's the plan?" she asked. "Or have you guys been waiting for me to come up with a plan?"

"There is no plan!" Kydar exclaimed. "There is no escape. They're going to kill us."

"Reith, what do you say?" Dema asked, ignoring her brother.

"There's nothing to do about it, Dema. We're trapped."

Those words bounced off the walls in a horrible echo, each repeat driving home the fact like a hammer pounding a nail.

"There is no way out," Vereinen added sadly.

"Hey, guards!" Dema yelled as she rattled the bars of her cell. "I know you can hear us! Let us out!"

Kydar snorted. "Like that'll work."

They all fell silent for several minutes, ones that seemed to flow on like a snail crawling across the ground.

"Reith, tell me your tale," Vereinen finally said.

"The morning you left, I went out hunting and returned to discover Coeden in ashes and everyone killed. I ran into the Gray Man, Solzar, I mean."

"How did you escape?" his master asked.

"A play on words." He explained the No One story.

"He was always a clever one," Vereinen remarked. "But to be so flippant about life and death …"

Reith told of his trip to Erador, but he left out the finding of sword. He didn't know who was listening or what they might do with the information. Vereinen was particularly interested in the grove of trees and the spring.

"I must have been right near it, but I saw nothing."

"They're magic," Reith said. "Perhaps they sprouted after you were gone."

"It's a mystery I would sorely like to know the meaning of," Vereinen said.

"The Gray Man, Solzar, he was there too. He was looking for a key."

"It must be this key for the restoration of Terrasohnen," Vereinen replied. "But why he would want to restore Terrasohnen, I don't know. Unless he means to destroy the key or the thing that is locked."

Reith continued his story but left out the details about the voice and sword. He felt guilty for it, but with the sword back with Cassius, he decided secrecy was the better course. He did tell of how he stole Aspen and traveled to find the survivors of Suthrond and their miseries among the elves of Crain, along with his travels to Sardis.

"How did you come to know of Shadows and Dark Powers?' Vereinen asked.

"I learned of the Dark Powers and the Guardians from Ellyn, the Lore Master and cleric of Crain, and from Ellamora, my travel companion. From my description of the Gray Man, they said he was a Shadow. The more I learned, the more sense it made."

"Indeed," Vereinen replied. "It is great evil to become a Shadow. It is to give up yourself to something dark and malevolent. Oh, Solzar!" There was a sob from Vereinen's cell.

For several minutes, the only noise came from Vereinen's cell as he cried. There in the darkness, Vereinen's grief became Reith's grief as he firmly placed himself in his master's shoes. At last, it died away.

"What times we live in." Vereinen sniffled. "Great and terrible things are happening and we are caught in the midst of them. It is not yet time for the three races to join together again, though I hope that time is soon. I perhaps would have cautioned you against going to the elves, but if you hadn't you would never have found yourself here. I am grateful for your company, though I wish it were under better circumstances."

"What do you think will happen to us?" Reith asked. "You've been here longer, so you must know the lay of the land."

"I wish I was more help. I don't even know why I am held other than a personal vendetta by Solzar. As for you, I fear that the king will try you for espionage or some other made-up charge and hold you prisoner or kill you. There's the off chance he may ransom you to the king of the humans, but I find that unlikely."

The talking died away, and Reith tried to think of a way out of this mess, but couldn't. *Cassius knows we're here, but what can he do?*

After what seemed like days, a light appeared down the hall, and guards came in with rotten vegetables and a bit of water for each prisoner. Reith drank the water but left the vegetables alone. He knew he'd want it later, but he wasn't nearly hungry enough for something so disgusting yet.

Reith had no knowledge of the passage of time as it was always dark there in the dungeon, save for the flickering torches on the walls, but he eventually laid down and attempted to sleep. He felt as though he tossed and turned all night, if it even was night out. Finally, he gave up and paced his cell. He heard snores from Vereinen's cell and similar noises of pacing from other cells. He inspected his cell thoroughly to see if anything could be used as a weapon. He found nothing, no broken bit of stone or piece of wood or anything.

There's the waste bucket. It wouldn't hurt someone physically as much as assault their nose.

Stale bread and water was brought and Reith assumed it was morning. This time he did eat most of the bread. Luckily for him, the darkness concealed the worst of it from his eyes.

Later, more guards came back. This time they unlocked one of the cell doors. He heard the door close again and they all walked by with Ellamora in their grasp. One was on each side of her, each holding an arm. She looked fleetingly at Reith, and there was fear in her eyes.

"Stay strong, Ellamora!" he called after her.

When the guards were gone, Kydar asked, "Where do you think they're taking her?"

"I think the king wants to question her," Reith said.

It was agony waiting in the cell while Ellamora was out there being questioned or worse. Hours seemed to go by, and Reith grew tired. He hadn't slept in many hours but knew he must remain awake for Ellamora's sake. Soon, the footsteps of the guards echoed on the stone and they were back.

He sat up on his bed and saw the guards dragging Ellamora between them. She dragged her feet and hung limply in the guards' arms and she had a smear of blood on her cheek. Her cell door opened and closed and then the guards were at Reith's door. He contemplated hurling his waste bucket at them, but he knew it would only enrage them and endanger himself and the others.

Two guards walked in and grabbed him by the arms before pulling him to his feet. Then they marched him out the door and down the hall. He managed to turn and see

Vereinen. He only saw him for an instant, but in that instant, Reith saw a man broken and aged.

Behind him, he heard Kydar and Dema trying to speak to Ellamora, but he did not hear a reply before they had turned and walked down a different hallway. They led him back to the throne room. The light from the windows was blinding at first, as used to the darkness as he was. Reith had a fleeting thought of the God of Light and whispered desperately toward the open windows, "Help me." He didn't know why he had done it, but the thought that the God of Light was there and cared about him and his friends locked in the dark gave him a spark of hope. The spark warmed him and he grew more alert.

The king was seated on his throne, slouched lazily to one side, dressed as he had been the other day. The Gray Man was to his right, as before. Neither the younger elf who Reith assumed was the prince nor the older elf were present.

"Welcome back, *human*. I hope your stay has been a pleasant one," the king sneered.

The Gray Man looked at Reith as a dog looks at a bone. Reith swallowed and braced for whatever came next.

"This is your trial, *human*," the king hissed. He pronounced 'human' like Pryderus did, full of contempt, as if he were tasting something foul. Reith remained silent.

"You are charged with war crimes against your people and mine. This crime is punishable by death. Let us begin."

Chapter Nineteen

"**Y**ou stand accused, Reith, of capital crimes against the good people of Terrasohnen," King Koinas said. "You are accused of committing arson, mass murder, looting, assault, espionage, and unlawful hunting in the king's forest."

"I didn't do any of that!" Reith protested.

"Silence! I will not stand for interruptions. Further interruptions will result in an automatic guilty verdict and a sentence of death. Do you understand?"

Reith hesitated, not knowing if he was allowed to answer.

"You may answer direct questions," the king said. "Do you understand?"

"Yes," Reith said. "I do." He could see Koinas waiting for him to add, "Your Highness" or something similar, but he held his tongue. *I'll win that small measure of satisfaction.*

"The chief witness against you is Sir Solzar. Sir Solzar, you may speak."

"I was but a lowly traveler when I sought lodgings in the city of Suthrond," he began in a tone that reminded

Reith of an actor giving a monologue in a play or a storyteller telling a rather unfortunate tale. "However, when I arrived, the city was burned to the ground and every inhabitant was killed. I was dismayed at this horrendous act." His words dripped with sarcasm.

How can the King believe this man?

"Who could do such a thing? So I sought out Coeden, hoping to find rest for my head and answers to my questions. When I came to Coeden, I witnessed the accused personally killing women and children of the town and ordering his men to do the same. Women and children!"

Solzar faked a sorrowful face that Reith could see right through.

"Furthermore, I heard him say to his men that he sought to invade the land of the elves. I knew this was a terrible thing, and I rushed here to Sardis to warn the good king. And then you did us the service of showing up here, unarmed and ready to be arrested."

"Those are the facts," King Koinas said. "Do you have anything to say in your own defense?"

"He's lying!" Reith cried. "He's a no good scoundrel who did all the things he is accusing me of doing!"

"Hmmm," said the king, stroking his chin. "I don't think that sways my mind."

"He is evil!" Reith exclaimed. "For crying out loud, he's a Shadow!"

For a split second, there was a change in the Gray Man's face. The glee dropped from it for just a second, but was soon back again.

"How very rude," the Gray Man said.

"A Shadow?" the king repeated, looking at the Gray Man. "Sir Reith, you have been listening to too many children's tales. Shadows aren't real."

A sinister gleam came to Solzar's eyes now as he stared down at Reith.

"What even is a Shadow, according to the old stories?" he asked in a show of fake ignorance.

"A Shadow is someone who has a spirit inside them," the king explained. "It can be a good thing or a bad thing. To assume that a Shadow is evil, if they even existed, is sheer ignorance and intolerance." King Koinas turned his eyes back on Reith.

Am I imagining it, or is there a gray gleam to his eyes?

"He is evil through and through! He murdered so many innocent people!" Reith yelled at the pair of them.

"It is not Solzar who is on trial here, it is you! He has given a satisfactory account of his comings and goings. It is you who is under investigation and trial."

Reith was boiling mad, and he could feel his face growing red. It was all so unfair, so sinister.

"Is the little baby who believes children's stories going to cry?" the Gray Man mocked.

Reith wanted to do exactly that, and yell, scream, kick, punch, and break something, preferably the Gray Man's nose. But he did none of those. He took deep breaths and mastered his emotions.

"Well it seems as though we should waste no more time," the king said. "I find the accused condemned on all accounts and sentence him to execution upon the conclusion of these trials."

"I didn't do it!" Reith pleaded.

"Silence!" Koinas bellowed. "Guard, take this murderer back to the dungeon where he belongs and bring up the next one."

Two armed elves instantly grabbed him. This time he struggled, trying to break free. All his struggles earned him was a blow to the head and then he knew no more.

Reith came to and found himself on the dirty floor of his cell. The guards had placed his head right next to the filth bucket, and he nearly threw up. He sat up and scrambled away, but this caused his head to throb, and he nearly fell back to the floor.

He sat against the wall of his cell taking deep breaths and rubbing his temple where he had been hit. The memory of his sham trial came back to him and the rage made his head throb even more.

"Who is on trial now?" he asked the surrounding cells.

"Kydar," Dema replied. "I was taken up after you were brought down."

"What happened?" he asked.

"Guilty on trumped up charges," Dema said. "Ellamora too. We're to be executed."

"Same," he said, gritting his teeth and clenching his fists at the injustice of it all.

"We will try to escape when they fetch us for the executions," Ellamora added from several cells over, though her voice betrayed how little hope she saw in the attempt. "Who knows? Maybe we will escape. Whatever happens though, stick together!"

"I am so sorry, Reith," Vereinen said.

"Have you been on trial?"

"Not yet. I don't know if I will be."

They all waited for Kydar to return. Reith positioned his waste bucket between him and the door so he could be ready when they opened it.

What's the worst that can happen? They're killing me already.

The knowledge of his impending death actually did not bother Reith much. He had always known that all eventually die, and he had assumed for his entire life that his own eventual death was well into the future. Now, faced with the imminent loss of life, his only regret was that it was coming by such an unjust means. He was strangely calm in the face of death. Logical, even. He thought of his prayer as he was taken to his trial.

Thanks for nothing, God of Light.

He was disappointed that the God of Light didn't seem to care about the injustice happening in the world he created.

Maybe this just means he doesn't exist. What sort of god allows all of this to happen? The Gray Man is the murderer, not me. And yet I'm in jail and he's advising—or controlling—a king, who himself might be turning into a Shadow.

Presently, Kydar was brought back, and then Vereinen was taken. When the guards were gone, Ellamora said, "Be prepared to run for it when they come back to take us."

Reith nodded grimly, then realized the silliness of replying this way to someone he couldn't see.

"I'll be ready," he said.

In a very short time, footsteps could be heard coming down the passage. Reith guessed that there were two or three elves coming toward them. He also heard the jingling of keys. *They're coming to take us.*

He prepared himself near the filth bucket, ready to throw it at the first elf who appeared at his door. A figure came into view, fiddling with the keys. He crouched, ready for action. The elf looked up, and Reith stopped in his tracks. It was the younger elf he took to be a prince. Gone was the silver circlet on his head. Instead, he was dressed for travel. Behind him was the older elf, no longer dressed in white but in a blue traveling cloak.

"There is no time," the prince said in a breathless voice. "We have to go."

"Go?" Reith asked, confused by the sudden turn of events.

"Yes, go! Away!" the prince urged as his keys jingled. He finally selected the right one and the lock clicked open. He moved over to the next cell, but Reith was hesitant.

Is this some sort of trap?

In short order, the cells of Ellamora and the two remaining humans were opened. They looked as confused as he felt.

"Let's go," the prince ordered.

"Hold on," Dema said. "Go where?"

"Away from here! This is a rescue."

"Why are you rescuing us?" Ellamora asked.

"Because I think it's terribly unfair what my father is doing to you. Solzar is a mad man and must be stopped, but first, we have to get you away from here. Ellamora, I have been in contact with your uncle. He has given me all of your possessions, they are packed, and I have horses waiting for us in the stables. There will be plenty of time to discuss this later, once we are out of the city."

"And who are you?" Reith asked the older elf.

"I am Myon, the king's chief advisor, or at least I was until Solzar came."

"Enough talk. Let's go," the prince snapped.

He did not go back the way they had come, but rather pushed ahead to what Reith appeared deeper into the dungeon.

"We will exit the palace through a side door that leads right to the stables," the prince explained as they hurried along the stone corridor.

The passage took them past several more cells. All of these ones further down were empty. They came at last to a sturdy wooden door with a small, barred window. The prince selected a key and fit it in the lock, but the lock did not turn.

"Come on," he hissed as he looked for the right key. He selected another, but this did not turn the lock either. Frantically, the prince tried a third key.

Reith had no idea how much time they had to escape, but he grew frantic as well. Thankfully, this key worked, much to everyone's relief. The prince pushed the door out and went first through it. They found themselves at the bottom of a spiral staircase. The prince went up two stairs at a time, the rest of them following his lead.

Are those our footsteps echoing or is someone following us?

At the top was another door, and this one too required a key. The prince selected the right one on the first try and they found themselves in a passage that had natural light from small windows high up on the wall.

"This way," the prince said, beckoning them onward. At the end of the passage was yet another door. Again the prince searched for a key and again he was lucky to select the right one on the first try. The door opened to reveal a flight of six stairs and the outside air. About ten feet beyond the top stair was a building that was evidently the stables. The prince looked both ways to ensure the coast was clear, then led them across into the darkness of the stables. It smelled of horse and waste.

Inside the stables were several horses with packs on them. Reith saw one horse with his bow and sword on the pack. There were two elves with the horses, evidently waiting for them.

"Everyone, mount up," the prince ordered.

"What about Vereinen?" Reith asked, suddenly remembering his master, who was probably before the king and the Gray Man right that second.

"Two of my men are going to extract him and meet us

at the gate," the prince replied. "They have Cassius with them, too." He looked to Ellamora with reassurance. "Now let's go!"

The prince swung up into his saddle. Reith belted his sword around his waist and put his pack on his back, then clambered up into the saddle of the large black stallion he was given. The horse shifted uncomfortably as Reith scrambled up. When everyone was mounted, the prince prodded his own beast, a dark brown battle horse, into a trot.

They soon reached the open air and began making their way through the city. Reith had no idea what time it was and therefore did not know if it were morning or afternoon. The sun was behind them, so he knew they were making for the east gate or the docks on the west of the city. Nothing looked familiar.

And yet even running for their lives, Reith felt alive, vibrant. He had hope again. The sunlight was pouring down on them, casting great shadows in front of them, which led the way toward freedom.

The prince took the lead, with Myon beside him. Next came Ellamora and Reith, then Kydar and Dema, and lastly to two other elves. They had scarcely been out of the stables for two minutes before they heard the blast of a trumpet behind them.

"Our absence has been discovered," the prince yelled back at them. "We must make haste!"

He took them to a main road crowded with people. Most wisely stepped aside to let the horses past, but it was so congested that the creatures had to slow to a walk.

Behind them, they heard shouts, and the prince yelled in frustration, "Move!"

The horses were able to get back to a slow trot through the crowded streets. Suddenly, an arrow whizzed over

Reith's head. It sailed past the prince and Myon and struck a cart. Reith chanced a glance back, trusting his horse to keep following. He saw several elven soldiers on horseback and a dozen more on foot chasing them. The arrow had been shot by one on horseback, and he was aiming at them again.

"Duck!" Reith yelled, and he crouched low over his horse's neck. An arrow went through the space that had just been occupied by his head. It sped past them all and struck a nearby elven bystander. The crowd began to panic and scatter. Screams filled the air. This actually worked to their advantage as the crowd seemed to surge between the escapees and the pursuers. They were able to continue to put distance between themselves and those chasing them.

For five agonizing minutes, Reith bent low over the neck of his horse, afraid of arrows from behind. *So far so good. I hope Vereinen is okay.*

After what seemed like hours, they reached the gate, which Reith determined was the eastern one as there was no river to be seen. The road stretched away from the city. The forest loomed large to the north of the road and there were plains to the south of it. Between them and freedom, however, were twenty confused guards waiting for them.

"My prince," their captain said. "What is the meaning of all of this commotion and trumpets?"

"There are villains and rogues at the northern gate. Go quickly and defend the city! I will maintain the gates in your absence."

The captain gave the order and the six elven guards trotted away toward the northern part of the city.

"That will take care of them," the prince said. "But where are the others?"

Reith saw no sign of Vereinen or Cassius, but he did

see that their pursuers were in sight, perhaps five hundred paces away up the main street.

"We need to leave," Myon urged.

"We can't!" Ellamora and Reith said together.

"I will give it a minute," the prince replied. "If they are not back then, we have no choice but to leave."

Reith and Ellamora scanned the crowd looking for their master and uncle respectively. Their minute was nearly up when Reith saw them. Two elves, Cassius, and Vereinen were all on horseback. They entered the main road from a side street and galloped toward them. Elves in the street jumped out of the way as they came.

But then Reith's heart sank. The pursuers were there too, nearly on top of them.

And then, from the side street Vereinen and the others had emerged from came a giant black war horse at full gallop. It's rider cared not for the elves on the street and ran over them with impunity. He was swift in pursuit of Vereinen and the others. There was madness and fury in those horrible gray eyes.

The Gray Man, Solzar, was in hot pursuit.

"No!" Reith yelled. Instinctively, he urged his horse to a gallop and raced back into the city, toward his master and toward danger. The pursuing palace guards were pulling out their bows and about to shoot at Vereinen. The Gray Man drew a sword and held it high, ready to strike.

Reith swung his own bow around and pulled an arrow from his quiver. He had never shot from horseback, but he felt the rhythm of the horse beneath him and timed his shot with it. He aimed and fired at the lead elf guard, and his arrow miraculously hit its mark, knocking the elf from the saddle. This caused the others to briefly pause their own arrow shooting to avoid the now rider less horse.

This slowed the pursuing elves so that Vereinen and

Cassius and their two guides put more distance between them.

Yet the great black war horse of the Gray Man leapt over the fallen elf and came on alone. There was no time to shoot again, so Reith drew his sword. Its metal gleamed as if on fire in the sunlight.

Reith could see the surprise and hunger in Solzar's eyes as he beheld his long sought for key. Solzar checked his great horse, which reared up on its hind legs. As it came down, he brought down his own sword straight toward Reith's head. Instinctively, Reith reached up with the sword and with two hands, received the terrible blow.

The force of the Gray Man and his horse came down upon him, but the sword held firm. Reith was as surprised as anyone. With an ordinary sword, Reith could not have hoped to receive that blow and remain unscathed.

The metal on metal crash earned a shower of sparks, making the black horse rear again, and Reith took the opportunity to swing a mighty blow at the Gray Man's side. The Gray Man managed to block it, just barely. But the force of Reith's blow and the rearing horse threw him off balance, and he tumbled backward out of the saddle.

Reith heard hoof beats behind him and found that all had followed him. Kydar, Dema, Ellamora, and several of their allies shot arrows at the pursuing elves who had caught up to them again. Then they all turned around and galloped toward the gate.

"Faster, faster!" the prince cried.

Arrows flew past them. Reith heard a gasp and saw one of the elves fall from his saddle to the ground, an arrow sprouting from his neck.

They were almost to the gate now. The two elves that had come with Vereinen and Cassius were in the lead now, with Vereinen and Cassius behind them. Then came the

prince, Myon, Ellamora, and Reith. Kydar, Dema, and the
two other elves were behind them. An arrow glanced off
of Reith's pack, but he felt the weight of it and knew he
would have a bruise there.

Ellamora shouted out. Reith looked to her and saw that
she had a red gash on her left arm where an arrow had
grazed her. "I'm fine!" she yelled to him.

More arrows sailed by them. They were a hundred
yards from the gate in an all-out gallop now. Ahead of
him, Cassius took an arrow to the back and fell from his
saddle. Cassius cried out as he fell, but his cry ceased when
he hit the road. Reith's horse swerved to avoid the fallen
body of Cassius.

"No!" Ellamora screamed when she saw her uncle fall.

"Don't stop!" Reith pleaded. "If you stop, you'll die!"

Ellamora reluctantly obeyed. They kept riding.

They were now fifty yards from the gate. Reith heard a
grunt and someone fall from their horse behind them and
he saw that one of the elves was down.

And finally they were through the gate and out on the
road. There were trees to their left. Reith heard another
grunt when someone else was hit. He turned his head and
saw that Kydar, Dema, and the other elf had all kept their
seats. But something was wrong with Kydar. He swayed in
the saddle and his eyes were distant.

"Kydar!" Dema cried, seeing that her brother was not
well.

They were out on the southern road, still galloping,
several hundred yards clear of the city. Reith turned again
and saw that their pursuers had stopped at the gate. He
looked at Kydar and his heart sank. Kydar was coughing
up blood, barely holding onto his horse. Reith slowed and
came in next to Kydar and his horse, reaching over and
grabbing the reins.

"Dema, help!" he called out, but Dema was already riding close on the other side. Their pace slowed to a trot and then a walk. Ahead, the rest of the party turned off the road to the left, going into the trees.

Kydar's breaths were coming in great shuddering gasps. Reith looked and saw an arrow buried several inches into Kydar's back.

"Kydar, stay with us," Dema pleaded. "You're going to be okay." Tears were streaming down her face and Reith found that his own eyes also stung.

They reached the spot where the others had turned off the road and found that they were in a small clearing in the trees. The prince, Myon, and Ellamora were off their horses and rushed toward them. The three of them helped Kydar down, and they laid him on his face. His breathing was ragged and uneven. *It pierced his lung.*

"Help him, please," Dema begged, sobbing now. Ellamora took her in her arms and squeezed her tight. Tears were in her eyes as well. Two of the unnamed elves had fallen in the city, as had Cassius. Those remaining were Reith, Ellamora, Dema, Kydar, Vereinen, the prince, Myon, and two of the other elves.

Vereinen was bent low over Kydar's back, and Myon was there with him.

"I am afraid that the arrow has done too much damage," Vereinen said sadly.

"Do something!" Dema yelled. She knelt by her brother's head and placed a hand on his cheek.

"I ... I ..." Kydar said, trying to speak. "I ... love ... you," he choked out.

Dema sobbed. "Take the arrow out, please!"

"If we take it out, he will immediately bleed out," Myon explained. "The arrow is blocking the blood right now. I am so sorry."

Kydar let out one final shuddering gasp and then went still. His eyes remained open, but all light had gone from them. Vereinen reached down and closed them.

Dema collapsed to the ground in a heap of tears, each cry shaking her entire body. Ellamora bent down and spread herself over the sobbing Dema as a blanket. Tears filled Reith's eyes and he knelt down to join the embrace.

He had never felt so empty.

Chapter Twenty

They were left alone to cry and hold each other for several minutes. Tears flowed freely, and Reith's fell on Ellamora, Ellamora's flowed onto Dema, and Dema's nourished the ground. There were no words for their grief. Eventually, the prince interrupted them.

"I am so very sorry, but we have to go."

"No," Dema said, shaking her head. "No. We can't."

"I'm afraid the king will send the whole palace guard after us."

"We have to bury him," she argued.

The prince looked to Myon, who nodded. "There is no time for a burial," the prince said. "Not a proper human one at least, with earth. Would you permit a burial by fire? It is the elven way."

Dema nodded.

"Good," he said. "Let us build an altar." For several minutes, Reith helped the prince and the two unnamed elves gather wood and stone. Soon, they had a heap of rocks, which they piled the wood on. Then they placed

Kydar on top. Dema put his sword in his hand and arranged his limbs so that it looked like he was sleeping.

"God of Light," the prince prayed, "none of us has life in himself, and none becomes his own master when he dies. For if we have life, we are alive in you, and if we die, we die in you. Whether we live or die, we are your possession. Care for this soul in your infinite life and light. May Kydar dance upon the fields of your kingdom. Comfort his friends and family in this time of sorrow and grief. Take him to be with you. So be it."

Just then, a light flashed at the altar, and Reith flung his arm up in front of his face to block it. But as soon as it appeared, the flash of light was gone. A fire was crackling on the altar, but Kydar was gone. *What on earth?*

"What happened? Where is he?" Dema demanded.

"The God of Light took him," the prince said as if commenting on the weather.

She sputtered, "Taken him where?"

"On," he replied simply.

"To a better place, where death has no more hold on him," Myon added.

Vereinen looked on in wonder. "Who are you?"

"I am Prince Romulus, heir to the elven throne and Knight of the King's Justice."

"Why did you rescue us?" Reith asked, still very confused as to why they had been saved.

"I am Knight of the King's Justice," Romulus repeated. "The king was going to make an unjust decision. It is my duty to oppose it."

"Is that all we are, an accomplishment of duty?" Ellamora asked indignantly.

"Not at all, good lady. It was the right thing to do. And if I am to have any throne at all, it is in my best interests to separate myself from my father and from Solzar. In the past few days, I thought I saw the darkness of the Shadow behind his eyes.

"I think I saw that too," Reith said. "During my trial. Is the king becoming a Shadow?"

"It would be the Dark Powers' greatest wish, to turn a royal. We can only hope that the God of Light protects him from the Shadow."

"That is all well and good," Vereinen said, "But what now?"

"As you may know, my father sent his forces north, one force by the northern path and one by the eastern path along the forest. This was Solzar's idea. I think they mean to invade the humans."

"What?" Vereinen asked sharply.

"Oh yes," Romulus said, shaking his head. "Solzar took care of Suthrond and Coeden, two towns that would have attempted a fight against an elf invasion. He cleared the way for my father to march troops deep into the land of the humans."

"So what can we do?" Reith asked hopelessly.

"We have only one course of action," Romulus replied. "We have no hope of reaching the humans in time to warn them. We must seek the dwarves. If we can win them to our cause, we can attack the invading troops from the rear."

"You would do that to your own people?" Vereinen asked, incredulous.

"It is my duty. We are all the children of the God of Light."

"And what about all the rest of you?" Reith asked, looking around at the other elves.

"We know a Shadow when we see it," Myon said. "It is a horrible distortion of the good created order for a Shadow to walk. We will oppose the Shadow, for

Terrasohnen and the God of Light. The king has forsaken my counsel, so I will forsake him. Brauron and Aytos are my willing companions in this." He gestured to the two other elves. "Shall we proceed on this adventure that the God of Light has called us to for the sake of our world?"

Reith asked, "What about the Gray Man? Solzar, I mean."

"His hand is stretched out to take the world. We must cut his hand down."

"It's his fault," Dema said, wiping her sleeve across her face. "It's his fault. For everything. For our family, for Suthrond, for Kydar, for Cassius, all of it." She stood up a little straighter, proud and strong. Weakened, but not defeated. "I will end him. If it's the last thing I do, I will prevent him from hurting anyone else. I swear it on my life."

"We'll be right there with you, Dema," Reith promised.

"Fighting by your side, till the very end," Ellamora added.

And with that, this group of humans and elves prepared to mount their horses. Reith pulled Vereinen to the side.

"I missed you, master." Master and apprentice hugged as they never had before. Reith realized he had not yet looked upon Vereinen's face properly since Coeden. It was more aged now, with deeper lines, but still there was a youthful appearance to his face.

"I missed you too, Reith," Vereinen said. "More than anything. And I am more proud of you than I have ever been. You have shouldered a burden beyond what could ever be expected of a boy, and you have borne it well."

"That is not all that I am bearing," Reith replied. He drew his sword and handed it to Vereinen.

"What's this?" Vereinen asked, inspecting the sword.

"I think this is what Solzar was looking for. I think this sword is the key."

"What makes you say that?"

"He mentioned that the key would be something with three metals woven together. And there's more. After I carried the sword, while I was still in Erador among the trees, I heard a voice. 'Save them. Serve them. Fight for them. Then find me.'

"Astounding," Vereinen said, holding the sword and weighing it in his hand. "I think you may be right. If so, sword bearer, you hold the key to the restoration of all of Terrasohnen. Bear it well."

Vereinen mounted his horse and Reith followed his lead.

The restoration of all of Terrasohnen? What a weight to bear.

With his right hand he held the reins and with his left he held the hilt of his sword, which felt warm in his palm. The sword felt warm to his touch. As he felt it, assurance that he was on the right path swept over him.

Reith might not know what was ahead, but he knew he was going the right way. The way was illuminated, and a little light was all that was needed to fight a Shadow.

Epilogue

The Gray Man watched the humans and the elves pass through the gate of the city.

It's too late to go after them, he thought. *I don't have the men. But the sword, the Sword! The boy had it all along! He knows not the power which he holds in his hands.*

He rode through the city, indifferent to the bodies of the fallen from the battle. But instead of the palace, he rode to the temple. He entered into the now familiar hall, carved of marble with fabulous stained glass filled with images of old. Along one side, near the back, he found his favorite. In this image a single figure stood. The red, orange, and yellow glass behind the figure gleamed in the sunlight, looking like it was on fire. The figure held aloft a sword, the Sword, toward a dragon sweeping down on him from the sky.

"My Masters," Solzar said aloud to the empty room. "The boy has the sword. Shall I follow him or shall I continue the path you have laid before me in your wisdom and power?"

There was silence for several seconds. And then, from

all around came a strong, deep, and ancient voice from Solzar's own mouth.

"Fear not the boy," the voice said from Solzar's lips. "He is weak. He is nothing. Turn your eye north. Our vengeance is near at hand."

"Yes, my Masters," Solzar said in his own voice. "I am your servant."

"You have done well," the voice said from Solzar's mouth. "You have been faithful and you will be rewarded beyond all others."

"Thank you, thank you, Masters," Solzar said.

"Go and find your men. They are across the river waiting for you. Then attack, as we have planned. The time of Light is over and the time of Darkness will soon come to pass. Even now, there is another Shadow rising in the East."

About the Author

N. K. Carlson is an author living in Texas. Originally from the Chicago area, he graduated from the University of Illinois before studying at Logsdon Seminary, where he graduated with a master of divinity degree. He has published two books.

The Things that Charm Us and the Smelly Gospel (which was co-written with Drew Doss) both came out in 2020.

His love of writing began in elementary school when each student was given a blank white book to fill with a story. In college, he took an interest in blogging and writing novels.